BEHIND THE LINES

WINGS 6

BEHIND THE LINES

Peter Leslie

First published in Great Britain in 1997
22 Books, Invicta House, Sir Thomas Longley Road,
Rochester, Kent

Copyright © 1997 by 22 Books

The moral right of the author has been asserted

A CIP catalogue record for this book
is available from the British Library

ISBN 1 86238 006 6

10 9 8 7 6 5 4 3 2 1

Typeset by Hewer Text Composition Services, Edinburgh
Printed in Great Britain by
Clays Ltd, St Ives plc

1

'You're quite sure this chap, whatsisname, will fill the bill?' The red-tabbed staff officer poked a heavy finger among the papers littering the desk. 'Blake. Yes, Blake. You're satisfied . . . ?'

'Absolutely, sir,' the adjutant said. 'First-class candidate. The only choice.'

'All very well for you to say that, Hesketh, but . . .'

'Trilingual in English, German and French,' the adjutant urged. 'Spent a year at Heidelberg before the balloon went up. He even collected a wound from that FE-2b training crash that could be a duelling scar!'

'Thought him a bit of a cissie, frankly. Chap came to the interview in civvies. Trifle foppish, if you ask me. Silk handkerchief flopping out of his breast pocket, and all that.' The staff officer – he was a brigadier – drew a large handkerchief made of red cotton from his sleeve and blew his nose loudly. 'He's not one of those . . . ?'

'Good God, no!' The adjutant was scandalized. He tapped a buff booklet lying among the papers. 'Fellow got eight out of ten for gunnery. Quite out of the ordinary for these flying wallahs.'

The brigadier picked up the document. Heavy black lettering on the cover announced: 'Army Book 425: Pilot's Flying Logbook'. The first few pages were divided horizontally, each column devoted to a particular exercise in the flying training programme. 'Only got five out of ten for propeller swinging,' he pointed out.

'Yes, but *nine* out of ten for Morse signalling aptitude,' Major Hesketh said. 'That's an absolute plus if the chap's to keep in touch with us from behind the lines, what.'

The brigadier grunted, ferreting among the official reports. 'I suppose so. If you people are quite sure.'

'*Quite* sure, sir.' Major Hesketh flicked a speck of dust from the green Intelligence flash on his khaki jacket. Outside the windows of the HQ hut, the sun-dried grass of Heston aerodrome stretched away towards a row of canvas hangars. Behind these were gasometers, a red-brick block of flats and a plume of factory smoke staining the blue sky.

'Patrice Blake, Lieutenant, Royal Flying Corps,' the brigadier read from the cover of the logbook. '*Patrice?* What kind of a Christian name is that?' He sounded personally affronted.

'It's French, sir,' the adjutant explained. 'His mother is descended from a Huguenot family which fled here in the seventeenth century. That's the other reason for his three languages.'

With the back of one hand, the brigadier brushed out the ends of his waxed moustache, which was modelled on Lord Kitchener's in the famous recruiting poster. He opened his mouth to reply, but the words were lost in a sudden juddering racket as mechanics outside the hut started up the radial engine of a scout plane with the metal cowling removed. In the middle distance, a BE-2c biplane lumbered across the field towards a wind-sock hanging limply from its pylon.

'How many hours' flying has your man had?' the brigadier yelled.

'Rather more than usual for a Western Front pilot.

Eighty-five as an observer, twelve and a half dual, twenty-six as solo pilot on patrol.'

'What's he going to fly on this madcap escapade of yours?'

Major Hesketh smiled. 'A Sopwith Pup. Partly because he's familiar with the machine, partly because the Hun has already captured several examples, so there'll be no secrets given away when he ditches it, but mainly because the RNAS use Pups and we aim to fly him off a boat.'

'Good God! But why?'

'Question of range and approach,' Hesketh said. 'Factory where Jerry is working on the device is too far inside Germany for a home take-off. But if he uses an aerodrome behind *our* lines . . . and then crosses no man's land to fly on into Hunland – well, they're going to be on to him from the start, aren't they? Supposed to be a secret foray, after all.'

'Quite.'

'If he flies in from the north and west, on the other hand – over Jutland, say – he's going to be over the river and into the trees before their observers even twig that the machine's not one of theirs.'

'And the ditched bus? No chance of him bringing it back?'

'None.'

'So what does he do when he runs out of juice?'

'We reckon he should get within twenty miles of the target. Forest in the valleys, moorland higher up. If he finds a landing place far enough away from civilization, he sets fire to the machine, which will carry no insignia anyway, and legs it into the sunset. If there's a town or a village too close, his orders will be to forget about destroying the aeroplane and set off as far and as fast as he can before the soldiery arrive.'

'And you really think . . . ?'

'We cannot go on having our chaps shot out of the sky at this rate,' Hesketh said. 'This is our only chance to catch up. Blake, in our opinion, is the sole candidate with a chance to succeed. For the reasons I have outlined.'

'How much of a chance?'

'Fifty-fifty,' Hesketh said.

'Hah!' the brigadier guffawed. 'Not familiar with your mount, my boy. Only met him once. But I wouldn't care to back him at those odds, by God!'

'You don't have a choice, sir,' Hesketh told him firmly. 'There's only one horse in the race.'

2

Heavy clouds building to an altocumulus hammerhead towered darkly above the low hills west of the aerodrome as the pilot flattened the biplane out for his tenth cross-wind landing on the undulating field.

The machine touched down briefly, leapfrogged a slight rise and staggered towards a group of canvas hangars before the 80hp Le Rhône rotary engine responded to a burst of throttle and lifted the plane high enough to circle the field and bank for a second attempt. This time there were no problems and the pilot of the single-seater scout taxied towards the group of officers standing on the strip of tarmac fronting the hutted headquarters of 200(N) Training Squadron, Royal Flying Corps. The racket of the engine wheezed into silence and the varnished propeller spun to a halt as the biplane pulled up thirty yards away in the long grass.

Major Hesketh strode forward and approached the cockpit. The pilot unbuttoned the flaps of his leather flying helmet and pushed up his goggles. Beneath the thin film of castor oil blown back from the hot engine, his young face with its precocious moustache was cheerful. 'Got it right that time, sir,' he called. 'Help us chaps if the Ministry of Whatever could make these aerodromes a mite flatter!'

'You'd better do a couple more, Blake,' Hesketh said.

'The brigadier wants to see how you handle a landing downwind.' He gestured towards the wind-sock bellying out between the hutments and the hangars. 'You won't have one of those tipping you off when you come down in Hunland, you know!'

'Just so long as the old bus herself doesn't tip the wrong way,' the pilot grinned. He looked dubiously at the sky. The storm cloud massif was spreading and there was a distant rumble of thunder. 'You don't think we've tested the old girl enough for one day?'

'It's your skill we're testing, Blake. Not the aeroplane. Two more circuits – and not so many bumps,' Hesketh insisted. 'And that's an order.'

'Right-ho, sir.' Patrice Blake slid a final glance at the hammerhead and refastened the flaps of his helmet. He pulled the goggles down over his eyes. Hesketh nodded to a rigger and two mechanics off to one side of the officer group.

The three men in their grease-stained overalls moved towards the plane. Once the disc wheels of the V-strut undercarriage had been chocked, the rigger turned the airscrew and the engine attached to it, sucking aviation spirit into each of the nine finned cylinders. Standing back, he looked enquiringly at the pilot. Blake shoved a gloved hand out beyond the padded leather rim of the cockpit and gave him the thumbs up.

The rigger nodded. He stepped up to the propeller. Grasping the higher half of the polished, sculptured blade, he swung it once with forceful, practised ease, jumping clear as the rotary caught with a shattering roar.

The mechanics pulled away the chocks. Blake kicked on full left rudder and fed power to the spinning prop. The biplane lurched around through 180 degrees and lumbered towards the far side of the field.

He throttled back the machine as a flight of slender-bodied BE-2 two-seaters planed down over the woods and hedges of Huntingdonshire to land in formation, then he turned towards the northern boundary of the aerodrome.

The wind freshened, blowing the wind-sock out horizontally. Large drops of rain spotted the tarmac in front of the headquarters hut. The thunder was loud enough now to rival the distant rumble of aero engines.

Patrice Blake's Sopwith Pup reached the airfield perimeter and turned once more through 180 degrees. The engine's stutter rose to a bellow.

'Christ!' Hesketh exclaimed. 'I told the silly young ass to try a couple of *landings* downwind – not to take off that way, dammit!'

He ran on to the grass, waving his arms frantically.

If the pilot saw him, he paid no attention. The Pup roared across the field, flattening the long grass in its slipstream. With the wind behind him, Blake was taking the longest diagonal. Even so, gathering speed, the biplane seemed unwilling to come unstuck. The tail rose, rose too high, dropped again as the pilot hauled back on the stick – too soon for take-off – then settled back firmly as the further boundary relentlessly approached.

When it became clear that the plane was not going to lift off within the confines of the aerodrome, Hesketh swore. 'What the devil is the young fool playing at?' the brigadier demanded angrily. The War Office intelligence chief, standing beside him in immaculate civilian clothes, raised his well-tailored shoulders in a shrug that was almost Gallic. Hesketh said: 'What we are seeing, gentlemen, is an example of Youth, subtly enough, flouting Authority. The actions of Lieutenant Blake – although, of course, we have no proof – could be interpreted as the equivalent of what a schoolboy would call cocking a snook.'

'Sassy young blighter,' said the brigadier. 'Hope you'll tear him off a bloody strip just the same.'

'You can rely on it, sir,' Hesketh said tightly.

The Pup reached the far side of the aerodrome, skipped nimbly over a hedge punctuated by blackthorn trees and raced across a paddock beyond, scattering cows. Then, at the very last moment, it rose almost vertically, clearing by less than twenty feet a copse of sycamores sheltering a farmhouse, and soared away towards the south-east.

It returned ten minutes later, circling the aerodrome at fifteen hundred feet. Rain was falling heavily now, and lightning flashed intermittently among the massed storm clouds. A last gleam of brilliance before the sun was finally eclipsed flashed from the doped fabric of the Pup's upper wing as Blake banked to lose height in a series of side-slips.

The downwind landing was perfect . . . until a stronger gust lifted the lightweight machine and almost tipped it over on to the bright circle of its aluminium engine cowling. But Blake, feathering his controls expertly, mastered the squall and brought the scout to a halt two hundred yards from the boundary. He turned into the wind and revved up the engine immediately for his second cicuit.

The Pup raced back across the field with the Le Rhône screaming, rising steeply, dangerously, into the air in the first part of a ground loop.

When the plane was upside down, Blake threw it into a half roll, completing a textbook Immelmann turn to fly back on an even keel the way he had come. After a final circle of the field, he glided in for an effortless downwind landing, taxiing again to a halt a few yards from Hesketh and his colleagues.

Snatching off his helmet and goggles, he vaulted from the cockpit and strode towards them. Beneath the dark moustache, his mouth smiled widely.

'If there were anyone else for this job, Blake,' Hesketh grated, 'anyone at all, I'd have you taken off flying duties and gated for two months. You're lucky not to be court-martialled for insolence, disobeying orders and disrespect to senior officers.'

'Very sorry, Major,' Blake said, not sounding at all penitent, 'but you did say it was my skill being tested. Thought maybe I ought to give you a taste.'

The brigadier whisked his red handkerchief from his sleeve and blew his nose. The young pilot couldn't be certain, but for a moment he had a distinct impression that the man was hiding a smile.

'No disrespect intended, sir,' he said tactfully – if untruthfully – to Hesketh. 'But I felt I had to show you that I knew what I was doing with the old bus. Especially if, as you keep telling me, I have to ferry her across the bally border and then put her down behind the enemy lines.' He stuffed his flying gloves into the inner pocket of his leather jacket and brushed a lock of rain-wet hair from his eyes. 'Any chance now of letting the cat out of the bag?'

'What?'

'Sorry, sir. Well, I mean, when am I, er, to learn exactly what's involved in this oh-so-secret caper I seem to be training for?'

'Right away, Blake.' Only partly mollified, Hesketh was curt. The shoulders of his dress service jacket were already dark with moisture. 'Two big guns from the War Office are waiting inside. You are to receive your

official briefing' – he glanced at his gold wrist-watch –
'in precisely three minutes.'

'Very good, sir. Thank you, sir.'

Blake sketched the beginning of a salute, remembered
that he was not in uniform and allowed his hand to fall.
He turned smartly and followed the senior officers into
the HQ hut.

3

It was uncomfortably close in the operations room. Rain drummed on the asphalt roof and the wooden walls still breathed a medicinal hint of creosote into the heavy air. From time to time, yellow light directed at the blackboard from an electric lamp was swamped by the livid glare of lightning flickering outside the windows.

Seven men crowded into the first two rows of chairs. Apart from Hesketh, Blake and the brigadier, the major-general in charge of the RFC's combat division, a cartographer from the War Office, a civilian representing the Secret Intelligence Service and the colonel who was Blake's station commander faced the dais in front of the blackboard.

The eighth man, a tall, languid individual with a pink face and feathers of silver hair above his ears, stood beside the desk on the dais. Despite the thundery heat of the late summer day, he wore a heavy tweed suit with Norfolk breeches. A row of pens and pencils was clipped to the breast pocket of his jacket.

'Sir Alan Ravenscraft,' the major-general announced by way of introduction. 'From the Prime Minister's economic advisory unit. Sir Alan will provide you with the background to this . . . rather special . . . operation. Lieutenant Blake may take notes, later to be committed to memory and destroyed. I'd be obliged if the rest of you would simply listen.'

Ravenscraft cleared his throat. 'I'll go right back to basics,' he said in a pleasing tenor voice, 'in case any of you chaps should doubt the necessity of the adventure we propose.'

He pulled a large-scale map of Belgium, Holland and northern Germany down from a wall hanger and turned to the blackboard to scribble two columns of figures in yellow chalk. Tossing the chalk on to a shelf below the board, he hitched up one hip on to the desk and sat swinging an elegant leg as he talked.

'I don't need to tell you,' he began, 'that the one big difference between the present show and the two previous spots of trouble in South Africa and the Crimea is the presence of flying machines. They're doing the job that observers in tethered balloons used to do: checking on the accuracy of our artillery fire and then telling the gunners where they went wrong and what they have to do to get it right. And they're doing it better because they can see further and report back more quickly. The only trouble is that the enemy are doing it too.'

He cleared his throat again. 'The obvious result is that each of us is now trying to stop the other doing it – in other words, trying to destroy his flying machines. We all know how it started. Small-arms fire: revolvers, rifles, *hand* grenades, that kind of thing.' He shook his head. 'Useless of course. The lieutenant here, who has himself been an observer, can tell you that firing a handgun from an unsteady moving base at a target that is equally unsteady and deliberately taking evasive action is, well, simply not on.'

Blake grinned. 'What-ho!' he murmured under his breath.

'An additional complication,' Ravenscraft said, 'is that your actual two-seater observation plane is a staid and stable old bus. Has to be, to give the chap a chance to spot his targets, take photos and that kind of thing. For stable, read non-manoeuvrable. The answer, of course, was . . .'

'Yes, yes,' the major-general interrupted brusquely. 'You can take it that we are all familiar with the progression. Use the nippier aeroplanes, the scouts, to do the firing. Which means a fixed gun – preferably a machine-gun, because of the greater fire-power – the pilot being, ah, otherwise occupied. Carry on, Alan.'

'Since the war started,' Ravenscraft continued imperturbably, 'it has become increasingly evident that each side has been obliged to concentrate on preventing its enemy carrying out reconnaissance flights, by shooting at the machines involved, either with anti-aircraft guns or from other aeroplanes. If you control the sky, you can make as many reconnaissance flights as you wish.'

Once again the throat was cleared. 'For efficient prevention, clearly, it is essential that the guns involved be both accurate and reliable. And this is where we come up against the great obstacle, and the reason for this mission.'

The major-general uttered something between a grunt and a snort. The Brigadier's eyes were closed and his chin had sunk towards the three rows of ribbons decorating his khaki chest. Blake scribbled as an extra-loud thunder crash shook the timbers of the building.

Ravenscraft went on: 'Machine-guns are not only heavy: they are also liable to jam. If one is to be fitted to a single-seat scout, therefore, it must be within reach of the pilot so that he can reach out and free the thing. This rules out wing-mounted assemblies, which are in

13

any case impossible to aim efficiently, and those on the centre section above the pilot's head. The only spot-on place is along the nose of the machine, directly ahead of the pilot, so that instead of aiming separately, all he has to do, so to speak, is point the whole aeroplane at the target, and then press the tit.'

'Hah!' The brigadier sat suddenly upright. 'There's your fly in the bally ointment, what!'

'Exactly. In theory this would be fine in the case of a pusher, where the engine and airscrew are behind the driver. But pushers like the FE-8 and the DH-2 are too cumbersome and unwieldy to be efficient scouts, because of that great cage of wood and wire joining the tail unit to the front of the machine.'

'There's another slight disadvantage,' Blake ventured. 'From the point of view of the johnny at the controls, that is. He's too damned exposed, with no engine block in front to shield him from a stream of bullets fired from dead ahead. And in the event of a crash he's going to be the first thing to hit the hard ground – with all the weight of the engine ready to flatten his back.'

'Quite. So you lay the gun along the engine cowling of a tractor machine . . . and as soon as you fire it you shoot off your own damned propeller!'

'Hoist by your own bloody petard, by gad!' the brigadier wheezed. 'Nothing like shooting yourself down in flames!'

'The French ace Roland Garros,' Ravenscraft pursued, 'who was the first man to fly single-handed across the Med, came up with a partial solution to the problem. He fitted high-tensile steel deflector plates to the lower part of each propeller blade, so that any bullets that fouled the prop as it spun were knocked out of the way instead of severing the airscrew. One disadvantage here, however, is that half your stream of bullets risk being wasted instead of homing on the target. Another is that one of Garros' modified machines was forced down on German territory – and the Hun at once seized on the idea and improved it.'

Ravenscraft eased himself off the desk and moved to the blackboard. 'Look at these figures,' he said, tapping a knuckle between the two chalked columns. 'They represent weekly aeroplane losses, ours on the left, the Hun's on the right, from the last quarter of '15 to June this year. You'll see that, within normal, acceptable variations due to climatic conditions, military requirements and so forth, the picture remains fairly stable. Here our chaps are more successful; there the Germans have the upper hand.' He tapped the blackboard again. 'Until the beginning of this month. You'll see from the last three figures that since then our losses have more than doubled – in one case trebled – against theirs.'

A murmur – of consternation? disbelief? – animated the seven men sitting below Ravenscraft, who returned to the desk.

'The reason for this is a Dutch gentleman by the name of Fokker,' he said. 'Supplier of high-class aeronautical machinery to the German Imperial High Command. Fokker was asked to examine the captured Garros monoplane and come up with something similar. In fact he went one better. The alarming increase in our recent losses is entirely due to the actions of one particular Hun scout – the new Fokker E-III monoplane.'

'Which incorporates . . . ?' the major-general began.

'Some kind of synchronization principle, so that the gun fires only when the speed of each bullet permits it to escape between successive rotations of each propeller blade.'

'So all the rounds fired are available for attacking the enemy – and the bloody prop's in no danger?'

'Exactly. The principle, of course, is easy enough. You've got one variable – the rpm of the blades, which depends on the engine revs – and two factors which can be fixed: the firing rate of the gun and the muzzle velocity of the bullets as they leave it. It's a simple enough equation to determine the right mv and firing rate for any given propeller speed, once you know the distance between the gun muzzle and the blades. Not even higher maths. It's the design of the interrupter gear that links these variables efficiently together under all conditions that gives the armourers their headaches. And the details of that, theoretical and mechanical, can be deuced tricky.'

'Perhaps,' Major Hesketh said, 'now that you have outlined the problem, it would be a good time to brief Lieutenant Blake on the manner in which he is going to solve it?'

'Oh, good Lord, yes,' Ravenscraft agreed. 'That's the simplest part of all. The brains here would solve it eventually, of course. Just a question of time. But that's a commodity in short supply this year.' He gestured towards the tell-tale figures on the blackboard. 'As you see, the matter's urgent. What you're going to do, young man' – he smiled at Blake – 'is fly yourself into deepest, darkest Hunland, submerge yourself in the local populace, locate and steal the plans of this Fokker device, and bring them back to us PDQ – preferably using an E-III as transport.'

4

The weather remained unsettled for the rest of that week. HMS *Furious*, the first warship in the world to be defined as an aircraft carrier – that is, equipped with a flying deck for the operation of land planes – ran into heavy seas as she plowed her way northwards off the coast of Holland on the Friday evening.

The 22,000-ton vessel, converted from a battle cruiser designed to mount a pair of enormous eighteen-inch guns, now boasted a hangar and a flight deck along her forecastle. With a top speed of 31.5 knots, the *Furious* normally housed six Sopwith Pups and four seaplanes. Tonight, however, the Royal Naval Air Service was playing host to a cuckoo: one of the Sopwith biplanes had been jettisoned from the nest to make room for the specially modified machine which was to take Lieutenant Blake through the hostile skies of Germany.

It was only weeks since the ship's Senior Flying Officer, Squadron Commander E. H. Dunning, had made the world's first aeroplane landing aboard a vessel under way – side-slipping on to the deck from a forward pass into a combined headwind of 48 knots when a crew of two petty officers and nine men ran up to grab straps attached to the fuselage and haul the machine to a halt. Five days later Dunning had been tragically killed attempting to repeat the performance into an even stronger headwind, when his Pup had been blown over the side into the sea. The RNAS experts were anxious to show Blake, the landlubber, that mistakes are not always the fault of the hired help and if the impossible takes a little while, at least the wet-bobs are liable to do it quicker than anyone else.

Blake himself was not over-anxious to consider the impossible. Hunched behind the canvas dodger in the eastern corner of the flying bridge, he exchanged occasional pleasantries with the sub-lieutenant on watch, glancing up from time to time to meet the impassive gaze of the steersman behind the wheelhouse windshield.

At six-thirty a chill breeze had blown in off some distant ice-cap, whipping the crest of each swell into crumbling foam. Half an hour later the water was more purple than blue, and by seven-fifteen the thin silhouette of the distant coast was awash in a platter of beaten gold. Inside the hood of his storm coat, the sub-lieutenant's tin-hatted features shone ruby red.

Blake listened to the hollow boom of some vibrating structure within the hull, the deep throb of the carrier's engines and the ringing slap of whitecaps against the steel plates. Once the sun had plunged below the western horizon, every shred of cloud had withdrawn from the sky, which now lay as pale and vulnerable as a woman naked on an operating table.

As darkness seeped in from the east, powdering an infinity of stars above the converted cruiser's upperworks, he wondered whether the sky would stay clear until his hazardous take-off soon after dawn, or whether the storms forecast would materialize before he crossed the enemy coast. For the hundredth time he repeated to himself the details of his final briefing.

* * *

It was the War Office cartographer who had provided the most illuminating details. Superseding Sir Alan Ravenscraft on the ops-room dais, he had gone at once to the map – a large, comfortable man with curling iron-grey hair and a loose uniform bearing the crown and flash of a brevet major. He was at present seconded to the Woolwich Arsenal as a ballistics expert, Ravenscraft said. Nobody explained why an authority on the trajectory of artillery shells should be briefing a would-be spy on the theft of blueprints from a German factory. Perhaps, in the corridors of the War Office, it was considered a normal progression.

The expert had picked up a small baton from the desk. 'The factory is in the Upper Hessen *Land*,' he said, 'west of the Teutoburger Wald, an extensive forest, on the outskirts of a small town called Siegsdorf-am-Lippe. The nearest centre of any size is Paderborn. Kassel's about thirty-five miles to the south-east' – he tapped the map with the baton – 'Münster about the same distance to the north-west.' Another tap.

'That's well clear of the Ruhr, I hope,' Major Hesketh interrupted.

'The headwaters of the *River* Ruhr pass through the region,' the cartographer said, 'but the actual industrial area's miles away. About sixty-five to the west. This is pretty much a rural area: woods and fields and that sort of thing. Cobbled streets and half-timbered houses in the towns.'

'And how exactly are you proposing to get my chap there?' Blake's station commander spoke for the first time.

'Somebody mentioned Jutland!' Blake himself interposed.

'Yes, well, that's a bit off the mark! We're flying you in

from the north, but not *that* far north. Planning wallahs in the War Office reckon the best take-off point would be somewhere off the East Frisian Islands, just past the old Dutch frontier. That gives you a southerly course past Oldenburg, between Osnabrück and Minden.'

'To within twenty miles of the target?' the brigadier said. 'In a Sopwith bloody Pup?'

'That's the thinking, sir. Remove the drums of ammo and the Lewis gun on the top wing, make up the weight with a supplementary tank and a few extra gallons. Plus, of course, the Pup's unusually generous wing surface, keeping you aloft higher up, in the thinner air, with less resistance and therefore a consequent saving of fuel. With the additional advantage' – he directed a wintry smile at Blake – 'that if you do run out of juice at that height you have that much longer a glide path before you hit terra firma. Add another five or six miles, I should say.'

The baton described a small arc on the map. 'With luck you should reach this area here, on the lower slopes of the Teutoburger Wald, somewhere between Hameln and Detmold. So far as we know, the factory's part of an industrial estate just outside Siegsdorf – one of half a dozen light engineering works installed to liven up a depressed agricultural region. A Krupp subsidiary, of course. I should add here that plans or blueprints of the interrupter gear being developed at the factory are even more important to the war effort than sight of an actual Fokker Eindekker – welcome though that would be! – because the technicians there are working on an improved version of the original design.'

'Thank you, Charles,' the major-general said. 'That gives us the broad picture, I think. You, young man, will, of course, receive very full local information, plans, maps, equipment, papers, etcetera, before you board *Furious* at Gosport.'

'Yes, sir,' Blake said. 'Thank you, sir.'

'There is one other thing,' the cartographer said, stepping down from the dais. 'Might or might not be useful to you. Still, knowing your background ... fact is, this area, deserted in the eighteenth century, was colonized largely by French Huguenot refugees and remains Protestant today. It's one of the few Hun regions with something of a French cultural tradition. If you get really stuck – well, with Huguenot ancestors yourself you might stumble upon a family not altogether hostile to the Allied cause. You could even get a chance to air your own French!'

'I can't wait,' Blake said.

Below deck, he sat in the narrow cockpit of the Pup and slipped his flying boots under the straps of the rudder bar. *Furious* was rolling heavily in the westerly swell, and he imagined himself already several thousand feet up as the tethered biplane rocked from side to side.

Through the tiny windshield, with its padded leather rim, he stared at the aluminium engine cowling, the single shining propeller blade that was visible and the polished filler caps protruding from the oil and petrol tanks. Two large dials gleamed beneath the leading edge of the cockpit rim – one, on the left, an altimeter; that on the right an airspeed indicator, somewhat optimistically peaking, white figures on a black ground, at 140. Additional fuel and temperature gauges had been installed in this modified machine.

Blake had already, not for the first time, admired the precision engineering of the rotary engine, each cylinder machined from a solid, drop-forged ingot, each cooling fin thin enough to cut a careless rigger's hand. Behind the nine knurled screw-heads of the front-plate, which was integral with the propeller shaft, a film of burned castor oil veiled the dull gleam of metal and copper induction pipes.

'We want to offload you at first light,' the skipper had said. 'Nothing personal, old chap, but we'll be pretty close inshore and there *are* coastal batteries. That way, in any case, you'll be at operational height before sun-up. Apart from denying the Hun gunners a sitting duck offshore!'

Privately, Blake was a little more worried about the Hun gunners on land, in particular those based at Osnabrück, on the northern fringes of the Ruhr – even if they weren't expecting to see enemy aircraft this far north. One of the Western Front maxims he and his observer colleagues had quickly learned in 1915 concerned the fallibility of gunners' eyes. At that stage of the war few could distinguish the difference between an Albatros and an Avro 504, or a Fokker Eindekker and a Morane Saulnier monoplane. An aeroplane, particularly since small bombs had started to be carried, was a potential danger; it was better to shoot first and let somebody else ask the questions afterwards. The FE-2b, whose demise had produced Blake's bogus duelling scar and a deformed upper lip which was masked by his moustache, had in fact been shot down by a nest of French machine-gunners as it planed in to land at Hesdin after a reconnaissance patrol.

Things had improved slightly after RFC roundels had replaced the Union Jacks originally painted on the wings and fuselage of British machines, but pilots remained wary. Blake's Pup in any case carried no identification marks: the doped fabric surfaces had been stippled with a Halberstadt-style camouflage pattern but there were no black crosses on wings or tail. 'I don't know how the rules of war apply to machinery,' the expert seconded from the Royal College of Art had told him, 'but if *you* masquerade in German uniform you could be considered a spy and shot. Better not take a chance, what!'

Blake grinned, thinking of the rigger who had supervised the job, a grizzled veteran known to the squadron's pilots as Rigger Mortis on account of his unvarying pessimism. 'Mark my words, sir,' he had said, eyeing the multicoloured lozenges with disfavour, 'no good will come of this. Dressing the old girl in borrowed clothes just will not do. I mean it stands to reason, don't it?'

'Think of it as going to a party,' Blake had jested. 'In fancy dress.'

'You don't wear fancy dress to crack a safe,' the rigger said gloomily.

Threading his way between the shrouded shapes of seaplanes and RNAS Pups jamming the hangar, Blake returned to the bridge. The marine engines thrummed, the bows smacked sheets of spray from the swell.

The watch had changed. A bearded lieutenant commander huddled into a duffle coat stood talking to the new duty officer, a fresh-faced boy indistinguishable from the last. The lieutenant commander, who was responsible for the stowage and readying of flying machines aboard the *Furious*, nodded a greeting as Blake joined them on the bridge wing. 'Have to drag your bus into the open air in a few minutes, old boy,' he said. 'Sky should be thinning out in the east at any time, and the skipper has a lunch date in Stromness!'

'What's our present position?' Blake asked. 'Approximately.'

'About five miles off the splendidly named island of Schiermonnikoog,' the young man told him. 'Forty miles or so past the entrance to the Zuyder Zee.'

The lieutenant commander was focusing his Zeiss field-glasses on a sector a few degrees off the carrier's starboard bow. 'Right you are,' he said. 'Just right of dead ahead to you.' He handed Blake the binoculars.

It took Blake almost half a minute, but at last – each time the ship rose to a swell – he could make out beyond the streaked tumble of the sea a darker blur imposed on the dark, a thin, black silhouette that must be the Dutch coast north of Groningen. And above this indefinite, undulating line there was a definite difference in the texture of the night.

The stars had faded and died. Stealthily as a sediment draining from a glass of water, the night withdrew from the eastern sky.

Ahead of the carrier, the seas assembled themselves into parallel ridges, markers of a groundswell swinging shorewards over the shoaling continental shelf. The four thin smokestacks of the *Furious* swept across the paling sky in crazy arcs as the carrier, beam-on to the advancing tide, wallowed in the swell.

Minutes later Blake saw that the wind had freshened towards the north, stirring up small waves that raced crosswise over the swell, whipping drifts of spume from the lacework of foam whitening the troubled surface.

'Soon as we have you shipshape and ready,' the lieutenant commander told him, 'we shall wheel offshore, head directly into the wind to ride the bloody swell and give you the maximum lift.' He produced a whistle on a white lanyard and blew three shrill blasts.

Things happened fast after that. Just like the beginning of a rugger match, Blake thought. Excitement, apprehension, fear of failure, a sudden frantic desire to go to the lavatory . . . then the whistle blows, the game has started and you don't think any more, you just do.

The aeroplane, held in position by the launching crew, stood at the inner end of the flight deck, looking curiously fragile in the cold, grey light, fabric wings trembling beneath the blustering wind.

The skipper had come down to wish Blake good luck and offer advice. The LSO – landing signal officer – had last-minute instructions for the take-off. The RNAS rigger breathed encouragement into Blake's ear. He checked the magneto and carburettor inside the access hatch on the metal panel behind the port side of the engine cowling. After shaking hands all round, he clambered into the cockpit.

The skipper swung around and signalled the wheel-house. HMS *Furious* leaned into the swell and sped away from the coast, leaving a broad wake to cream among the whitecaps.

Gauges were scanned, quadrants set, levers trimmed. After an exchange of signals, the propeller was swung. The rotary engine caught with a shattering roar and the Pup shuddered in anticipation against the restraining chocks.

Five minutes before, Blake had noticed a cutter being swung outboard from one of the lower decks, ready to be lowered into the sea. A glance below and a raised eyebrow had stimulated a response from the lieutenant commander. 'In case you tip her into the drink, cock,' the bearded sailor had explained. 'Nothing to be done, in that case, for the bus. But orders are to fish you out, if living, and parcel you back to base.'

This was not an eventuality that Blake wished to consider in any way at all. He wished he hadn't seen the bloody boat.

He had made two trial take-offs from the flight deck of *Furious* when the carrier was in Portsmouth harbour, one of them when she was under way and heading for the Solent. There was no point wasting everybody's time with a deck landing when he wasn't going to be expected to make one. He had simply flown across the water to the aerodrome attached to the flying-boat base at Calshott and then returned to the ship for his second attempt.

The experience had been alarming, but not as alarming as a dawn take-off from behind the lines at Hesdin, in the middle of an artillery barrage.

Jockeying a machine into the air from a stable platform on a sunny day in port – even if the platform was a trifle short on length – had nothing in common, nevertheless, with the same exercise on a heaving battle-cruiser a few miles from the enemy coast in a North Sea gale.

Blake gritted his teeth, listening to the rotary warm up as he kept one eye on the dials and the other on the LSO, immobile in his niche at the far end of the flight deck.

The horizon sank away and then floated up again as the carrier rose, hung, dropped and then rose once more, breasting the swell. The Sopwith Pup's tail was being held up by the crew. The engine bellowed. Arms waved on every side.

The LSO was scything get-on-with-it signals into the air above his head.

The rigger nodded and the chocks were whipped away from the wheels.

Shuddering momentarily, the Pup surged forward.

Blake gave the sturdy biplane everything he had. Hunched over the control column, thighs plastered to the seat, spine in tune with the vibrations of the wood and fabric fuselage, he fed maximum power to the labouring rotary, feet and fingertips alert to every bounce and twitch of the speeding machine as he willed it into the air.

The ship's bows rose three times during the Pup's short run to the end of the flight deck. On the first heave the plane lifted for an instant, but it was still well below its stalling speed, crashing heavily down on to its undercart as the planking dropped away.

Blake was ready for the next swell, holding the machine down to allow the acceleration to build, feathering the stick as he sensed the wings' reaction to the altered wind pressure.

The final lip was terrifyingly near, a blur against the steel-grey waves. The LSO whipped backwards, with open mouth and windmill arms. The aeroplane had nothing more to give. Once more the deck rose, thrusting the Pup away. Blake eased back the stick, praying, clasping the leather top lovingly to his belly.

The Pup hopped into the void. Sank like a wounded bird.

For a deadly instant, he thought they really were going to hit the water. Then the airspeed and the elevator lift combined and they were climbing, clawing their way into the sky ahead of the dwindling carrier, banking steeply to turn south.

'Christ!' Blake yelled into the slipstream. 'Oh, *Jesus*!'

A long, low island slid into view beneath the lower starboard wing. Below and behind, *Furious* was a white arrowhead heading for Scapa Flow. Climbing still, the scout flew on towards the German mainland.

'I hope, gentlemen,' Field Marshal Sir Douglas Haig said to a conference of senior officers at Aldershot in July 1914, 'that none of you is so foolish as to think that aeroplanes will be usefully employed for reconnaissance in the air in any future conflict. There is only one way for a commander to obtain information by reconnaissance and that is through the use of cavalry.'

Fortunately the views of Britain's Commander-in-Chief Land Forces were not shared by everybody, and there were enough adventurous pioneers who had obtained the Royal Aero Club licence to form the nucleus of the Royal Flying Corps in 1912. The original organization was based on the Central Flying School, at Upavon in Wiltshire. The purpose of the CFS was not the basic training of pilots; neither the Army nor the Navy had funds to spare for that. Its role was to convert existing flyers into military aviators. Officers who applied to join had been required to pay their own way through flying centres at Hendon or the motor-racing circuit at Brooklands before they qualified for a course in military flying. If accepted by the RFC they received a refund of £75 towards these costs, but they remained officially on the strength of their old regiments and were only 'attached' to the new military arm.

Patrice Blake, then a junior Territorial officer in the

City of London light infantry regiment quaintly called the Honourable Artillery Company, had been one of these men. But he did not receive an order to attend No. 9 Course of Instruction at the CFS until late 1915, by which time he had been sent to France with the HAC and received a machine-gun bullet through the ankle at the first Battle of Mons.

Instruction at Upavon was tame. The commanding officer, Captain Godfrey Paine, RN, was known throughout the RFC as Bloody Paine because of his vitriolic command of foul language when scolding his pupils. But this violence of approach did not extend to the training programme. At that stage of the war stability and not getting lost were all that was required of the military pilot. The role of the flying machine in war was to provide an aerial observation platform, so most training flights took place in the early morning or late afternoon, when the prevailing winds on Salisbury Plain offered no hazards to flyers.

Suave circuits of the aerodrome, with occasional cross-country forays at a constant altitude in level flight were all that military pilots were expected to master. Abrupt or violent manoeuvres were discouraged: they might tear the wings off the aeroplane. Stunts were actively discouraged, positively forbidden below two thousand feet.

Luckily for Blake, his first posting was to 23 Squadron at Gosport. And the new Squadron Commander was Major Louis Strange, an anti-establishment rebel who got results, a man who was a passionate believer in what he called advanced training. Basic airmanship, in his view, demanded not only the ability to maintain level flight but the skill to evade attack and to launch it.

Before the war Strange had been a barnstormer touring the country with air circuses, club races, competitions to see which pilots could drop bags of flour nearest a ground target from a height of five hundred feet. And he used all the skills learned in this rough-and-tumble profession as part of his military training programme. Strange's pilots were not forbidden to indulge in aerobatics: they were taught them. Instead of avoiding the problems of flight – crosswind take-offs, spins, side-slips and stalls – pupils were encouraged to provoke them deliberately. In this way they should be expert enough to deal with technical difficulties before they had the added embarrassment of a hostile Albatros on their tail.

During his two months as a pilot on the Western Front with 2 Squadron, Blake had profited from this instruction. Major-General Trenchard's maxim – 'No empty seats at RFC front-line mess tables' – had meant that as soon as a pilot was lost he must immediately be replaced from a Home Establishment pool, no matter how inexperienced the newcomer or how small the number of flying hours he had chalked up. In a situation where the RFC was losing more pilots and machines through accidents than through enemy action, Blake's expertise had been something of a marvel to the young men whose expected days of survival were too often counted in single figures. He was no ace – his score was a modest three victories and one probable – but he always brought his plane back. And he was still there.

He hoped fervently, nevertheless, that he would not be called upon to demonstrate these skills afresh during this crazy trip over German territory in an unmarked machine.

Ten thousand feet below, the bleak brown wastes of the peat moors east of Aschendorf and Papenberg glided slowly astern. Oldenburg was a smudge of factory smoke between the Pup's port wingtips.

A long way ahead the flat land rose into a line of low

hills, and above these a distant cloud front drew a dark line across the entire horizon.

He stared at it with mounting concern as the biplane forged ahead through the rarefied air. The forecast had promised clear skies at least until midday, by which time, with luck, he should be back on solid ground. The only cloud formations, they had said, might be forming up behind him, blowing down from the north. The front ahead, he supposed, must be due to some freak or unexpected climatic condition over the industrial furnace of the Ruhr.

The ragged, undulating surface of the front's eastern end suddenly paled, grew a silver edge. A nimbus of glaring light seeped westward. Small drifts of cloud broke free, floated upwards in rosy light, turned white and then dissolved against the aching luminosity of the sky. A blazing arc, incandescent in the early light, hoisted itself above the sombre horizon.

Very slowly, an outsize orange observation balloon, the sun rose brilliantly into the serene, existing day.

Blake wiped the mist of castor oil from his goggles and checked his instruments. Bright shivers trembled the fabric of the wings as the headwind plucked at the stiffened surface. He had been in the air exactly half an hour.

Major Louis Strange had described himself as a 'ragtime flyer'. Blake, curiously enough, had applied the same term to himself when he first started to take flying lessons – although in his case the reference was strictly musical. He had in fact divided his time, when he left school, between the drudgery of an insurance office in the City, the blessed relief of weekend flying at Brooklands . . . and evening work with a group of friends forming a ragtime band in which he was the trap-drummer. It was the wristy skill he had acquired perfecting his rolls and paradiddles that earned him such unusually high marks for 'Morse aptitude' during his flying training. Quick, neat, separate taps at the wireless key were no problem to a man versed in the elite syncopations of *Shimmy-Sha-Wobble* and *Tiger Rag*.

'You'll find it a boon, lad, when you're on the run in Hunland,' Major Hesketh had told him enthusiastically at the end of his very first briefing. 'Particularly comforting when you make first contact with your cut-out.'

'Cut-out?'

'The agent in place. Buffer between you and us. Can't risk only a single bird with the mission at his fingertips. The cut-out forwards your stuff our way, passes on our instructions to you. Buffer between you and the Hun too, if it comes to that. If Fritz latches on to info coming in from us, traces it to the cut-out . . . well, that's only one in the bag. Leaves you free to continue. Even if . . . persuaded . . . the cut-out can't finger you. Can't tell what you don't know, eh?'

'You mean our only contact is through the wireless? We never actually meet?'

'Absolutely. Morse communication only. In code, of course.

'Well, it's nice to know one won't be totally alone,' Blake had said.

He was alone now. Eleven thousand two hundred on the clock and the spars groaning a bit, the cloud front ahead extending, reaching towers of cumulus up into the sky. A couple of teased outliers drifted across the sun, whipping sudden shadow across the wings of the machine.

It was penetratingly cold. The rotary roared reassuringly. Far below, green fields and dark woods sprawled.

He saw a small town with railway lines, a turreted castle on a hill, a loop of river glistening. Off to the east, the shadow of one of the breakaway clouds sculpted a rocky ridge from the flat country.

For the tenth time Blake felt behind his seat to check that the miniature wireless transmitter with its Morse key was there. Contacting the cut-out was all.

It was then, banking slightly to scan the sky below, that he saw the two-seater with its ring-mounted observer's gun and the black crosses on its wing.

Strange and Blake had first met on a special occasion when their two brands of ragtime coincided. It was at the Royal Automobile Club in Pall Mall on 16 January 1914. The occasion was the famous 'Upside Down Dinner' held by the brighter spirits in the flying fraternity to celebrate the exploits of two Hendon pilots – the first Englishmen successfully to loop the loop and also to fly intentionally in an inverted position.

The dinner invitations were printed upside down and back to front, the tables were arranged in the shape of a loop, with upside-down tables on top of normal ones and there was an inverted figure in an upside-down fuselage suspended above. The banquet itself was similarly 'about face'. Starting with coffee, liqueurs and cigars, it progressed through dessert and cheeses to a main course of roasted snipe. After this came lobster, soup, and finally hors-d'oeuvres.

One of the loopers – who had dared to perform his feat a second time with a brave lady passenger – drank half a bottle of champagne from an inverted glass. The other sang 'Two Lovely Black Eyes' standing on his head.

Blake's ragtime band, proudly showing off examples of the new 'jass' specialities imported from the United States aboard the *Mauretania* and other luxury liners, played suitable music in an ante-room throughout the evening.

He didn't see Strange again until he was sent on a course to the tented camp at Hythe which housed Britain's No. 1 School of Aerial Gunnery . . . and found there that the major was his new CO.

Flying alone over northern Germany many months later, he wished fervently that one of the Lewis guns with which he had proved such a fine shot was with him now.

Yes, it was an Albatros all right. One of the C.II reconnaissance versions with the upper wing mounted high above a slender fuselage. The upright engine, projecting through the nose, and the triangular rudder were unmistakable.

Blake cursed. He could out-climb the two-seater, probably outrun it, but an escape would certainly alert them; they would report an unidentified aircraft – and the whole of the north German defences would be on the lookout. All the more so because, according to the latest front-line gossip, many of the German reconnaissance machines were now equipped with wireless installations linking them to their base.

Better avoid that if possible, continue along the straight and level until the cloud cover was reached. Maybe, seeing the Idflieg-style camouflage, they'd think the Pup was a prototype, some kind of experimental machine, without crosses because it wasn't yet in military service.

If, that is, they had seen him at all.

Lowering the starboard wing, he peered over the cockpit rim again.

They had, of course. The German two-seater was climbing, fast. The observer had hauled the machine-gun around on the ring mounting and was crouched over it, squinting up into the bright sky as his pilot coaxed the Albatros aloft.

What the deuce were they doing over this part of Germany anyway, hundreds of miles from the battlefront? Blake thought irrationally. He had been tooling along practically at cruising speed, husbanding the juice in the hope of getting that much nearer the target. Better a ride than a walk in hostile country! But now . . .

Gritting his teeth, he slammed the throttle fully open. The clattering roar of the Le Rhône rose to a bellow. The slipstream punished his oily cheeks and tugged at his helmet.

Below him, the Albatros steepened its climb.

Many people, most of them experts in their own way, had contributed information, analyses, character evaluations, reports and advice on Blake's suitability for a secret mission behind German lines. Along with this wealth of personal opinion went the documentary material – the training reports, the war service, Territorial experience, a military dossier – added to by successive commanding officers – detailing his entire career in uniform. Along with this wealth of intelligence, the competent authorities considered such matters as his physical appearance, his proficiency in the right languages, his sense of loyalty, his initiative and his excellence as a gunner and wireless operator using Morse code.

Curiously, though, what was perhaps the most significant facet of all – certainly to the young man himself – had passed completely undetected through the fine mesh of this official screening. But the fact nevertheless remained: No. 1902818 Blake, Patrice D., of the Honourable Artillery Company, presently on attachment to the Royal Flying Corps, was a physical coward.

6

It was a fact that consumed Blake with self-loathing, but something he had always found it hard – sometimes impossible – to master.

Only twice had this failing been publicly exposed, once when he was fourteen years old, once, much later, at a Territorial camp. But the many hells he had been through, desperate to hide it on subsequent occasions, had scarred him almost more than the original humiliations.

In his final term at an expensive preparatory school, in front of a jeering crowd, he had funked a fight provoked by a younger, smaller but more aggressive boy – panicking to run home and fake an attack of flu that would keep him away for the few remaining days of term.

The affair at the Territorial camp was worse. It was during an exercise on Salisbury Plain. Blake and a fellow cadet were running to intercept an 'enemy' soldier driving a lightweight scout car. The driver saw them, swung the vehicle brutally around to make a getaway and tipped it over into a deep ditch, where it immediately caught fire.

Blake and his friend raced towards the blazing wreck. But once they were within reach of the scorching breath of the flames, Blake stopped dead. His friend dashed on, plunged into the inferno and emerged, smoking, dragging the injured driver.

Blake had no idea why he stopped. It was no conscious decision. He just did.

On subsequent occasions fear had driven him now this way, now that, sometimes into what appeared a logical course of action, sometimes not. But he had always contrived to conceal that basic, innate motivation – the dry-mouthed impulse to turn and run that no argument of the mind, however fierce, could overcome.

Hide it successfully, that is, from others; not from himself.

He had more than once manoeuvred himself into situations liable to provoke the craven reaction, believing until it was too late that meeting the danger halfway might annul it. He had allowed himself to be placed in positions where his activities were controlled by others, imposed upon him by authority, and not the results of his personal decisions. Joining the Royal Aero Club and forcing himself to learn to fly was an example of the first of these ploys; becoming a member of the HAC as a 'Terrier' of the second.

After the fluid, not quite believable campaigns of Mons and the Marne, he had welcomed the bullet which had invalided him home from the hell of the static trench warfare which followed. And he had volunteered to join the RFC as a panic alternative – any alternative – to avoid a return to the shell-torn desolation of the Somme.

In the air the danger was somehow not quite so personal: as an observer, control of his movements was out of his hands; as a pilot, his skills were sufficient to keep him largely out of trouble, especially in single-seaters.

And then this . . . this damnable mission. At first his fear of being thought a coward if he refused it had overcome his trepidation at the idea of actually doing it.

And then it was too late: here he was, smack in the middle of it.

Being stalked by two Huns with machine-guns. Flying an unarmed aeroplane.

Blake was already at an altitude not far short of twelve thousand feet. There was the risk that the south-westerly headwind which had proved the forecasters wrong and was piling up the clouds ahead of him could start draining fuel from the tanks. Lack of oxygen was already causing him pain in the chest. And if he did squander fuel climbing still higher there was no proof that the German might not match him. He had no information on the ceiling of the two-seater Albatros: the black crosses were widely spaced; the wing surfaces looked generous, practically as spacious as the Pup's. It was certainly possible . . .

Better to increase speed by losing height and make for that cloud.

He pushed the throttle up to maximum and eased the stick forward. The scout's bulbous nose dropped and the engine screamed. They streaked down towards the towering mountain of cumulo-nimbus.

The Albatros, perhaps no more than two hundred feet below, changed course to vector on an interception course which would bring it up under the Pup before Blake reached the clouds. The observer's ring-mounted Spandau was already canted up at its steepest angle.

The cloud mass was expanding at an alarming rate. Below the frothed white billows roiling upwards into two separate hammerheads, the colours and texture of the barrier altered dramatically. The darkest, most menacing sector, at a height perhaps of five or six thousand feet, was in constant movement, writhing from a pearly tint through slate grey to a black that was almost purple. As he watched through his tiny screen,

Blake saw blue lightning fork to the sombre landscape beneath.

Beneath the leather of his flying helmet, hairs on the nape of his neck tingled. His feet felt heavy and cold as ice. Nausea clawed at his stomach. But whether he was running because he was scared or because the priorities of the mission demanded it was a question that was purely academic now. No time here for introspection, doubts or self-interrogation. Just do it, man . . . and hope.

The storm clouds raced towards him. Strips of fabric flicked from the port wing, fluttering wildly in the slipstream. Blake looked over his shoulder. He saw holes in the tailplane, a long tear in the rudder. The Albatros, still a hundred feet below and half as much again astern, was firing at him!

He banked steeply, rolled once in the hope of fazing the Hun pilot, then dropped the Pup into a dive that was almost vertical.

Wooden spars in the fuselage behind him shuddered as a stream of bullets from the German two-seater – now level with him, now slightly above – ploughed through the stressed fabric skin.

Then wisps of teased-out grey were racing past, the darkened cumulus above blacked out the sun . . . and the visual world vanished: he was alone in a world that was totally black.

He kept the throttle wide open and continued on a compass course approximately south-west by south.

The aeroplane dropped sickeningly and then was buoyed up as arbitrarily as a ping-pong ball on a fountain jet. It was hopeless trying to keep control of it. He was completely at the mercy of the storm centre into which he had flown. All he could do was take advantage of every little chance allowed him by the elements, throttling back when the bracing wires screamed, keeping the stick held slightly forward if there was a momentary lull.

Sometimes, when the thumping of the machine abruptly ceased, he felt as though he was floating alone in the void, with only the weight of his body thrown against his safety belt to connect him with the structure of wood and metal and doped fabric he was controlling. Then he could think of nothing but what to pull, push or swing in an attempt to roll it back on to an even keel. Once, aware of a disastrous side-slip only by the howling hurricane tearing at his left cheek, he was convinced that the Albatros had miraculously caught up with him and was peppering the plane from all sides. The thunder and shriek of the weather was momentarily eclipsed by a violent tattoo on the aerofoil surfaces as they dropped through a violent eruption of hailstones the size of frozen loganberries.

Fear was as much of an abstraction as logical thinking in this maelstrom; the will to survive, something welling up from deep in his being, had seized control of the motor reflexes, willing them to act as experience dictated.

Blake knew that they must have been losing height for an eternity, and he throttled down at last, waiting for the ground to appear through the curtain of torrential rain.

All at once he was aware of light, and the stair-rods of rain were silver. A church spire, an onion dome with a sharp steeple, upside down, appeared above his starboard wingtip. Surprise was beyond him. All he could think of was to set it back the right way up. Automatically he handled his controls.

The spire flicked out of sight and reappeared, correctly aligned, below the Pup's port wing.

He slammed forward the throttle, pulling back the stick

as the machine roared into bright light. He was less than a hundred feet above a stretch of waste ground, with a line of trees, a huddle of gabled houses beyond a river ahead. Ant-like figures scattered across a stone bridge as he zoomed up and over the steep, tiled roofs.

And then, astonishingly, above a range of low hills in the east, there was a flood of golden light, an arc of brilliance, and the sun rose splendidly into view to bathe that peaceful post-storm landscape in the luminescence of a new day.

'What-ho, what-ho!' Blake cried aloud. 'A chap for whom the sun rises twice in the same day can do no bloody wrong!' He pulled back the stick and started to climb.

The violent loss of height which had afforded him two separate views of the rising sun filled him suddenly with a confidence both in the aeroplane and in the mission as a whole which until then had been noticeably absent. Alone in the narrow cockpit as he nursed the machine back up to ten thousand feet, he began to sing.

Falling away beneath him, the lush green curves and rectangles of the summer countryside dwindled to a random patchwork sewn together by the bright threads of metalled roads and an occasional shining railway line. Once he saw dark smoke from a freight train blown across a scorched brown field dotted with tiny haystacks.

Far away to the east, blue hills rose into the sky. The Harz Mountains, he supposed. And, a little nearer, the multiple twists and turns of a broad river in a valley that must be the Weser on its tortuous way to Bremen and the North Sea.

There were more clouds ahead, but they were of the white, cotton-wool variety and there were patches of clear sky in between. It was two hours since he had left the flight deck of the *Furious*. Studying the map fixed below the windshield with its chinagraph arrows and symbols – and allowing for loss of time and wastage of fuel because of the Albatros and the storm which had enabled him to escape it – he estimated that he was probably halfway between Hanover and Osnabrück in the east–west sense, perhaps a dozen miles short of the waterway linking the Weser with the Dortmund–Ems ship canal.

And, yes, cloud shadows skipping over woods and pastures below, undulating now across the roofs of larger towns, were running into a smoky haze veiling the land to the west. Dark fumes belched from factory chimneys above the serrated glass roofs of workshops in a spider's web of railway lines. He was approaching the eastern fringe of the Ruhr.

This would be the area of maximum danger. The Ruhr, cradle of the Kaiser's entire war effort, home of the armaments industry, the Krupp complex, most of the aviation works, was Germany's most vulnerable target after the submarine pens at Kiel and the shipyards of Hamburg and Bremerhaven. It would certainly be heavily defended, even if it was far out of range of normal aircraft based on the present battlefront. And the Albatros observer would by now have reported an unidentified aeroplane flying that way, even if the burgomaster of the village Blake had so narrowly missed had not.

He didn't have to wait long to find out the truth.

He had just located the canal, a leaden ribbon, ruler-straight across the misty landscape ahead, when the Pup lurched suddenly, dropping like a stone for fifty feet as he wrestled with the stick. He hadn't heard the explosion and it was only afterwards that he remembered the smoke whipping past his face.

That near miss had been a freak chance for the gunners below, but the sky was now pock-marked with shell bursts, on either side and as far ahead as he could see – brown, white, black pricked out with scarlet, a series of cracking detonations that drowned the rotary's steady roar.

They hadn't quite got the range yet – that first one had been a lucky miss – but the way ahead was laced with spinning shrapnel. Archie, as flyers nicknamed the fire from ack-ack or anti-aircraft batteries, was flinging up everything he had.

Blake's mouth was dry. He felt as if all the blood in his body had drained to his feet. His safety belt clawed at his queasy stomach as he hurled the Pup into a dive to get up enough speed for the steep climb he needed. The murderous sky continued to erupt all around him. Air shrieked through tears in his lower wing. And after Archie, he knew, fighters would be waiting to pounce. At the top of his climb, for the second time that day, he ran for the clouds.

This time he was equally blinded, but by brightness and whiteness rather than the sombre gloom of the hammerhead. Pale scarves and streamers and ribbons of livid mist, ripped apart from the seemingly solid cloud mass by the scything disc of his propeller, flicked between the wings and past his goggled head. The engine laboured, gaining height.

And then suddenly he was drenched in warmth. Through the uppermost layer and out into the aching blue, he saw the sun, high now in the sky, dazzling the eye with the magic vision no flyer ever really tires of. Level as a marine horizon, the bubbling snowfield stretched as far as he could see in every direction.

As he skims this continent of ice-white cloud, the earth

below becomes to the flyer an abstraction, someone else's dream. Blake forgot his fear, forgot the danger, allowed the priorities of the mission to fade from his mind. The compass bearing was a shaking blur, the fuel level was menacingly low, but he lived only in the joy of his weightless existence, in the mastery of the elements granted to him by the contraption of wood and wire and metal that he controlled. The haphazard patterns of brown and blue and green visible through the occasional gaps in the cloud floor were as one-dimensional, as lacking in immediacy, as the printed symbols on his map.

Until he saw the German planes.

There were three of them, flying in close formation, perhaps three or four hundred feet below among isolated tufts of white which had torn free of the main cloud mass.

Two Pfalz D-III scouts led by a Halberstadt single-seater. The leader was unmistakable, with its single elevator and small rudder on an isolated pivot, the crescent-shaped exhaust projecting vertically above the exposed engine block. The Pfalz fighters, with their trapezoid strut formations, also had exposed in-line engines high above their pointed noses. They were silver, with thick black lines painted horizontally between the propeller boss and the cockpit, and red stripes zigzagged from cockpit to tail. The Halberstadt fuselage was pearl grey, with wings and tail in a stipple camouflage not unlike Blake's own.

The formation was flying on a course only a few degrees off the Pup's. Their bracing wires and control cables glinted in the bright sunlight . . . until the fleeting moment when the shadow of Blake's scout passed over the German leader and one of his wingmen.

Both the German fighter types had been designed with

the upper wing very low down and close to the fuselage. This restricted forward view from the cockpit, which was set fairly far back; but a semicircular cut-out in this upper wing allowed the pilot excellent upward vision.

Automatically, each man glanced above. They saw the stranger at once. The leader waved, banked and set the Halberstadt into a steep climb.

Cursing, Blake went cold all over. His machine was lighter than the Germans', but the Halberstadt was powered by a 120hp Argus engine, the Pfalz by a 160hp Mercedes and his Le Rhône peaked at no more than 80hp.

The Germans carried wing-mounted 7.92mm Spandau machine-guns.

He was two hundred, three hundred yards from the far side of the gap. Certainly he could dive down, plunge back into the clouds before they were within range, but by the time he was lost to sight they would have arrived at the same altitude. They would expect him to take evasive action once he was invisible. If he was the flight leader, Blake thought, he would direct one of the wingmen to veer left, the other right, in the hope of locating him once visibility returned. Perhaps the leader himself would keep roughly the same course, but lower down, where the cloud carpet thinned and broke up.

Playing a double bluff, Blake took no evasive action at all: he maintained his original course, height and speed.

He flew out into the next break much earlier than he expected, much sooner than he had hoped. The sun was tiresomely bright. He wiped oil mist from his goggles with the back of one glove. One of the Pfalz scouts was a speck far away on his left. There was no sign of the other. But the Halberstadt – he saw with horror, dipping the starboard wings – was immediately behind him, about fifty feet below. A perfect position for the sucker kill, coming up from beneath the tail, the machine's blind spot, with guns blazing.

There was only one thing Blake could do. The next bank of cumulus was half a mile ahead. If he dived he would offer his belly to the German's Spandaus. It was too late for the classic banked turn on wingtips. On full power, he hauled the stick back and sent the Pup shooting up into the first half of a loop.

At the zenith of the manoeuvre, when the plane was upside down, he half rolled it on to an even keel and flew back the way he had come, completing a perfect example of the aerobatic stunt turn invented by the German ace Max Immelmann.

Facing this way, the clouds were much nearer. Blake put the nose down and dived.

Anticipating this, the Halberstadt pilot had wheeled steeply. Blake had an instant vision of flaming guns as he plummeted past. There was a sudden heavy jolt from somewhere amidships. And then he was shrouded again, thankfully blotted out by the merciful cumulus, gift-wrapped in cotton wool!

He emerged at about six thousand feet, the compass swinging wildly, and gazed desperately right and left in an attempt to relocate his bearings. Was that wide waterway dotted with a string of barges the Dortmund–Ems canal? There was no sun here to help. But, yes, those rolling, wooded heights on his right must be the Teutoburger Wald.

Except they should be on his left.

He swung the Pup around in a wide turn and began easing the stick back to coax it out of its dive.

Wind whistled and shrieked through the wires. The

engine roared. Tears in the wing surface flapped frenziedly. And from somewhere below the floorboards there was a heavy thumping, punctuated at intervals by a metallic rasp.

Blake bit his lip. The machine wasn't answering to the controls as swiftly as he expected. She was sluggish to react, with a tendency to yaw, the starboard wingtips canted up.

He was sweating, a thousand feet lower down, by the time he straightened the Pup out. It was then that he saw one of the Pfalz scouts, a mile away on his port quarter, heading directly for him.

And it was then that the rotary, having squandered what was left of its fuel in the past few hectic minutes, coughed, choked, caught again for an instant and finally whined into silence. The airscrew spun to a halt.

For a hundredth of a second, Blake froze. Then the experience gained through dozens of lessons, of lectures, of mock dogfights and aerobatics, took control. The expertise of the instructors at the Central Flying School, Major Strange at 23 Squadron, the 2 Squadron battles over the hell of the Somme – from the depths of his combat memories an automatic evaluation of the situation, a consideration of the options, a decision on the right course of action took over.

Jockeying the control column, feet fighting the rudder bar, he sent the powerless machine into the famous height-losing escape known as the falling-leaf stunt – a series of alternating side-slips, right and left, that gained no ground but brought the earth near with frightening speed.

Wind sighing through the struts and wires now hummed an alto descant.

The Pfalz drew closer, preparing to circle . . .

Perhaps, seeing that the machine was crippled, the German pilot would hold his fire and simply watch it die? A kill was a kill, whether the final crash was due to the death of the aeroplane or its driver.

On one of his more violent side-slips, Blake felt an extra-heavy thump from beneath him . . . and saw with disbelief a wheel, two V struts and part of an axle whirl away below. Shots from the flight leader must have wrecked his undercarriage, and now part of it had broken away.

He gritted his teeth. A crash landing with half the undercart still in place implied a ground loop unless he was very lucky.

But a crash landing where?

He was over open country. A village with a tall church spire, sliding rapidly away on his right. Cornfields separated by twisting lanes. Woods, too many woods, carpeting the high ground on each side of a river. A stretch of moorland in the distance – but it looked as though the heath was strewn with boulders.

Nose down, the Pup was corkscrewing into a spin. With a supreme effort, the sweat coursing into his eyes, Blake flattened the machine out two hundred feet above a mill-race where a turreted manor spanned the stream. The Pfalz circled a respectable height overhead.

There was no choice now: he was into the final glide with no lift available to him. It would have to be the slanting field of cabbages . . . no, perhaps the stubbled meadow beyond. Trees, hedgerows, a weeded pond with a flurry of ducks, hurtled towards him.

Blake's hands were steady on the controls. He dropped the Pup on the far side of a blackthorn thicket. It pancaked with a rending crash, bounced into the air, nosedived with enough force to tear off a lower wing, then cartwheeled into a haystack.

Silence.

And then the small sounds, near and far, defining the time and place. The tick of cooling metal, rooks cawing in the distance, a creak of wood as the wreckage settled, wind blowing. Somewhere above, through the cloying stench of hot castor oil, he could hear liquid dripping.

And above that the regular beat of an aero engine.

Blake had to think very quickly. The briefing, dealing with forced landing, had not bargained for an enemy spectator, circling several hundred feet above.

There were two priorities: get away fast; and at the same time let the Pfalz pilot think he had perished in the crash. That way, until salvage teams called from the nearest town discovered there was no body, he might stave off a manhunt for long enough to get clear of the immediate area.

Whether or not he destroyed the Pup, they had told him, was of less importance.

Blake thought he might use that third factor, nevertheless, to help with the other two.

But first, quickly, he must have freedom of action. He was upside down in the open cockpit, hanging from his safety harness. In that situation, according to the CFS drill, the unfortunate pilot waited for rescuers to run up and free him. Suspended so close to the ground, a man fumbling with buckles could drop out on to his head and break his neck before he could reach down arms to cushion the fall.

No rescuers here, though. He had seen no workers in the fields, but the whole thing must be over before peasants or people from the manor hurried to investigate the crash.

There was a Very pistol beneath the seat. Blake reached above him to free this and allowed the heavy weapon to fall. He dropped the small rucksack which contained his maps, the proofs of his new German identity, and other necessities thought up by the intelligence experts at Gosport. Then he wedged his toes beneath the two sections of the rudder bar and felt for the buckles.

The Pfalz was still circling above.

Cramp in his left instep, agonizing in its intensity, seized the muscles of that leg. He felt the toe slipping from its hold as he wrestled with the harness. Why were these *bloody* belts always so difficult to free?

The cramp moved on, knotting his calf. He yelled, feeling the foot swing stiffly free. His whole weight was depending on the flexed muscles of his right foot now . . . and he could sense the preliminary indications of cramp flickering there too.

With a gasp of relief, he felt the straps loosen and slide away. He withdrew his right foot, snatched out his arms and reached above his helmeted head.

Blake hit the ground in a shoulder roll, backing away at once in the shadow of an undamaged upper wing, dragging the pistol and the rucksack with him.

He hoped the wreck as a whole would conceal his movements. How long was it since they hit? It seemed an eternity but was probably less than a minute. They didn't always burst into flame on impact; sometimes it took time for the volatile fumes to ignite. He just hoped the Hun pilot was aware of that.

There were two rounds with the Very pistol, one green and one red. Although the tanks had run dry, he reckoned there should be enough petrol fumes still evaporating to combine with the air and form an explosive mixture – especially in the heat of a magnesium flare.

The red one, he thought. Face down at the extremity of the sheltering wing, he supported himself on his elbows and sighted the long-barrelled gun. Bristly stalks from the stubble pricked through his trousers at the knee. His left foot was still giving him hell.

Aiming up into the cockpit, between the controls, he pressed the trigger. And then swung around at once to fire the green flare into the centre of the haystack against which the remains of the aeroplane were leaning. The results were spectacular.

For an instant the cockpit glowed a blinding, incandescent crimson. Then the tanks exploded with a dual thump and the entire nose of the plane, from the smashed propeller where it had dug into the ground, erupted into a blazing fireball. Milliseconds later the fuselage was afire.

The longerons and formers of the tail, along with the struts and every single aerofoil section supporting the doped, inflammable fabric of the wings, were made of wood. All at once the Pup was no more than a fiery cross, flaming to life at the same time as the tinder-dry haystack in a crackling inferno.

From the foot of this towering holocaust, where the oily engine burned, a column of black smoke marbled with red leaned away across the meadow as the west wind blew. Beneath it, fleeing the scalding breath of the fire, Blake raced for the nearest hedgerow.

He lay flat in a ditch, watching the Pup's funeral pyre as he massaged the cramp from his foot. Soon the Pfalz overhead banked to turn north and flew away.

Blake crawled through the hedge, crossed a sunken lane and vanished into a wood. For the third time that day he ran – but this time under orders and not from a panic beyond his control.

7

'The aeroplane is – was – a Sopwith. There can be no doubt about that,' the area *Kommandant* announced.

'But, sir, how can we be sure? There was nothing left of the machine – nothing but a pile of smoking embers. And, of course, the damaged engine.'

'Precisely. A Le Rhône rotary. Favoured by Sir Thomas Sopwith for many of his designs. Two brass plates with series numbers which survived the fire relate to the Boulton and Paul factory in the city of Norwich, and to Britische Caudron of Cricklewood. Both companies are subcontracted to produce Sopwith machines – at least according to your own service, *Herr Hauptmann*,' the *Kommandant* said acidly.

The young officer who had rashly interrupted flushed. He had only recently been seconded to the foreign intelligence branch of the German secret service and had yet to learn that the wise agent told very senior officers only what they wished to hear.

'It is true that those concerns also fabricate parts for other machines,' the *Oberst* in charge of the local defence squadron observed. 'But the pilot from my No. 2 Flight who pursued the aeroplane through the clouds and eventually shot it down is convinced, despite the lack of markings, that it was a Sopwith. And an observer on a training flight in an Albatros Doppeldekker reported from a sector further north that he had sighted an unidentified intruder flying on a course approximately south-east by south. He too was convinced that the machine was an *Englander*, although he was unable to specify what type.'

The three men, together with the area police commissioner and a civilian from the Ministry of Defence in Berlin, were sitting around a refectory table in the great hall of Hohenstein Castle, a turreted fortress on a spur overlooking the Upper Weser district. The *Kommandant* had requisitioned the castle as his staff headquarters.

'A Sopwith then,' he repeated now, 'although we do not know whether it might have been the so-called one-and-a-half-strut version, an example of the new scout they call for some reason a camel, or the small dog . . .'

'The Pup,' the *Oberst* said.

'Exactly. The Puppy-dog. How absurd the *Englander* is, with his unhealthy regard for animals!'

'One of our agents reports that the Sopwith company is experimenting with a prototype that possesses *three* wings,' the *Hauptmann* put in rashly.

'Indeed. Well, here we are contenting ourselves with two.'

'But, with respect, *Herr General-Major*' – the civilian spoke for the first time – 'how can an enemy machine, an *Englander*, possibly be seen over that part of the Fatherland?' He glanced at a typed report on the table in front of him. 'Between Vechta and Diepholz, flying *south*? And then, further still, down here in Lower Saxony?'

'You have read the reports,' the *Oberst* said. 'They are factual.'

'Oh, I do not doubt that a machine was seen, that it was shot down near Detmold. But a *British* machine?

Could it not possibly be an intruder from the east, from the Russian front?'

The *Oberst* laughed. 'Your geography, my friend! From Osnabrück, where our observers first sighted the intruder and where it was fired upon by the defence gunners – from Osnabrück to the nearest part of the Russian frontier is more than one thousand kilometres. And at that point the machine still had enough fuel for a further ninety or a hundred!'

'It is not so much the damned machine,' the police commissioner objected. 'That is an academic question. It is the past. An aeroplane was here; it was destroyed. The question now is: what happened to the pilot? Did he perish with that machine, or did he somehow escape? If so, where is he and what is he doing? Why was he coming in the first place? And who was he?'

'It was a single-seater,' the *Kommandant* said. 'At least all the reports agree on that. So he was alone. It is clear, moreover, that he must have been flying to a predetermined plan, that he *intended* to penetrate the country as far – or further – than he did. This was no erring fool or overzealous scout. Particularly as the Sopwith appeared to be unarmed. No, he meant to come – and from wherever he came, whoever he was, he must have known he could never get back. What does that imply?' He looked at the *Oberst*.

'Bearing in mind that the machine bore no distinctive markings,' the aviation chief replied, 'a most ungentle-manly departure in my opinion, and remembering that the camouflage resembled our own, I would say that the purpose of the flight was indubitably clandestine. Clearly the man is – or was – some kind of spy. As my colleague points out' – he glanced at the policeman – 'the question is which. Is or was?'

'There was no body in the wreckage,' the *Hauptmann* said. 'Surely that implies that the man got away?'

'Could a man, even an uninjured one, have escaped such a blaze?' the *Kommandant* asked.

The civilian, who was an arson investigation inspector, nodded. 'It is not impossible,' he said. 'Unlikely but not impossible.'

'We are talking of the possibility of a *body* in the wreckage,' the *Kommandant* pursued. 'But there was no wreckage, not in the usual sense. Just a heap of ashes around an incinerated rotary engine. I have been to the site; I saw this myself. Wouldn't a body naturally have been consumed in such an inferno?'

This time the civilian shook his head. 'Not necessarily. Largely consumed, yes. The fire was extremely fierce . . . but it did not last long. Even if the corpse was destroyed as such, the flesh etcetera, there would be indications: bone perhaps identifiable as part of a skull, a watch case, the metal rims from a pair of goggles. Something that could positively be said *not* to be an aeroplane component.'

'And there was nothing?'

'Not a thing,' the policeman said. 'My men combed through the hot ash three times. Nothing.'

'Then we must assume,' the *Kommandant* said heavily, 'that we have an infiltrated spy in the area. A spy at large. Your dispositions, *Herr Inspektor*, must be based on that assumption.'

'The entire *Polizeikräfte*, every station, every substation, each individual agent in the region will be alerted,' the commissioner promised. 'There would be "Wanted" posters on each tenth telegraph pole – if we knew what the man looked like.'

'Exactly. If we knew. But we are only *assuming* he exists at all.'

'The population will also be warned. Every stranger, each man below a certain age, any person not known by sight must be reported. Clearly the intruder will be young: aviators are required, after all, to have a certain standard of fitness. And there are not too many able-bodied young in this region after almost three years of war.'

'Exactly,' the *Kommandant* said again. 'It must be remembered, however, that the *Englanders* are not altogether fools. They will not have gone to all this trouble without finding someone who has at least a chance of passing unnoticed. You will not, that is to say, be looking for a straw-hatted pipe-smoker carrying a cricket racket.'

The man from the Ministry of Defence smiled dutifully, and said: 'Most importantly, of course, it must be discovered *why* he is here. Militarily, this is not after all a "sensitive" area. But it is almost equally urgent to discover precisely *how* such a machine could penetrate this far, from that direction. The spy must be closely interrogated. If necessary with severity.'

'Naturally,' the police chief said. 'As soon as he is captured.'

8

Blake had watched the staff cars arrive at the castle, flat on his face in a grove of alders on the far side of the river.

Two open Mercedes 28/95 tourers led the parade, their sharp V radiators glinting in reflected sunlight as they rumbled across a stone bridge a little further downstream. The young officer lolling on the rear seat of the first was accompanied by only his driver and a steel-helmeted NCO holding a carbine upright between his knees. The second car flew from its offside front wing the pennant of 12 squadron. The *Oberst* ramrod-straight in this one had a four-man escort: one man beside the driver and two more perched on tip-up seats in the rear. The car was closely followed by a green police saloon.

It was five minutes before the last arrival appeared around a distant bend in the riverside lane: a huge black Maybach landaulette-limousine. The uniformed chauffeur behind the wheel in the open, doorless front wore polished leather buskins and a peaked cap. The single passenger in the closed rear section was a civilian.

Parting leaves, Blake noted the alacrity with which the black and gold iron gates of the castle were swung open, the crispness of the sentries' salutes as the big car swept through, and assumed the newcomer was someone of considerable importance. He had no way of knowing that the hastily called conference was in connection with his own appearance – or lack of it – in the area. But it seemed a fair guess anyway that it was an area to get out of quickly if top brass from the army, the air force and the police were meeting in what was clearly some kind of staff headquarters.

The river was not very wide here, the fast-flowing water dappled with sunlight filtering through the trees overhanging it on either side. But the castle itself, soaring above a double loop of steeply climbing drive, was iron-hard in the midday glare. Judging by the amount of military movement visible beneath its multiple turrets and pepper-pot spires, the garrison must be important. Through the arched entrance gateway he saw two squads of soldiers, and then a third, marched to roofless transport lorries. The throb of their engines carried clearly across the river. As the first truck emerged through the archway he pushed himself back from the alder clump and moved hastily further up the wooded slope of the valley.

Blake had covered twelve miles in a south-westerly direction in the two and a half hours immediately after his crash landing, mainly across fields and through sparsely forested uplands. Crouched low behind the uncut hedgerows, he had bypassed the few country folk he had seen working on the land. Only twice had he been obliged to make circuitous detours to avoid a village.

Reaching the valley, he had found an empty wood-cutter's cabin among the trees and remained there for the night. Now it was time to push on again.

Once you're in a town of any size, they had told him, come out into the open, have a meal, a drink in a bar; take a bus, a train. Your German's perfect, your cover good. But stay hidden in the country, keep off the roads, travel only at night if you can. It's there that a stranger will show up like a flashing lamp – and that's what they'll be on the lookout for.

The cover, he supposed, *was* pretty good – although he hadn't yet been called upon to test that. His stomach turned over at the thought.

He was dressed in genuine German clothes, garments that might have been worn by a minor official – a belted jacket in thick cloth, with breeches, heavy stockings and laced ankle boots. The labels in the outer garments were those of a Hamburg department store. He hadn't asked how the intelligence people had obtained them.

Because of his 'duelling' scar and his German accent, it had been thought better to give him a cover as a bourgeois rather than a worker. Beneath his tweed hat with its shallow brim, the moustache that masked the second scar was now bushy rather than clipped in the RFC fashion.

The genuine bullet wound, visible in his left ankle, which had left him with a genuine limp, sufficed as an explanation for why he wasn't in uniform. And if asked he could supply a perfectly truthful account of how he got it, for the army discharge papers with which he had been supplied were those of a soldier from a regiment in action during the first Battle of Mons.

He carried a small expandable briefcase containing documents and technical material establishing that he was one Gerhardt Ehrlich, representative of a Hamburg electrical firm, on a permitted promotional tour seeking orders from factories engaged in domestic production in central Germany. Factories whose own supplies might have been compromised by scarcities caused by increasing demands from the front.

The rucksack, the Very pistol and every non-German

item Blake had carried on his flight had been wrapped in his leather flying coat, weighted with stones and sunk in a pond in the middle of a dense wood.

He had about forty miles to cover before he reached Siegsdorf-am-Lippe. Detmold, Paderborn and Lippstadt were the only towns of any size on his route.

By far the most dangerous obstacle, however, was the miniature wireless transmitter with which he was to contact – and subsequently report to – his intelligence cut-out.

True, it was German-made, and bore on its underside a stamped intaglio serial number and the information that it had been manufactured in 1912 by Radifonik Schwerzel GmbH of Bielefeld. Certainly it fitted inside the briefcase without making it too bulky. But what was he doing with it? What did he use it for? How could he possibly explain it if he was searched or it was discovered in any other way? It could not in any way be said that it had a connection, however tenuous, with any of the equipment he was supposedly trying to sell to companies supplying installations to the domestic market, whether for the home or office.

The obvious answer would have been to find a hiding place for it, only removing the thing for the hour, early each evening, during which the cut-out would be listening in, waiting for his message.

This would have been fine if he had already arrived at Siegsdorf, or had any other static base, but was clearly a non-starter for anyone constantly on the move.

His first transmission, the important initial contact, was due that evening.

It was hard going at first, working his way upstream from the castle; the sides of the valley grew increasingly steep, the underbrush beneath the densely packed trees increasingly thick. And there was the additional consideration, forcing his way between branches and briars, that he must keep his clothes looking reasonably respectable for when he did finally appear in public. This would be at Detmold, five miles down the wooded slope of the Teutoburger Wald, on the far side of the saddle at the head of this damned valley. Before then, nevertheless, the transmission must be made.

In fact he reached the saddle long before he expected. This was because of an error in the generalized, small-scale sketch map of the whole region supplied by the intelligence briefers in London. He had thought the river much less 'important' than its reputation warranted. But it was only when he started to use the detailed, large-scale German map that he considered it safe to carry that he discovered the truth: this was not the Weser at all, but a tributary west of it, running in a parallel valley towards a confluence just south of Hameln.

He was therefore one ridge of the Teutoburger Wald nearer to Detmold than he had planned for. Unless he wanted to spend another night in the open, he would have to push on as fast as he could and send his message from the town itself.

Ahead of schedule now, he quite enjoyed the rolling alternations of forest and meadow which dropped steeply down on the far side of the saddle. Detmold, the capital of the Westphalian principality of Lippe, lay sprawled across the lowest slope; it was a pleasant market town grouped around a rectangular Renaissance castle.

Once on the outskirts, of course, he had for the first time to use the roads, but traffic was light – farm carts piled high with vegetables, horse-drawn drays, an occasional bus, very few private cars. Nobody seemed to notice the young man in the Norfolk-style suit with his neat briefcase and heavy moustache.

The centre – narrow cobbled streets full of tall, half-timbered houses with steep, dormered roofs – was busier, as it was five o'clock. The railway station, he thought, was the most believable place for a stranger to appear. He loitered beneath a bridge until a train was due, then left in the middle of a crowd of passengers who had just arrived from Hanover. He went into a *Weinstübe* across the street and ordered a glass of white Franconian wine.

Not surprisingly, the gossip around the sawdust-floored bar was largely concerned with the aeroplane crash beyond the wooded heights the day before.

'It was between Barntrup and Bad Pyrmont – you know: where there's a weir and that fortified mill built across the stream.'

'Shot out of the sky by one of the aces from the Boelke Jagdstaffel. Went up like a . . . well, like a house on fire!'

'They say it was coming from the *north*! I must say that's a bit . . .'

'Nonsense. It couldn't have been. I think . . .'

'Well it couldn't have got here from the *Western* Front, that's for sure.'

'Just the same, it was an *Englander*. My nephew told me he saw the . . .'

'There were no markings on the machine. That's official. Frenzel was talking to the training squadron observer who first saw it. It was definitely British though.'

'I don't believe it. Not *here*. If you ask me, it was a Tsarist aeroplane – a Russian spy, an anarchist.'

'*Russian?* You can't be serious! Do you know how far . . . ?'

'Fact. One of the firemen told me. It was the melted snow from their boots put out the flames.'

Laughter. And then: 'Good old Ernst! Trust him not to miss an opportunity.'

'You say *their* boots,' someone observed, 'but it was a single-seater, a scout.'

'That's what I mean: so what was it doing out here?'

'I don't believe it was a scout. It carried bombs. That's why it went up with such a bang. It was on the way . . .'

'Karl! Three more Steins, a Pils and a schnapps for doubting Thomas here!'

'. . . to one of the Krupp factories in Dortmund.'

'They'll never know. I suppose the pilot was killed in the crash.'

'That's a funny thing, my friend. An intern told me that no meat wagon went out from the hospital; nothing from the morgue. For me that means no body in the wreck.'

'Nobody could have got out of that. My God, I saw the flames across the fields. High as a church tower, they were. No, the poor devil must have been burned to a cinder, and that's the truth.'

'Even so, there'd be *something* they could scrape up and bury. There'd have to be.'

'Not at Verdun there wouldn't. Hilde's brother said the shell holes . . .'

'Anything can happen in this damned war.'

And suddenly everybody was talking at once. More drinks were ordered. Then a more authoritative voice called out: 'If the pilot didn't escape, why have the police been given special orders, top priority, to watch out for strangers? Why have a squadron of

Uhlans been sent down from Hameln to comb the woods?'

'Of course he escaped,' someone scoffed. 'Two school-girls from my village saw him. A huge bearded fellow. He chased them across a meadow.'

'With an axe?' This was Ernst, the joker. 'If the girls had been from *our* village, *they* would have been chasing *him*!'

Blake dutifully joined in the laughter this time. Thankfully, he was now well enough away from the immediate crash area. The gossip, as always, was too vague, contradictory and far from the truth to be disturbing. He paid for his drink and left the bar. It was time to find a quieter place – somewhere he could test the 'aptitude' of his Morse wrist for real.

The transmitter was halfway between an outsize desk stapler and a miniature, one-key typewriter. A single earphone, with no headband, was the only receiving unit. In a small velvet pouch in Blake's pocket were half a dozen crystals numbered from 1 to 6. Each crystal vibrated at a different frequency, and in case the German security forces somehow fixed on transmissions, he had been told to change crystals every transmission, starting with No. 1, working through to No. 6 and then using them again in reverse order.

The dry battery installed in the device would provide up to two hours' continuous transmission, rather more in the case of a series of short broadcasts, at a maximum range of twenty miles – although this tended to diminish as the power faded. Blake wondered what kind of person would be listening for him, and where. Why would they be doing it, and how would his reports be passed on? If the cut-out was within twenty miles, why go to all the trouble of sending a man from England? Why not have the man in place penetrate the factory at Siegsdorf and steal the plans?

Because he was too well known in the area and his presence would alert the authorities? Because for some reason he was physically incapable of moving around? Because he was psychologically unfitted for burglarious activity (a cold spasm chilled Blake's guts as the idea occurred to him)? Maybe the chap was just too old. Or was it that they felt it was a hundred per cent essential that the spy must himself be an aviator, someone who would understand the implications of blueprint designs, who could be trusted not to make off with the wrong bumf? On the whole that seemed the simplest – and the most likely – explanation.

Blake had found an ideal place to transmit: a disused timber yard surrounded by a high wooden fence, whose sagging gates had been left ajar. Stacks of rotting wood still lay piled beneath the corrugated-iron roof of a shed at the far end of the yard, and he settled himself down between two of these.

The air was spiced with the tang of ancient sawdust. Through a gap in the rear fence he could see evening sunlight gilding a row of semicircular pediments above the dormers of the Fürstliches Residenzschloss, the castle. Through a gateway below, there was a view of a courtyard with a corbelled gallery linking two of the corner towers. He took the machine from his briefcase. It took only a moment to set it up.

Suddenly everything was very real. He was a spy in an enemy country, preparing to steal military secrets. This was where the story proper began: he was about to contact another illegal, a clandestine agent in place. Everything he was doing, even the fact that he, an army officer and a pilot, was wearing civilian clothes, carried the death penalty if he was caught. Spies were executed if they were unmasked on the territory of all belligerents, including that of his own country.

Blake licked his lips. He was aware of the pounding of his heart, shaking the vulnerable ribcage. He was very much aware of the alien noises of the town too: a squeal of brakes, somebody cursing, the clip-clop of horses' hooves, the steady tramp of booted feet and guttural commands. Beyond the dilapidated fence a car or a lorry backfired, and a bird flapped heavily away from the girdered rafters supporting the iron roof over his head.

Breathing deeply, he started, cautiously at first and then with more confidence, to tap out the dots and dashes representing the four letters of the agreed call-sign.

They had decided on the word 'land' because it would announce his aerial arrival and at the same time meant something quite different in German. The cut-out would reply with 'cont', which would signify, first, that it was safe to continue, and secondly instruct Blake to proceed with his message.

He had Morsed the call-sign a dozen times at one-minute intervals according to plan, before there was a response in the small round earphone held to his left ear.

And then, scratchy, faint but unmistakable, came the dots and dashes spelling out the cut-out's reply. Pulse racing, Blake hammered out his first clandestine communication. He had been told never to transmit for more than two minutes; ninety seconds would be better, seventy perfect. For information had been obtained from the Flanders front that German counterintelligence experts had developed a system of triangulation which enabled them to home on transmissions very fast.

This, he realized, apart from the clarity of the dots and dashes, was why Hesketh and his superiors had been so impressed with the speed of his Morse transmission.

His message was brief: 'ARRIVED STOP PUP DESTROYED PILOT SAFE STOP DETMOLD.'

There was no need to sign off. He simply keyed the acronym OTY – over to you – given to him by his instructors.

His unknown correspondent shortened his replies even more by using truncated words in the manner of the cablese favoured by newspaper correspondents reporting from abroad. If the meaning was clear, why waste time and money spelling out a lot of unnecessary letters? The message Blake transcribed read: 'EXPCT YOU PADWARDS MORROW STOP THENDORF STOP TTT STOP PSE ACK.'

That was clear enough. They expected him to reach Paderborn the following day, and Siegsdorf the day after that. 'TTT' stood for 'this time tomorrow'.

He acknowledged as requested and confirmed that he would make his next report at the same hour by tapping out the single expression 'WILLDO'.

Concentrating on the correct reading of the incoming Morse, and the speed and accuracy of his own, Blake had forgotten his dry mouth and the thudding of his heart. But he was aware, dismantling the apparatus and packing the crystal away in its pouch, that he was sweating heavily.

The Bavarian fob watch supplied with his suit told him that the entire transmission had taken one minute and eight seconds.

He replaced the transmitter in his briefcase and left the yard on the far side from the entry gates, through the gap in the fence offering a view of the castle. Two uniformed policemen watched him sidle through on to the sidewalk beyond.

Blake stood stupidly staring at them with his mouth open and rivulets of sweat running into his eyes from beneath the headband of his hat. One of the policemen was tall, with a 'Kaiser Bill' moustache; the other was shorter, a plump man with a red face.

'What the devil do you think you're doing?' Redface demanded roughly. They wore holstered pistols clipped to their belts.

'I . . . I . . . I was . . .' The officers' green brimless headgear, he saw, was exactly the same shape as the hard hats worn by English postmen. What could a reasonably well-dressed man believably be doing in a disused timber yard at six o'clock on a weekday evening? Blake felt as if he was choking. 'I had to take a leak,' he said desperately. 'It . . . it was the only place I could find.'

'There are public conveniences at the station,' Moustache said severely. 'Most of the bars . . .'

'Yes, but it . . . it comes on me suddenly, you see. On account of my wound,' Blake explained with a flash of inspiration. 'I don't know the town and I had to find somewhere quickly. It was the only place I could . . .'

'Your papers,' Redface said. He held out his hand.

Blake produced them, along with his army discharge book. With luck, they might have noticed that he limped *before* he saw them.

'Where did you stop the enemy bullet?' Moustache demanded, flipping through pages.

'The left ankle. It was . . .'

'No, no. *Where?* Which *front*, God in Heaven?'

'Oh. Mons in '14. We were moving up to . . .'

'You must have been glad to get out of that, just the same,' Redface said.

'Afterwards, yes. At the time it was hell. They poured neat carbolic acid through the hole at the field dressing station.' Blake's shiver was only partly contrived, though the emotion producing it had nothing to do with the Western Front.

'Better here than there, eh? What have you got in that briefcase?'

He told them.

'Show me.' This time it was Moustache who held out his hand.

Blake started to remove promotional literature, documents, a prospectus, but the policeman took the briefcase from him. 'A salesman, eh? Got any orders yet?'

'A small one in Hanover.' He knew there was, among the papers, the carbon of an invoice confirming this.

'Rather you than me,' the policeman said. 'And what exactly is this?' He held up the chassis of the transmitter.

Breathing hard, Blake was ready for that. 'A new line,' he said. 'So new that it's not in the prospectus yet.'

'Yes, but what is it?'

'Instead of the telephone. You know how – excuse me – how the military monopolize the lines. You know how the lines available are jammed. Well, this is kind of a bypass for factory heads – not much more than a toy, really – but if they really need to contact a subcontractor, expedite an order or check on a delayed delivery, they can do so directly with this, without going through some damned operator. In their own code. It works by wireless, you see.'

'Sounds pretty far-fetched to me,' Moustache said. Privately Blake agreed. He hoped fervently that they wouldn't ask to see how it worked.

'More like something criminals would use to communicate secretly,' Redface said. 'Or spies.'

Moustache laughed. 'We're very careful not to sell them to any Russians,' Blake said as lightly as he could.

Both the policemen laughed. 'Where are you staying?' Moustache asked, handing back the briefcase, transmitter chassis and papers.

Blake swallowed. 'I . . . I haven't found a place yet. I only just arrived on the train from Hanover. I was on the lookout when . . . when I . . .' He gestured towards the fence surrounding the timber yard.

'There's the Fischerhaus,' Redface told him. 'That's where most of the commercial travellers stayed before the war. On the other side of the castle. Or the Badischer-Hof – if you like Bavarian food.'

'Thank you. I think I'll try the Fischerhaus,' Blake said.

'Which firms are you calling on here in Detmold?' Moustache asked.

'None, actually,' Blake said truthfully. 'The next ones on my list are in Paderborn and . . . and Siegsdorf-am-Lippe. I'm simply staying here because I arrived too late to go on further: the connections are not suitable.'

'But the train you were on, the Hanover train, continues to Paderborn.'

'*What!* Oh, that damned ticket clerk!' Choking back a spasm of nausea, Blake feigned indignation. 'I was in too much of a hurry to check myself . . . the idiot told me I'd have to change here and wait for over an hour . . .' He shook his head.

'That's the trouble in wartime,' Redface sympathized. 'All the efficient ones are fighting; all you get at home are the temporaries, the infirm and the dullards – amateurs seasoned with an occasional cripple . . . Oh. Excuse me, sir. No offence, I hope.'

Blake shook his head, managing to raise a smile. That stupidity about the train was the first serious mistake he had made. Check, check, check, they had urged him, before you give an explanation for anything. And he hadn't.

'There is just one thing, Herr Ehrlich,' Moustache said. 'If your . . . need . . . should take you again, be more careful where you go, eh? It may be disused, but there have been many thefts of wood from this yard. You could easily have been taken for a petty criminal.'

'Thank you, I'll remember that,' Blake said.

The policemen saluted and walked off. Blake headed for the castle and the hotel. It was only then that he realized that this – apart from the perfunctory ordering of one drink – had been the first time he had spoken German since his clandestine arrival. On the whole he thought it hadn't gone too badly. If only he hadn't allowed himself to be caught out on the question of those bloody train times . . .

The Fischerhaus was a pleasant enough hotel, a tall, narrow, five-storey building with half-timbering. Through the dormer window of his top-floor room, he could see the reddened western sky above steep slate roofs, hear the rattle of wheels on cobbles in the small square below, voices from a nearby bar and the strains of a brass band somewhere. The room had a boarded floor of scrubbed pine, a feather bed, one chair and a washstand with pitcher and basin. In the morning, he was sure, a maid would bring hot water in a copper jug.

Blake was exhausted. He was looking forward to an early night in a real bed for the first time since he had left England. His papers had, according to the regulations, been handed to the receptionist when he arrived. His luggage, he said, had been mislaid in Hanover. He was to retrieve it at the station the following morning.

It was after a dinner of rationed stewed pork with the inevitable potatoes, washed down with a litre of local beer, that he heard the familiar voice.

He was on the third landing, on the way up to his room; the voice came from the hallway below, beside the reception desk. Cautiously, he approached the wooden banister and leaned over. Yes, in the light of the oil lamp on the desk, a familiar green uniform.

'Frau Schipp, do you have a traveller from Hamburg staying with you? A certain Gerhardt Ehrlich, a man with a limp?' It was Moustache's voice.

'Why yes,' the elderly owner of the hotel replied. 'He arrived not long before dinner. Do you wish to see him?'

'No, that will not be necessary.'

Blake, whose hands had started to tremble, released the breath he had been holding.

'His papers, perhaps? They are here with the other . . .'

'No thank you, Frau Schipp. Merely a routine enquiry.' The policeman moved away from the circle of light. The front door closed.

Blake stole up the remaining flights of stairs to his room, nodding to himself. There was a lesson there for him.

Just checking.

9

Paderborn, according to Blake's pre-war Baedeker, had been an important stage on the ancient commercial and strategic Hanseatic route linking Flanders and Saxony. Well, that was fine by him: he was linking Flanders and Saxony himself – the war in the air in Flanders, his own aerial entry by way of Saxony. What interested him much more was the sight of a small aerodrome just east of the town. He saw hangars and dispersal huts as his train slowed to enter the station, then, through the opposite window after they had rumbled across an iron bridge, a field strewn with many different types of machine.

Glancing rapidly right and left, Blake identified Albatros scouts and two-seaters, a Pfalz D-III, several Fokker M-8s and a Halberstadt-LVG Type C-5. The machines were dispersed in no particular order, some of them with a stippled or lozenge camouflage, others painted in bands or zigzags of bright colour. The only sign of regimentation was a flight of three Fokker Eindekker monoplanes, warming up their engines in formation outside a hangar.

Before the train ran into a cutting between high brick walls, Blake glimpsed two civil aeroplanes: a Hansa–Brandenburg biplane lettered with the insignia of the Austrian postal service and a Luft–Reederei biplane with a curious five-seat cabin behind the pilot's open cockpit. Just beyond this, mechanics were wheeling out a very small scout with a rotary engine and *three* wings! Apart from the gleam of dope on fabric stretched over wings and fuselage, this machine was colourless and without insignia. Some kind of prototype perhaps?

Blake wondered if the field was being used by the Imperial German Air Service for the assembly of one of the new Jagdgeschwadern formations creating such havoc among British and French squadrons on the Western Front. These massed groups, composed of successful pilots from several different squadrons, had become known to the Allies as 'circuses' because of the vivid colours distinguishing their aeroplanes. They included such aces as Boelke, Immelmann, Ernst Udet and Werner Voss. The most successful, and the most feared, was the ex-Uhlan cavalry captain Rittmeister Manfred Freiherr von Richthofen, who started his deadly career flying Fokker biplanes and Albatros scouts.

Paderborn was no more than a stage on the route to Siegsdorf. Apart from the story he had fed to the police in Detmold, there was no reason for Blake to remain. Having seen the aerodrome and the variety of machines assembled there, however, he decided to backtrack if possible for a closer look. There might be information he could glean of use to his superiors; the Eindekkers he had seen might be equipped with the improved interrupter gear; it could be useful – possibly life-saving – to know something of the routine on the field in case he had an opportunity, or was forced, to steal a plane as a getaway ploy.

The unknown quantity in his personal equation was nevertheless the reaction of the Detmold policemen, if any, to his story.

On his way to the station that morning, he had bought a cheap suitcase at a secondhand shop and filled it with newspapers and magazines. Arriving without luggage at a hotel could be explained away once, but it would look odd if a sales rep were to leave town carrying nothing but a small briefcase!

His forethought was justified. He was ten minutes early for the train, sauntering towards the ticket barrier when he saw them. Redface and Moustache, standing idly by the door to a small kiosk where travellers could buy sausage, beer or acorn coffee – but in a perfect position to oversee everyone who came and went.

Fifteen yards from Blake, they nodded gravely and raised languid hands in salute.

Swallowing the lump in his throat, he nodded back and contrived a smile. He went through the barrier and crossed the bridge to the down platform.

Coincidence?

Were they there as part of the general alert he had heard about in the *Weinstübe*? A routine posting to keep their eyes open and check anyone they thought looked suspicious? In which case this was an advantage: they had checked him already.

Or had they decided – or been ordered – to confirm that Herr Gerhardt Ehrlich really was going to Paderborn? If so, would they have alerted colleagues to check that he did leave the train there?

There was no way of knowing, no way of telling whether or not they were there specifically for him, no chance of removing the chill which settled on his stomach the moment he saw them. He was just thankful he had thought of the suitcase.

There *were* police at Paderborn, of course, coldly eyeing everyone who passed. But again that could simply be evidence of an area alert. No direct connection with the pair at Detmold. Was it his imagination though, or did one of them murmur something and hurry to the stationmaster's office just after he passed?

He had, of course, no factories to visit. But he had a list. He thought it prudent to ask the way to one, and enquire about a hotel, in the hearing of the remaining officers.

There was a small hotel in the shadow of a massive tower pierced by many Romanesque bays which over-looked the thirteenth-century church. The restaurant was closed for the duration, but they did have a room. He booked in for one night. What the hell. It would support his story if by chance they were checking on him – and he would have more time to take that closer look at the aerodrome and the machines there. Siegsdorf would have to wait for one more day.

By the time he came out of the hotel, the sun, bright in the early morning, had retired behind a bank of cloud blowing up from the west and the huge tower no longer cast a shadow.

The company whose address he had been given was by the river, on the way out of town, but one of the others on his list was on the road to Bad Driburg and Brakel, and that he thought should pass fairly close to the aerodrome.

With his briefcase under one arm, he set out on foot in that direction. Even if he was being watched, there was after all no logical reason why he should necessarily go first to the address he had requested. *Was* he being watched? He was fairly certain that a man he had seen in the street just before he went into the hotel had still been there, across the road by the porch leading to the church, when he came out again. But there were a dozen valid reasons which could believably have explained that.

He steeled himself not to keep glancing behind as he left the town centre, but on the one occasion he did look – just before crossing the street – he experienced a thrill of alarm, thinking he saw the man threading his way through a queue of housewives with ration tickets, outside a bakery. On the other hand the follower's dress, if he was a follower, if it was the same man, resembled that of many other men in the street: a green loden jacket and paler breeches. And the bakery was at least a hundred yards away. By the time Blake had allowed a two-horse wagon piled high with hay to pass, and skipped aside to avoid being run down by a fat hausfrau on a bicycle, the possible tail was nowhere to be seen. Without increasing his pace, he continued on his way.

A.G. Wunschefabriek, according to the faded lettering on a signboard above the entrance to reception, were experts in sanitary engineering. The factory, a row of workshops with serrated glass roofs, stood on a slight rise about half a mile outside Paderborn. Below it, the white, dusty country road twisted away between fields of cabbage and ripe corn. Above the hiss of blowtorches and the hammering of metal, Blake could hear the distant roar of aero engines from the far side of a wood crowning the skyline to the north.

He looked back as he climbed the slope leading to the factory's reception. He saw a figure in the distance, apparently loitering by a farm gate, but it was too far away to make out the cut or colour of clothes. He opened the door and went inside.

An elderly woman with frizzy grey hair and spectacles sat behind a desk in a small, wood-panelled room crammed with teak filing cabinets and shelves loaded with tottering piles of documents. 'Who are you and what do want?' she snapped, glaring at him over the steel rims.

A little nervously, Blake brought out his cover speech.

No, the woman said, cutting him short, they had no need for – nor any interest in – the supplies offered by an electrical manufacturer in Hamburg. They had quite enough trouble trying to make companies in the Ruhr honour their delivery dates.

She stopped him producing his promotional material and sales brochures and refused point-blank to call in a manager or even a foreman to see him.

Blake was thankful. He had been dreading the effect of his sales pitch, such as it was, on an expert. It was with a sense of enormous relief that he backed out and hurried away down the slope. At least, so far as his cover was concerned, he had gone through the motions. If he had been turned down without arousing suspicion, so much the better: in a sense it strengthened his story.

He stared back down the road. The farm gate was open. There was nobody in sight.

It was still early afternoon. Clearly the aerodrome was approaching peak activity. Above the trees, he saw a number of low-flying machines circling, rising and falling as the engines bellowed and the bracing wires sang. Halberstadt, Pfalz, Albatros, even an ancient Rumpler came and went in turn. Circuit and bumps for beginners, he thought, or perhaps in some cases experienced pilots familiarizing themselves with a new machine.

He turned again. The road remained empty. The factory still hissed and hammered.

The hell with it, he thought for the second time. It was surely reasonable enough that a sales rep, turned down and thus with time on his hands, should be interested in new-fangled flying machines in wartime. He strode off towards the wood.

A footpath led circuitously through the belt of trees. On the far side, crouched behind a screen of bushes, he looked down a long slope of meadowland, past the embankment and the railway line, to the hangars and the dispersed aeroplanes. The field was a hive of activity, with scouts and reconnaissance craft taking off and landing, it seemed, every few seconds.

Blake took notes in his own personal shorthand on the routine so far as he could make it out. He had been there perhaps fifteen minutes when there was a shattering roar and the three Fokker Eindekkers he had seen from the train began warming up in unison, surrounded by a group of mechanics and a single officer in uniform. Each of the monoplanes, he could see, was equipped with twin Spandau machine-guns, sited just behind the engine cowling.

Soon the Fokkers taxied to the middle of the field and took off, still in formation. When they had reached an altitude of perhaps a thousand feet, the two wingmen broke up the V and fell in behind the leader one after the other. They circled above an undulating stretch of moorland two or three miles to the far side of the aerodrome.

Then the leader banked steeply and dived to five hundred feet, flying in a much tighter circle above a pale scar visible between two swells of the dun moor. After four circuits he climbed again to fall in behind his two companions. The manoeuvre was followed by each of the other Fokkers in turn. After twenty minutes, the trio returned to the aerodrome.

The scar, Blake assumed, was the lip of a sandpit or disused quarry. There would presumably be a target, probably in the shape of a plane, pegged out on the floor of the pit. Certainly, from where he was, the stutter of the Spandaus was clearly audible above the roar of the machines' Oberursel rotary engines.

They were much too far away for a visual check, but he had had plenty of time to study them before they took off: there were no wing-mounted guns; *and the guns of the single-engined scouts were definitely firing forward through their propeller arcs.*

'Very interesting!' he said aloud. And suddenly his mission sprang into sharp focus in his mind, hardened into a vital imperative instead of a problem that had been almost academic.

Over the muddied desolation of the shell-torn Western Front, these machines – as the intelligence officers had told him – would be lethal for the Allied observation planes and their crews, and equally murderous opponents for escorting scouts with their antique, angled-off Vickers or wing-mounted Lewis guns.

The urgency of the task, the recognition that the responsibility of obtaining the plans of the Fokker interrupter gear was his and his alone, were all at once agonizingly acute. For the first time since he had left Gosport, self-preservation took second place to the dictates of duty.

He hurried back to his hotel.

The clouds which had been extending from the west now covered the whole sky with a lowering canopy, and before he was halfway to the outskirts of Paderborn flying from the aerodrome had stopped. A few minutes later it began to rain.

Blake's shoulders were dark with moisture and his breeches were clinging to his knees by the time he found a shop where he could buy a cheap raincoat.

There was a ruddy-faced man in pale breeches and a loden coat sheltering in the church porch opposite the hotel entrance. Blake walked straight past and found his way to the address he had asked for at the station. At this moment preservation of his cover was paramount.

The building was a converted water-mill. A huge vaned

wheel still turned slowly, channelling the swift-flowing current of a stream into the River Pader. A weathered board by the roadside bore the faded information, addressed to pre-war tourists, that this was the site of the Paderquellen – a collection of more than two hundred small springs which bubbled from the ground to form the stream powering the water-wheel.

Blake's list stated that the converted mill housed the shop-floor premises of Eberbach–Klammerhein GmbH, manufacturers of household equipment, mangles, kitchen utensils, etc. But it was evident at once that it was out of date. The windows of the two top floors were boarded up, a bare patch on the ivy-covered wall showed where a signboard had been removed, and a rusty chain barred the entrance to a loading bay. The only occupant now appeared to be a small watchmaker and repairer. Through a plate-glass window, Blake saw an old man with white hair and a leather apron peering through half-moon glasses at a table strewn with cogwheels, springs, pendulums and weights. The wall behind him was lined with empty clock cases in mahogany and bird's-eye maple. Clearly this was not an enterprise likely to be interested in the products of a Hamburg electrical supplier.

In any case there was nobody to notice whether or not he went in. He looked over his shoulder. A carter was whipping the horses of a brewer's dray across a bridge over the river. A Daimler-Benz saloon, probably a taxi, growled past in the other direction, spraying mud from the wet cobbles. No pedestrians were visible beneath the dripping trees that lined the street.

For the second time, Blake headed for the hotel.

The man in the loden coat was still there.

Blake bit his lip. Could this *still* be some kind of

coincidence? Was it possible, for instance, that the fellow was indeed on the lookout, but not for him? Was he just a loiterer? Unemployed? In militaristic wartime Germany that was hardly likely. There was nothing he could do about it anyway. It was time now to signal his cut-out.

In view of the weather, he reckoned it would attract less attention if he dared to transmit from his hotel room. Heavy rain drumming on the roof above would mask the light, scarcely audible thump of the key every time he pressed it down, whereas if he set out in the downpour in an attempt to find a secluded spot, even if the man across the street was not a watcher . . .

He shrugged and went in, stamping his feet and shaking drops from his raincoat in the narrow hallway.

As soon as his call had been acknowledged and he had received the safe-to-continue acronym, he tapped out: 'DAYLATE SDORF DUE VALBLE AERO INFO PBORN STOP PSE ACK CONFIRM.'

There was a long wait before the reply came. He was distinctly uneasy by the time he heard: 'ACCEPTED BUT BASE INSISTS PPRS NEC URGENTEST STOP ACK.'

Was it because of the dangerous time-lag – he supposed the cut-out had contacted London or some superior nearer – or did he detect implied disapproval in the fact that he had been told curtly 'Acknowledge' instead of the customary 'Please acknowledge'?

That was something else he could do nothing about. It would be too complicated to explain that it was mainly to strengthen his cover that he decided to spend the day in Paderborn. He simply transmitted the word 'UNDERSTOOD', and signed off.

Before he left the hotel again to try and find something to eat, he stood inside the entrance door peering through the coloured-glass panels in its upper half. But water streaming down the outside exaggerated the effect of the frosted glass and he could see nothing clearly. He opened the door and went out into the rain. The church porch was deserted. There was no sign of the loden coat left or right.

He found a small, down-at-heel café around the corner where he could sit at a scrubbed table and order half a litre of watery beer to wash down a meal of unrationed wurst and dry bread. The place was poorly lit, rancid beneath the layers of smoke with the odours of cheap tobacco and acorn coffee. Three old women in black huddled together in the far corner, screeching with occasional laughter. All the other customers were elderly men, some with crutches, one in a cast-off army uniform. Four of them, conversing in low voices, were playing some kind of game with cards.

The man in the loden coat sat at the next table to Blake's.

He couldn't be certain that it was the man he had seen outside the bakery or the person by the farm gate, but it was certainly the one from the porch – a thickset individual with heavy features and fleshy moist lips. As Blake thumbed back the metal lid of his pottery beer mug and raised it to his mouth, he saw that the man was looking fixedly at him, raising his own tankard. The man smiled.

What did this mean? Simply that the man was indeed a watcher, that he was playing cat and mouse with Blake? See, I have you where I want you: you cannot escape me? Or was it that he simply happened to have noticed Blake a couple of times that day and was doing no more than acknowledging him? Perhaps he himself was a stranger in town and recognized in Blake a fellow outcast.

Whatever he did, Blake couldn't ignore the approach:

the stare was too direct, the smile too personal. He nodded in a distant way, drank some beer and looked down at his plate as he ate some sausage.

The regard was unwavering. He couldn't just ignore it. The man was smiling more broadly than ever now. Blake was reminded of something he had read somewhere about the unwanted intimacy which developed between the torturer and the tortured, the executioner and his victim.

The stranger had pushed back his chair and risen to his feet. He was carrying his tankard across. He sat down at Blake's own table, next to him. 'Wicked weather if one is alone in town,' he said, the smile remaining in place.

Blake swallowed. 'Most unpleasant,' he said as coldly as he could.

'Especially for a young person. After all it is not as if there was anywhere stimulating to go – not in Paderborn anyway.'

Blake ate a mouthful of sausage. He drank more beer, making no reply.

'And in your case not even comrades in uniform to share a joke.' The man leaned closer, his beery breath warm against Blake's cheek. 'I couldn't help noticing, seeing you pass, that you walked with a slight limp.'

'I was invalided out,' Blake said shortly. 'The . . . Battle of Mons.'

'Ah. That was something for the brave ones.' The man pulled his chair even closer to Blake's. There was a slight dew of sweat on the flushed face. 'A shame that a young man – a good-looking, attractive young man such as yourself – should be deprived of the joys of youth, the companionship, the games, by an infirmity inflicted in the service of the Fatherland.'

A heavy hand descended on Blake's thigh, midway

between the knee and the hip. The moist lips were very close to his face. 'Perhaps sometimes an older man . . . someone aware of the infelicities, at times the callousness, of youth . . . can help to assuage the spiritual if not the physical wounds of war.' The fingers of the hand moved slightly higher, tightening on the resilient flesh.

Oh, *Christ!* Blake thought. Not this! This is one thing I could really do without . . .

Shoving back his chair violently, he left the remains of his meal, slapped money down on the bar and pushed his way blindly through the swing doors, out into the night.

The man had called something after him, but he was too angry to hear what it was. He ran through the heavy rain, footsteps splashing through puddles in the uneven flagstones, and burst into the hotel.

Snatching his key from the old woman behind the reception desk, he took the stairs two at a time, still panting with exasperation as he thrust the key into the lock.

The door of his room was unlocked.

Pushing it open, he stumbled across something on the floor, fumbling to find matches so that he could light the oil lamp on the bedside table.

As the light brightened and spread from the flaring wick, he saw that what he had stumbled across was his suitcase. The lid was open, and the newspapers and magazines he had stuffed inside to weight it were scattered across the floor.

For the first time in his life he experienced the sensation described as the blood running cold . . . He flung himself at the bed and hauled up the mattress.

The briefcase, containing the documents supporting his cover and the incriminating transmitter, had gone.

10

Once again there was a conference in the great hall at Hohenstein. For the second time, five men sat around the sixteenth-century refectory table. *General-Major* Rudolph von Sonderstern still sat in the throne-like chair at the head of the table.

But this time all of the participants wore uniform. Two Uhlan NCOs, with spiked helmets, thigh boots and drawn swords, guarded each pair of double entrance doors.

Oberst Klaus Frodenburg, commander of the local air defence squadron, was once more accompanied by the area police commissioner and *Hauptmann* Erich Schneider, the young foreign intelligence officer from the German secret service. The fifth man, however, rather than a ministry official, was a *Kriminalkommissar* – the equivalent of a CID Detective Inspector from Scotland Yard – brought in from Dortmund, the nearest big city.

He sat shuffling a sheaf of papers, some typed, some handwritten, others printed forms which had been filled in here and there with ticks or crosses.

'The investigations requested, *Herr General-Major*,' he said to Von Sonderstern, 'have duly been made. The Hamburg company cited did indeed have on their books as a war veteran sales representative a certain Gerhardt Ehrlich, but' – he picked up one of the forms – 'the man was killed in a car accident.' He glanced at the form again. 'In the spring of 1915. In Bremen.'

'So. We know then that the man here is an impostor.'

'Exactly. The difficulty, *Herr General-Major*, is that . . .'

'What we do not know,' the *Oberst* cut in, 'is whether this impostor is in fact some kind of domestic criminal or whether he is connected with the *Britischer* aeroplane crash.'

'Surely that is unlikely?' the *Hauptmann* said. 'At least insofar as the identity of the pilot is concerned. One would not normally fly a machine all this distance dressed as a minor sales representative!'

'Young man,' Sonderstern said acidly, 'the *Englander* secret service is not staffed by complete fools. If they are infiltrating a spy into the Fatherland, they will hardly have him running around wearing a leather helmet and goggles! If this impostor is indeed the escaped pilot, I have no doubt that everything he wears will have been fabricated in the German fashion, with suitable labels.'

'Unless of course there are two of them,' the local police chief said.

'The machine was definitely a single-seater, a scout,' the *Oberst* told him. 'There is no question of that. Five of my pilots individually confirm it.'

'No, I mean the pilot and a second man *already* here, an agent in place. This is always possible, distasteful though it may seem. In which case the bogus Ehrlich would most certainly, as the *Herr General* says, be . . . equipped . . . as a German. Even if he is not anything as unthinkable as an actual countryman, a traitor.'

'The man we are investigating is almost sure to be an

Englander – or an individual from the so-called United Kingdom,' the *Kriminalkommissar* said.

'You are sure of this?' Sonderstern asked.

'Practically certain, *Herr General-Major.*'

'How so?'

'Through a remarkably perspicacious piece of observation on the part of an officer working for my colleague here.' The detective nodded graciously in the direction of the local man. 'I have questioned this officer personally, and it seems that two of his companions in Detmold had already become suspicious after a routine identity check following the area alert.'

'Indeed? Why was this, if his cover was as good as we have been told?'

'There was an error in one of the documents he produced. An army pay book, I believe. In one place where our German text required a ß, a double S had been used. This led the officers to believe not only that the document might be a forgery but also that it could well have been fabricated by a non-German.'

'Very astute. And then?'

'Rather than arrest the man at once, the two operatives decided to keep a covert watch on him. Having spent the night in Detmold, the stranger took a train to Paderborn, and the policemen requested their colleagues there to continue the surveillance.'

'Why not arrest him at once?'

'They felt it might be more useful, if he was indeed an impostor, to find out why he was there and what he was doing first.'

'Very well. And so?'

'They decided that overt surveillance might provoke a more rapid result, perhaps frightening the suspect into making an error. And this proved to be the case. One of the Paderborn agents assumed the identity of a degenerate, one of those pests who hangs around public places and follows personable young men in the hope of . . . striking up an acquaintance. Apparently in an attempt to avoid such unwelcome attention, the suspect hastily crossed a crowded street.'

'That seems prudent enough,' the *Hauptmann* commented.

Sonderstern simply said: 'Well?'

The *Kriminalkommissar* paused for effect, and then continued: 'Before venturing into the stream of traffic, the man looked first to the right and then to the left.'

The information was greeted with a puzzled silence.

The police commissioner sighed. 'Because traffic is obliged by law to keep to the right-hand side of the road,' he explained, 'pedestrians here naturally look to their *left* before crossing a street, because it is from that direction that the nearest vehicles approach. Afterwards they look in the other direction. But a person looking *first* to the right is automatically expecting traffic from that direction – that is to say traffic keeping to the left-hand side of the road.'

Another pause.

'There is one place where that is the rule,' he continued impressively, 'and one only: England and the adjoining territories.'

Sonderstern cleared his throat. 'Excellent. Admirable reasoning. The officer is to be commended. So our man is an *Englander*, and very probably the pilot of the crashed aeroplane. Why was he not immediately arrested and interrogated?'

'Because, *Herr General-Major*, the officer did not at first make the connection. The suspect made several calls which corresponded with his assumed identity.

It was only after it began to rain and he repeated the manoeuvre that the officer realized the significance of what he had seen. Accordingly he followed the suspect into a café and engaged him in conversation so that colleagues could search his room in a nearby hotel.'

'What was the result of the search?'

'The suitcase supposedly containing what travellers would normally carry – clothes, additional shirts, night-wear, shoes – was stuffed with newspapers.'

'Well, that certainly proved that he could not have come from far afield, and definitely not from Hamburg!' the *Hauptmann* said.

'That in fact he was from the immediate area, perhaps no further than the field where the foreign aeroplane crash-landed?' the police commissioner added drily.

'The searcher also found a short-range wireless receiver equipped with a key which could be used to transmit Morse signals. Unfortunately he was disturbed before he could look further, because the suspect returned earlier than expected.'

'Followed, I trust, by the disguised police officer?' Sonderstern said.

'Yes, sir, indeed.' The *Kriminalkommissar* coughed. 'Alas, he was a shade too late to make an arrest: the suspect had already escaped through the window of his room.'

11

The window was a dormer, projecting from the steepest of grey, wet, slate roofs. There was a hint of the massive church tower off to the left, and between a chaos of chimneys and shining slopes a gleam of cobbles beneath the diffuse street lighting five storeys below.

Blake leaned out over the broad sill, his heart thumping wildly. From the foot of the stairwell, he had heard the harsh tones of the man in the loden coat, unmistakable now as a peremptory, hectoring voice of authority, demanding which room the receptionist had allotted the stranger. Heavy footsteps already pounded the ancient stairs.

For the first time since he had set foot on German soil, the lethal progression – arrest, imprisonment, trial, firing squad – assembled itself in his mind. What had been almost a game, a jape, a story to tell later in the mess, was now suddenly a terrifying reality. He scrambled on to the edge of the sill.

He was unarmed; the policeman would certainly have a gun. There was no chance of forcing an escape within the hotel. This was his only opportunity.

Below the sill was a short slant of tiling, then the gutter, and six feet under that a string-course – a narrow brick ledge running along the vertical face of the building. Panting, he turned, grasped the sill and began to lower himself face down across the tiled slope.

Escape now was his only priority, survival the sole target. If this was the route and there were no alternatives, he was taking the route whatever the obstacles. Blind determination, fuelled by a kind of savage, obsessive anger, obscured every other emotion, leaving no place for fright; even the fear of death was momentarily submerged.

His feet touched the gutter. He lay at the full stretch of his arms.

This was the critical moment: it was only by clinging to the gutter and lowering himself down the wall below that he could hope to wedge his toes on to the string-course beneath.

Was the gutter strong enough to hold his weight?

He shifted his body experimentally on the wet slate, loading it first on one foot, then the other. Through the lit window above, he heard the locked door of his room burst open. A familiar voice cursed in German.

Between the sole and the upper of one boot, cold rainwater soaked Blake's sock. The gutter seemed firm enough: water gurgled past his feet towards a downpipe ten yards away. He tested it one final time, allowing all his weight to pivot around one leg. He felt no evident slackening, no give in the solidity of the metal channel. Very well. This was it. He relinquished his grasp of the sill so that his body could slide.

Above his head, the shaft of light glinting through a curtain of bright rain dimmed. A man's head and beefy shoulders were blocking out half the dormer. 'Don't be a damned fool, man,' he cried. 'You'll fall to a bloody death!'

The rain drummed on Blake's sodden coat, needling

his scalp with icy points. Hunched at the foot of the slope, he clenched fingers and thumbs over the curved rim of the guttering. Water swirled around his knuckles.

'Come back; I'll lend you a hand,' the policeman shouted. 'You're twenty metres above a row of spiked railings there. You can't possibly . . .'

The rest of the sentence was drowned in a sudden, more forceful squall of rain and the slither of Blake's body scraping past the lip of the gutter.

There was an agonizing wrench at his shoulder muscles as his outstretched arms and clamped hands supported his entire weight, and then his feet found the string-course.

On tiptoe, he could still just hold on to the gutter. Very slowly, hand after hand, he began inching crabwise towards the downpipe.

The ledge was no more than three inches wide. With nothing but that strip of weathered stone beneath his toes and the cold, wet metal of the gutter above, the ten yards of that traverse was a perilous journey. He was excruciatingly conscious of the void yawning below him, the possibility of rotted stonework above and ahead. Even if the guttering held, could the iron staples cementing it into the wall pull free? Would his weight, even supported from above, risk crumbling the fragile ledge? A rising wind plucked at his clammy trousers; rain plastered his hair to his skull.

Worse was to come when he arrived at the downpipe. The policeman would have run from the hotel, rounding up reinforcements to surround the block. Blake had hoped to shin down the pipe and somehow make his getaway at street level before the cordon was in place. But if the gutter held, the pipe it sup-plied would not. The metal was corroded, and as he reached out thankfully to grasp the curved tube, two of his fingers sank through the rusty, paper-thin surface.

Panic suddenly seized him. There were no more dormers above the guttering. Beyond the rotted pipe, the gutter itself was discontinued. The wall of the building turned in at a right angle to circumvent the three sides of a narrow rectangular air shaft. Beyond this the steep roof, with three more dormers, continued.

Blake swallowed. Sweat mingled with the rain to run into his eyes.

He peered around the corner. The string-course continued around the air shaft and beneath the next row of dormers. But there was nothing above it except a blank face of vertical brickwork; the adjoining building was one storey higher than the hotel.

Blake's knees were trembling. Could a man edge around that narrow ledge changing direction four times, and reach that immeasurably distant line of windows? He quailed at the thought. It was impossible, it was insane, it was too dangerous even to consider.

But what were the options? He choked back a cry as he supplied himself with the answer. None.

As they used to say at school, it was do or die; in this case probably both.

He remembered the tough Scottish officer who had given him the three-day crash course in breaking and entering. There had been a special lecture on the subject of ledges.

'Oh, aye, ye could come across one,' the Scot had said. 'Sometimes the only way in, forbye. In theory there's no' a problem. A strip of stone four, three, even two inches wide should be wide enough for a man to walk along. But when that ledge projects from a sheer wall, there ye have trouble.'

There had been diagrams on a blackboard at this point, Blake recalled. 'In such a case,' the officer had continued, 'the bulk of the body becomes critical. For if the centre of gravity moves too far away from the median line of yer ledge, that body will overbalance and fall. To succeed, a man must either face the wall and move on the balls of his feet, with his heels stickin' out in space; or rest on those heels with his back to the wall.

'In which case,' the Scot said genially, with his moustached smile, 'he is shit-scared of his exposed position and will probably suffer from vertigo.'

Blake chose to face inwards. Without the gutter to support him, he was only able to remain balanced on the string-course because he was thin enough not to have much body overhang – and because he had run from his room without the voluminous raincoat he had bought that afternoon. He didn't even remember taking a conscious decision to continue: the Scottish officer had carried him around the downpipe and the right angle beyond it. Now, with arms flung wide and his lean, wet body pressed to the streaming brickwork, he inched forward, thrusting upwards and inwards with the tortured muscles of his toes and calves. With his cheek against the wall, he concentrated his gaze ferociously on the inner part of the shaft, just discernible in reflected light from somewhere below. He knew that if he looked down he was doomed.

There were two more downpipes at the far end. Without them, Blake would have been lost: he could never have transferred himself, twice, across ninety degrees of nothing without the slightest projection to grab hold of.

As it was, the fifteen feet to the first pipe were hell. Perhaps because death had never seemed nearer, he was reminded acutely of the first few seconds after the death of the Pup. Once again sounds became exceptionally important. He lived with the scrape of his soles along stone, the rasp of his jacket on brickwork, a rattle of wheels on far-off cobbles.

When at last he fell forward to grasp the first pipe, he clung to the smooth, cold casting with a sob of relief.

It was then that luck turned suddenly his way.

Dreading the next two deadly traverses, he discovered with a flood of joy that was almost indecent that they were not going to be necessary. The corroded hotel downpipe was for rainwater only; this one, linked at each floor to feeder pipes, clearly carried away waste from kitchens or washrooms. And it was solid, rock-hard and yielded nothing when he tapped it.

Blake wrapped his arms around it like a lover.

Normally, the idea of lowering himself five floors down a slippery drainpipe, lashed by driving rain and in flight from the police would have filled him with horror. After the torture of the string-course, it was almost a joyride.

Fortunately the soles of his boots were inset with cleats of composition rubber. With these clamped to the curved surface of the shiny, nine-inch pipe, he was able to halt or at least minimize the slide each time his hands slipped on the wet metal.

Cautiously, like a slow-motion frog in reverse, be began his descent.

There was no immediate danger of his falling. The pipe was ridged with iron junctions every ten or twelve feet where the outflows from each floor slanted into it, and at each of these he could wedge a foot into the angle and rest. Physically, therefore, the drain on him was relatively light. He divided the descent into five stages, at each of which he could momentarily take the weight off his hands and feet and relieve the strain on the muscles of arms, wrists and calves. Mentally, however, the problems remained, and were in fact intensified because physically he was less traumatized.

He had no idea what he would find at the foot of the shaft. He didn't know whether or not he could get out easily. He knew the man in the loden coat would have alerted colleagues, but he didn't know how far they would have got or whether the block would already be cordoned. Most importantly, he hadn't the least notion of where he could go or what he could do if he did escape the police net. The closer he got to the ground, the more these problems seemed insurmountable.

The wind plucking at his drenched clothes slackened, the rain fell less heavily. He had arrived – he could see now, glancing warily over his shoulder – in the shelter of a high wall blocking off the small yard at the foot of the shaft.

His feet rested on hard ground.

Blake was panting hoarsely. His arms shuddered. He was trembling behind the knees and one calf had locked into a painful cramp. His chest heaved as he sucked in lungfuls of air like a drowning man. Over the distant sounds of traffic he heard a tramp of heavy feet, a shouted command.

Panic again.

He stamped the cramp from his leg and ran for the wall. There was a door but it was locked. At one side of this was a row of dustbins. He clambered on to the top of the nearest and pulled himself up to the top of the wall. As he levered himself away from the bin, the lid rolled off with a deafening clang and slid noisily away across the wet yard.

Someone, somewhere threw up a window and shouted angrily. But Blake was already on the far side of the wall and running.

And now, suddenly, after the agonizing slow motion of his escape from the hotel, life moved into top gear; he seemed to himself to be moving with the accelerated jerkiness of a figure in a cinematograph film.

There was a service lane on the far side of the wall, running right and left. He turned right because as far as he could tell the sounds of pursuit had come more from the left. The lane was rough, cobbled and pitted with holes awash with rainwater. Light from a gas lamp eighty yards away, where it ran into a side-street, illuminated the shafts of rain bouncing off the polished stones and pock-marking the yellowed surface of the puddles.

Blake splashed to the far end of the lane. The street was narrow, twisting away in either direction between tall gabled houses. He turned right . . . and froze.

A block away, uniformed figures in capes and hard hats had appeared beneath another lamp where streets met. Naturally. The police were circling the block in two different directions.

Blake heard a shout, then another.

The whole group sprang into motion again, ducking out of the pool of light and clattering towards him in a single, menacing mass.

For the third time the voice bellowed, and he thought he heard the phrase 'or we shoot'.

He whirled to his left and raced away.

The street curved left and then right. Judging by the yellow light reflected up on to the low clouds, it was heading in a circuitous way for the centre of the town. Blake was out of sight of the pursuers now, but the pounding of their feet from around the last corner was terrifyingly close.

He hared between shuttered houses for the bright lights of a square a hundred yards ahead.

The square was busy. It was not yet ten o'clock in the evening. As he ran nearer he saw trams, a couple of horse-drawn cabs and a crowd of pedestrians around the brightly lit entrance to a *Weinstübe*. A convoy of canvas-topped military motor lorries was leaving the far side of the square.

In the centre of the wide space there was a triangle of wet grass surrounding a deserted bandstand. Iron railings, of which only the bases cemented into the ground remained, had been cut down to go to the smelters and aid the war effort. Blake dodged behind a Benz touring car and crossed the grassy strip.

The pavements beyond were more crowded. As he registered the sounds of pursuit erupting from the side-street, he threaded his way through a queue outside a grocer's and stepped into a dark alleyway.

Ten yards inside this, the open door of a small restaurant splashed a band of light across the alley. Just inside the door an earthenware tube acted as an umbrella stand. On an impulse, he reached inside and snatched one of the wet umbrellas. This was in fact the smartest thing he had done since he left the hotel. He was still panting but his mind, sharpened by danger, was ice cold. What were they looking for? Somebody running, someone running away. A hatless fugitive with no raincoat, a man already noticeable on a night like this.

So give them what they were not expecting.

He put up the umbrella, a large, black affair, and emerged from the alley to saunter slowly *towards* the square and the pursuit. He held the umbrella low, slanted to conceal his head and upper half. He joined the end of the grocery queue, where he was immediately joined by two housewives complaining about the rise in prices.

His back was turned, but he heard the voice – presumably that of an officer – roughly questioning passers-by. 'A man, bareheaded . . . probably wet through . . . from that direction, running hard . . .'

And amid a babble of voices, conflicting, doubting, assured, the confident assertion: 'Yes, yes. I saw him. That way: down the alley and past the restaurant . . .'

The police posse vanished into the alleyway.

After a few minutes, Blake mimed a man exasperated by an interminable wait and left the queue. Consciously mastering his genuine, frenzied impatience, he walked slowly to the far side of the square, turned into the street taken by the army convoy . . . and then hurried away as fast as he could.

At eleven o'clock he was crouched, on the inner side, at the foot of a wooden fence around a goods yard west of the station.

There was a loaded train fifty yards away, the locomotive panting wisps of steam into the rain while the engineer and fireman manhandled the trunk of a hose feeding water into the saddle tanks.

It was not until midnight that a green light glowed beside the signal-box and the train pulled slowly out of the yard and puffed away down the track in the direction of Siegsdorf, Lippstadt and Dortmund.

But by this time Blake, oblivious of the downpour thundering on the tarpaulin which concealed him, was deep in an exhausted sleep on a pile of sacking in one of the wagons halfway between the locomotive and the brake van.

12

Six trucks – flatbeds loaded with what looked like crated machinery – were attached to the freight train at Lippstadt, and two closed vans later at Siegsdorf. Blake, surrounded by what felt like sacks of potatoes or turnips, remained beneath his tarpaulin.

He had decided to make no attempt to disembark before the train arrived at Dortmund. This in any case was the destination of the truck he was in, according to the waybill pasted to the exterior. But he was convinced, first, that a city goods yard would be easier to escape from than a siding in a small town, and secondly that it would be more prudent, for the moment at any rate, to stay well clear of Siegsdorf.

Clearly, the police now knew that there was something bogus about Herr Ehrlich of Hamburg; possibly they even suspected that he might be the foreign pilot of the crashed aeroplane. There was no way Blake could know. Equally there was no way *they* could know why this suspect stranger was in the area or where he was heading. So the less he was associated with his target town the better. To approach Siegsdorf from Dortmund, in the west, would therefore give him a better chance of remaining undetected than if he arrived from Paderborn in the east, where there was already a hue and cry.

That was fine in theory. It was easy enough blithely to think of an 'approach'. But the practical details were for him quite terrifying. He still had the Ehrlich identity papers and army pay book, but unless they were used in a region where he was not known as a wanted man, they could be more of a liability than an asset. He still had money. The street plan of Siegsdorf and such information about the factory as he had been given were sewn inside his jacket. But the jacket itself was now filthy, soaked through and torn in two places. His boots were badly scuffed. He was unshaven and the palms of his hands were grazed where they had too fiercely gripped the downpipe during his escape from the man in the loden coat.

He looked in fact thoroughly disreputable, the kind of tramp unthinkable in a regimented wartime Germany. He was hungry, he had a blinding headache, and he was sure that he was getting a cold.

Worst of all, with the loss of his Morse transmitter he was now totally alone, cut off from his contact, with no means whatever of communicating his plight to cut-out or base.

It was a problem the initial stages of which he had hoped to deal with while it was still dark. But the shunting at Lippstadt took an age; there were several halts to allow what were presumably troop trains to pass; and they waited over half an hour outside a signal-box a few miles outside Dortmund. Shivering below the steady thrum of rain on his tarpaulin, Blake ground his teeth in fury as he listened to the ribald pleasantries exchanged between the engine driver, his mate and the signalman. The quiet panting of the locomotive, shining in the red glow of the signal lamp, served only to fuel his impatience each time he lifted a corner of the heavy cover.

Although the rain had by then ceased, daylight was already assembling the grey rectangles of warehouses, the long lines of shunted trucks in the yard, by the time the clatter of buffers ceased and the train finally stopped in the city.

Ten, twelve tracks away, between the lines, lorries were backing up to another train. He heard men shouting.

Blake lifted the edge of the tarpaulin higher.

Twelve tracks? Ten? With all those lines of wagons and trucks in between?

He squeezed out under the stiff sheet and dropped to the ground. Overhead, the clouds were racing. A long way ahead two figures in blue overalls – the driver and his fireman? – trudged towards a roundhouse bristling with locomotives and steam.

Doubled up, he ran the other way, stumbling among cinders. The sleepers were never the right distance apart for running.

Rounding a corner behind a pair of hydraulic buffers, he climbed to the open platform of an empty brake van. He saw a wooden hut, an oil lamp that still burned behind a window, smoke curling from beneath the conical top of a metal flue. Beyond the cabin was a wall of dark planking, a stockade, with a telegraph pole and an attached street lamp on the far side.

Blake jumped down from the van, ran past the hut and pulled himself to the top of the wall, wincing as the coarse wood bit into his damaged hands.

A door thumped open. A man shouted. Blake dropped down to a grassy bank, crossed a narrow street and started to run again.

He was in a mean neighbourhood of grimy, two-storey houses. Horse droppings littered the street. Smoke blew from only a few of the chimneys outlined against the hurrying clouds.

Over the rooftops, though, black smoke belched from a brickwork kiln visible in the distance. Blake followed a group of elderly men on bicycles pedalling slowly towards the factory. Two hundred yards further on he found a barber's shop on the corner of an alleyway. He went in and asked for a shave.

The barber, a white-haired man of about sixty with a wooden leg, settled a white sheet around his shoulders and neck. 'Just signed on at the factory, have you?' he asked, stropping an open razor as he nodded towards the smoking chimney.

Blake had allowed his cancelled army pay book to be seen as he stripped off his wet jacket. He shook his head. 'No, I was hoping to find something in Lippstadt. Not always easy, though, with this.' He patted his lame leg.

'I know what you mean,' the barber said sympathetically. 'If my old man hadn't had this business . . .' He sighed, stirring up a lather. 'The Western Front – the leg, I mean?'

Blake nodded. 'Mons. Thank God, though: it saved me from Ypres and Verdun!' He tilted back his head as the razor began to scrape.

'You want to go further than Lippstadt, just the same, if you're looking for light work,' the barber said. 'Try Siegsdorf, a few miles further on. There's an engineering company there makes spare parts for aeroplanes.' He chuckled. 'Machine-guns for the Freiherr von Richthofen to shoot down the *Englander* swine, eh?' He wiped lather from the blade. 'Good God! What happened to your hands?'

'Motor accident,' Blake said curtly. 'On the road from Essen. I was bumming a lift from an empty troop carrier and this fool of a carter . . .' He shook his head again. 'Scraped my hands getting out of the wreck, but I lost my stuff. Had to walk fifteen kilometres through the damned rain.'

'Tough,' the barber said. 'I'll put a touch of disinfectant on that for you. But you want to get out of those wet clothes. You'll catch your death. There's a secondhand shop nearby if you have the necessary.'

'Thanks,' Blake said. 'And thanks for the tip about Siegsdorf. I'll try there.'

As he limped away from the alley, the factory hooter was blaring its call to duty over the rooftops. Seconds later, further to the north, it was followed by another, shriller, more insistent. Even on the fringes of the Ruhr, Blake thought, the Kaiser's war machine was running in top gear.

The secondhand clothes shop was a godsend. The owner, a bespectacled woman wearing a flowered overall and a turban, was rolling rails of coats and suits out on to the pavement as he arrived.

Blake went straight inside. The facial blemish that resembled a duelling scar was useful as an apparent Teutonic badge, but damning as part of a wanted man's description. The less he was seen on the street the better – especially choosing a change of clothes.

In the gloomy recesses of the shop he found a table piled high with odds and ends of army uniform. He chose a high-necked tunic with the insignia and badges of rank removed, and a greatcoat of the type issued to private soldiers. Nearer the door were piles of rough cotton shirts and workmen's baggy corduroys. Blake slung the grey-green coat over his shoulders and had the rest of his purchases parcelled up in brown paper. Then he set off in search of a cheap shoe shop.

By nine o'clock he had bought thick-soled brogues, found a public baths and wash-house, and transformed himself into an out-of-work ex-soldier looking for an easy job. A worn, slightly greasy forage cap, found doubled up in the greatcoat pocket, completed the picture.

Gerhardt Ehrlich's sodden suit, boots and underclothes, packaged now in the brown paper, were discarded among dustbins in a lane behind the baths. Blake's ID, army pay book and the papers recovered from the torn lining of the Norfolk jacket were buttoned into a pocket of the private's tunic.

He walked to the railway station near the city centre and joined a queue in the booking office.

For him, this was the moment of maximum danger. Had he reasoned correctly, travelling beyond Siegsdorf and then doubling back?

There were, of course, police outside the doors leading to the platforms. But there probably were at every station in Germany. And not just because of a minor manhunt east of the Ruhr.

There was nothing for it but to go through, hoping for the best.

He was standing in front of the ticket window.

'*Eine Tagesrückfahrkarte nach Detmold, bitte,*' he told the woman clerk. A day return, he thought, might just direct their attention away from Siegsdorf if any questions *were* asked later.

The woman was piling small change on top of the pasteboard ticket.

'*Wann fahrt der Zug ab?*'

'*Halb zehn.*' It leaves at nine-thirty, she told him.

'*Von welchem Bahnsteig . . . ?*'

Platform three, she interrupted, already raising an enquiring eyebrow at the passenger waiting behind him.

Blake nodded, scooping up ticket and change. There was nothing for it, he thought again. He would have to walk past those policemen and push through the doors. Dry-mouthed, he walked.

The officers – there were three of them – scarcely glanced at him as he trudged lamely past. He crossed a footbridge to platform three and waited behind a pillar, his heart thudding painfully, until the train came in.

Perhaps fortunately, all the carriages were crowded.

Laden housewives who had been to the market, soldiers on leave, workers in overalls. Blake was ready to jump down from the footboard as the train steamed into the station at Siegsdorf.

There were police there too, but their attention was concentrated on a local arriving from Paderborn; passengers from Dortmund were waved straight through.

So far, so good, Blake thought. It was encouraging to note that his reasoning, at any rate in the short term, had been without fault.

A man in uniform was barring his way.

Momentarily, he felt the blood drain to his feet. He was unable to draw in breath.

'This ticket is a return to Detmold,' the collector said accusingly. 'That's another three stations.'

'I . . . I know,' Blake said huskily, feeling relief flood through him. 'I changed my mind, that's all. Someone . . . a man I met on the train told me I'd have a better chance of a job here.'

'A fat chance, if you ask me.' The ticket collector was dismissive. 'You won't get a refund, you know. And you can't continue later on the unused portion. No breaking the journey on a day return.'

'Yes, yes. I know. Thank you. I . . . it doesn't matter,' Blake stammered as the ticket was torn across and he was handed the return half.

The official grunted. 'People who throw away their money,' he said angrily to a colleague standing beside him.

Thankfully, Blake made his escape. Just so long as he didn't throw away his life, he thought.

The factory – a two-storey administration block and four separate workshops with serrated roofs and a lot of glass – glittered and sparkled against a background of dense woods in the sunshine which had dispersed the clouds at midday. There was no landing field attached to it, but a new Fokker Eindekker E-III still without a squadron identification stood on a motor trailer just inside the entrance gates.

Blake felt his heart beat faster. At last his goal, the physical reality surrounding the abstract paperwork he had come to steal, lay before his eyes. Finally he could begin to work out the steps he must take to overcome the ultimate obstacle barring the successful end to his mission – or examine the alternatives to those particular steps if his first plans proved unworkable.

He had wondered idly, walking the two miles from Siegsdorf, whether he might not pursue genuinely the course he had trailed as part of his cover on the way there: walk boldly right into the factory and ask for work. Even if the answer was no, he would at least get a glimpse of the interior layout.

But a single glance at the site, once he had breasted the last rise and seen the place close to, slid that one straight into the tray marked 'unworkable'.

There was a military presence, for a start. He could see armed soldiers inside the tall iron gates, a sentry box and what looked like a guardhouse. More men, walking in pairs, patrolled between the single-storey workshops, and once he thought he saw dogs.

There seemed to be no other entrance breaking the close-linked wire fence which surrounded the factory. Perhaps Mynheer Fokker's aeroplane interrupter gear was not the only military secret being developed below those flashing roof slopes of glass?

One thing, he felt, was certain. An installation requiring this amount of protection would not be left unguarded at night.

Between fields of root crops and ripening corn, he pushed on towards the wood behind the factory. The road led eventually to a village signposted as Salzkotten. He looked only once up the slope that led to the gates as he passed. He could have been a war invalid returning home, any kind of poorly paid worker. None of the soldiers paid him any attention.

Once he was out of sight, he doubled back through the wood to reconnoitre the site from behind.

From this point of view it was slightly less formidable.

It was more obviously a factory, less like a military installation. No patrols were visible and shop-floor noises competed with the birdsong and creak of wind-tossed branches above his head. From the nearest building he could hear hammering, the chunter of belted machinery, a sudden screech as metal bit metal on a lathe.

Trees grew to within ten feet of the wire fence, and a ragged carpet of underbrush encroached further still.

Perhaps the military presence was routine, almost perfunctory, rather than a security imperative? If the factory was engaged in the very topmost of top-secret work, surely the ground would have been totally cleared for at least fifty or even a hundred yards all around the site, and not just in front? It was dangerous, nevertheless, to draw conclusions that happened to suit you from data that was incomplete.

Blake climbed up into the branches of a sycamore tree to watch and wait.

The information he had been given on the factory was, or at any rate seemed to be, fairly complete. He knew that the workshop where Fokker's gear was produced was the third of the four strung out behind the gates. Among the papers buttoned into his pocket was a floor plan of the building with benches and assembly lines clearly marked.

A smaller sheet – of rice-paper which could be chewed up and swallowed in an emergency – sketched the interiors of a foreman's office and design bureau at one end of the shop-floor. Here, the position of filing cabinets, draughtsmen's equipment, worksheets and drawers of planning diagrams, so far as was known, was indicated. He wondered how those who had prepared his papers *had* known. Surely, with information as detailed as this, they must have had some kind of inside access?

And if this was so, why fly out an amateur all the way from England, with all the attendant risks – to the mission as well as the amateur? Why not simply instruct the inside contact, the man already there, to grab the material required and send – or bring – it home?

It was a question he had posed before. And the only answer he could think of was a chilling one. Because if the inside man did that he would be exposed as an Allied agent, and it was more important to the people in London to keep him there incognito than to risk this one particular mission.

Whereas the amateur, if he was caught, was . . . well, expendable?

Better, Blake thought, to stop hypothesizing and get on with the job.

How, first, to penetrate the site?

It would, of course, have to be after dark, when the workforce was absent. The fence was about seven feet high. Even if it was not electrified, it could virtually be ruled out as a crossing point, particularly if the place was guarded at night, and especially if there were dogs. The trees, then, seemed the best bet.

Several of them spread low branches towards the fence; there were one or two places where an agile man – if he could find a branch that would hold his weight – might swing out and drop down on the inner side of the wire. This, on the other hand, would leave him in the same position in relation to guards and/or dogs as if he had found some way to climb over. He would have a better chance if he could somehow reach the two-storey admin block, and from there approach across the roofs.

From his perch in the sycamore, Blake allowed his eyes to rove the perimeter.

The block was just that – an industrial module, rectangular in plan, with a flat roof, two double-square and two treble-square façades. A narrow gap, spanned at ground-floor level by a covered passageway, separated it from the nearest workshop. And, yes, so far as he could see, there were at least two possible trees that might provide a jumping-off base.

From Blake's vantage point, the block was about a third of the way around the perimeter. He dropped from his branch and hurried through the undergrowth to a spot opposite the rear wall of the building. From here he was still out of sight so far as the guards on the gate were concerned, but he could see the gravelled turning area where the trailer with the Eindekker was parked.

The trunk of the first tree grew within twelve feet of the fence, with a complex of trailing branches sweeping towards the site. But the far ends of these, drooping close to the wire, offered no chance of a leap or climb to the roof of the block, even if they would bear his weight. In addition to this, the tree was some kind of pine, with a scaly bark that oozed resin – not the most suitable material to smear over the hands and clothes of a man whose life depended on undetectability.

The second tree was set much further back. But this one was a sturdy oak, taller than most of the others on the fringe of the wood, with heavy branches jutting horizontally towards the site from quite high up.

Blake eyed it speculatively. From the topmost of these, was it conceivable that a man could leap to the roof of the block?

Absolutely not. Not even the finest athlete. On the other hand . . .

He stared. If a length of rope was looped from that branch, perhaps seven or eight feet of it, and a man swung out and over on the end of that, could he . . . ?

No again, so far as the roof was concerned. But he could drop right beside the wall of the building, as far as possible from the fence, without the need to cross that potentially dangerous strip of open land in between.

And from there, via two rows of arched window embrasures, it would surely be possible to climb to the roof? Blake thought it would. Whether it would be better to use the techniques of breaking and entering that he had been taught from there, or through one of those windows, was a question he would consider later, once he had worked out the logistics of the rope and the tree. For the moment it would be enough to shin up there and test the branch.

The branch was solid. But if he was going to get enough momentum to swing himself as far as the block wall, he would need more like ten feet of rope. More difficult still, if he was to work up enough back-swing on the pendulum, in the right direction, he would have to remove one of the lower branches on the tree. And that meant a sizeable saw, for the branch was more than six inches thick at the base.

Two soldiers emerged from the alley between the admin block and the first workshop. Once behind the block, they leaned against the wall to light cigarettes, shielding match flames against the wind with cupped hands. Were they in fact a nonchalant patrol? Or two men dodging out of sight for an instant to enjoy a forbidden smoke?

Shrinking back among the foliage above, Blake realized he would have to keep watch for much longer if he was to find out exactly how the factory was guarded and how often the surrounding territory was liable to be watched.

Somewhere inside one of the workshops a bell shrilled insistently. The rumble and clatter of machinery dwindled and then died away. Suddenly the late afternoon air was alive with voices. Three motor buses ground up the slope and parked beside the trailer. The day's work was evidently over.

Overalled women and elderly men in dungarees streamed out through pass doors in the tall wooden blinds closing off the loading bay in each factory block. They filed past the gap between these and the admin block and headed for the parking area.

Blake was about to climb down from his tree and take a closer look at the installation's security routine when movement around the buses froze him astride the branch.

The home-going workers were approaching . . . but as many more, mainly men this time, were crowding out of the vehicles and hurrying towards the workshops.

Blake bit his lip. Inwardly he cursed. How stupid! Of course he should have thought of this himself. In a militaristic country with insatiable battle demands for men and machines, they were not going to halt production just because darkness fell. Especially when the machines that could fly were knocking enemies out of the sky almost as fast as they could take off. The English catch-phrase 'Don't you know there's a war on?' came to his mind.

Clearly the Siegsdorf assembly lines were working round the clock, in eight- or twelve-hour shifts.

He had thought, naively, that once he had eluded any guards posted at night he could safely take his time, working inside throughout the hours of darkness until he had located the information he needed and if possible discovered completed parts of the new Fokker design. But if the factory was working full blast all night the task was going to be twice, three times, ten times more hazardous. If it was going to be possible at all.

The engines of the buses coughed into life and they rattled away towards the gates. The incoming shift, after a certain amount of ribaldry and badinage with the men and women they were relieving, had been swallowed up within the workshops. The bell was shrilling again. Soon the machinery was tapping and thumping as before. Two soldiers with rifles slung over their shoulders circled behind the buildings, glancing cursorily right and left as they walked.

There was a sick feeling in Blake's stomach. How could he be expected to find and then steal papers from a place that was guarded outside and staffed inside night and day? Why hadn't the people in London warned him? Why had they not arranged a personal contact with his cut-out, so that he could at least seek help or advice or even discuss the damned problems?

His earlier thoughts about his expendability returned, and gnawed away at his resolve. He became sorry for himself, and then furiously angry. It wasn't fair. He was a scout pilot and not a professional bloody burglar! Why should he be plunged against his will into this ridiculous, *dangerous* situation, stuck with this lethal operation which had become impossible through the incompetence of those sitting safely in London, sipping whisky and soda before they were chauffeured home to their soft beds?

Then the sense of outrage swung the pendulum of his emotions the other way. Damn them all! Very well, he would show them. They couldn't push him around all over the shop and then wash their hands of him just like that. He would get their damned plans by hook or by crook and throw them in the face of . . . well, someone with red tabs and a lot of rank!

If he was to have any chance at all, he reflected when his rage had cooled a little, the attempt would have to be made at night just the same. At least darkness would allow him, with luck, to approach the outside of the buildings unseen. The strip of ground between the fence and the factory would no longer be a danger. And, for reasons of safety and silence, he would still use the rope. Two questions, however, were vital. How often did the two-man patrol, with or without torches, circle the perimeter during the hours of darkness? And was there at any time during the night the equivalent of an English tea-break for the German workforce? If there was, that had to be the time during which he launched himself across the wire. Because it seemed to him that only if workers were eddying around away from their machines would he have a reasonable chance of getting inside the block where the Fokker gear was made.

Both questions, of course, demanded that he remain on watch until the next change of shift. Blake prepared for an uncomfortable night.

It could have been worse. He wedged himself into a fairly comfortable fork lower down the oak, with enough support at the sides to stop him falling out of the tree if he fell asleep momentarily. Discomfort in any case was not the major problem. Along with an aching hunger, drowsiness was, for this was his second night without sleep.

There was no moon. Visually, there was practically nothing to attract the attention: light escaping through the slanted glass roofs of the factory cast a dim yellowish glow on low clouds scudding overhead. Only an occasional hum of conversation from the guardhouse punctuated the monotone of distant machinery, the soothing night sounds of creaking branches and the rustle of leaves.

Twice it was only a sudden freshening of the cool wind that jerked him awake as the darkness intruded and he slid into nothing. Once, as he was overwhelmed, his head snapped back to hit a sharp projection on the trunk and he felt a warm trickle of blood on his neck. The fight to keep awake was hell.

By the time the yellow glow faded against brightness spreading from the east, Blake was in possession, nevertheless, of four essential items of information.

The interval between successive passages of the patrol was on average half an hour, occasionally more, never less.

The soldiers patrolling did carry torches, sweeping them outside and inside as they marched.

The factory worked twelve-hour shifts.

There *was* a thirty-minute break – between eleven forty-five and a quarter past midnight – during which the machines were stopped and the workers flooded into the open air to smoke a cigarette, or filed into what he assumed was a canteen on the ground floor of the admin block. This might or might not coincide, he gathered, with the interval between patrols. On this particular night there was an overlap of ten minutes: the patrol passed at five past midnight. Something he could work out in advance if he took up his position early on the night he made his attempt.

It was during the change of shifts early in the morning that he climbed stiffly out of his tree, threaded his way through the wood and limped back along the road, past the workers milling around the buses, towards Siegsdorf.

It was a difficult day. Aching in every limb, Blake crammed black bread and acorn coffee into his belly at a workers' café near the railway station. He dare not order anything more substantial because he was running out of small coins and the high-denomination banknotes which could have passed without comment in the hands of Gerhardt Ehrlich would instantly arouse suspicion proffered by an out-of-work ex-soldier.

He had the same problem buying the saw he needed. The shopkeeper at once asked the direct question. Eyeing Blake, unshaven, unkempt, dressed in the clothes of a down-and-out, he demanded: 'What do *you* want with a thing like that?' as soon as Blake indicated the tool he had chosen.

'Some woman outside town offered me half a day's work cutting up logs,' he stammered. 'Her own saw's useless, rusted practically through. She gave me this with orders to buy her a new one.' He offered the man the single note he had got ready for just such a situation.

Before he reached for the saw, the shopkeeper examined the note carefully.

'And I'm to ask for a receipt,' Blake added. 'The old bitch is afraid I'll buy a cheap tool, say it was expensive and pocket the change.'

'I don't blame her,' the shopkeeper said. He counted change on to his counter and scrawled figures on a slip of paper.

'Nobody trusts anybody these days,' Blake said bitterly.

'With reason. Who is this lady anyway?'

'Frau Schneider,' Blake improvised. 'On the Belecke road.'

'Never heard of her.'

'That doesn't mean she won't need logs when it turns cold again,' Blake snapped. He snatched the saw and walked out of the shop.

His skin was crawling with fatigue, but he had to try half a dozen small shops before he could find a length of rope that was small enough not to be conspicuous but strong enough to bear his weight.

Before he left England he had been given a small bunch of flat skeleton keys, which he carried next to his skin, attached to a cord around his waist. But he still required several small household utensils which could be put to use in burglary if necessary. This again meant an odyssey involving several different shops in different parts of the town.

He was virtually at the end of his tether by the time he bought a loaf of bread and trudged away from the shops. The rope was coiled around his waist beneath the army tunic, the small tools lay inside the pockets of the greatcoat, the saw was wrapped in a piece of sacking he had found in a side-street.

So far – an extra toll on his dwindling reserves of energy – he had managed to dodge away or change direction each time he saw a policeman in the distance. But anyone who stopped him now, looking the way he did, and found what he was carrying, would have taken him instantly for a thief.

He was forced to drag himself more than a mile out into the country before he found a suitably deserted field which had already been harvested. Scrambling through a hedge, he hurried to the furthest haystack, dropped thankfully to the ground . . . and was asleep almost before his back had touched the straw.

13

Just before night fell the wind freshened again, flattening the stalks of ripening corn, roaring like distant surf through the upper branches of the trees in the wood.

The clouds, escaping into the higher reaches of the sky, moved more slowly from west to east. Blake wondered how long it was since they had crossed the English coast.

He had raised one arm to shield his face from the punishing gusts as he climbed the rise before the factory site, hoping that the suspiciously bulky bundle of sacking under his right arm would not draw the attention of the guards on the gate. The Eindekker and its trailer had gone, he noticed – presumably now equipped with the latest modification of the Fokker interrupter gear. The buses bringing the night shift should in any case be arriving at any minute.

He was almost level with the first line of trees when he heard the grinding of gears from the hill behind him. The soldiers had been too busy opening the gates to bother with the tramp on his way to the next village. By the time the factory bell signalled the stoppage, he was out of sight, pushing through the bushes towards the oak.

He would make fast the top end of the rope now, he had decided, but not allow the rest to drop until after dark. The tree was moving uneasily in the wind, the lower branches threshing as he climbed. Moving out as far as he dared beneath the tossing leaves, he uncoiled the rope from around his waist and knotted one end firmly. Then, edging back along the swaying branch, he looped the rest loosely around the gnarled wood. It was time now for one of the most delicate parts of the operation.

Extraneous noises, he had reasoned, would be more noticeable after dark; the best time at least to start sawing would be during the change-over, while the guards were occupied with the departing shift and the engines of the buses were running. There wasn't much time left, he saw: the day workers were already boarding. The moment the bell shrilled for the newcomers, he would begin.

The lower branch was crooked, with many leafy offshoots. It was going to make the devil of a noise when finally it fell, crashing through twenty feet of healthy wood. The treetop agitation caused by the wind would help to mask this, of course. But the wind would also carry the sounds of sawing, one of the most easily identifiable of all noises, more clearly to the workshops. Positioning himself carefully with his legs wrapped around a neighbouring branch, he stroked the curve of rough bark experimentally with the shining teeth of the new saw.

A pale drift of sawdust fell, and then was whisked away by the wind. The teeth bit into the bark with a satisfying ease. But once the harder wood was reached, he had to use a great deal more force and the familiar alto rasp shivered out from beneath the trees. When the buses had gone, he would have to limit himself almost to a single stroke at a time. And this would make for trouble when he was halfway through and the edges of the cut wood tended to close in over the blade. Without the impetus of continuous, forceful strokes, Blake knew, sawing through to a point where the branch was ready to fall was going to be a long job.

What the hell: he had until eleven forty-five!

The buses drove away, the sound of their exhausts swallowed in the continuous rumble of factory machinery as they coasted down the far side of the hill. Slowly, the light faded. Two soldiers circled the site, stopping behind the admin block to light cigarettes.

Beneath the restless treetops, Blake sweated, pushing his saw hard in and down, waiting until the next gust blew, withdrawing with as much force as he could muster, pushing again. After ten minutes of these single strokes, the cut was less than an inch deep. Grunting with impatience, he varied the rhythm and changed to an in-and-out pattern: one-and-two ... pause ... one-and-two. A quarter of an hour later, he was forced to move to the other side of the trunk and shift the saw to his left hand. His grasp on the wooden grip was rubbing the grazed palm raw. The branch was penetrated to a depth of two and a half inches.

Light splashed into the gathering dusk through the glass roof of each workshop. Another patrol passed. Thankfully there were no dogs. Through slatted shutters on the ground floor, Blake could see that the canteen was illuminated. The arched windows on the upper floor remained dark.

When the branch was sawn halfway through, he rested, panting after the combined tensions of force and restraint. The palms of both hands ached abominably.

It was completely dark now. He was marooned in a world of wind, relying only on his sense of touch to keep him from overbalancing as he thrust and pulled. All around him invisible branches creaked and swung.

Shafts of brilliance lanced the blackness as a patrol passed, probing the strip between fence and factory.

The work became harder with every stroke now that most of the blade was submerged in the cut. When his fingers told him that he was three-quarters of the way through, Blake rested again.

The wind, which had blown less fiercely for some time, now redoubled its force, savaging the trees in the wood with an express-train roar. Abruptly, Blake found that his saw was moving in a widening gap. The weight of twigs and foliage at the outer end of the branch, blown this way and that by each blustering gust, was wagging the whole unit up and down.

With a sudden splintering crash, the branch broke free, ripping away to leave a long scar marking the trunk. To Blake, frozen halfway up the oak, the noise as it plunged to the ground, tearing off leaves and smaller branches with it, was louder than an artillery barrage.

One of the workshop pass doors was flung open, casting a band of light across the strip. A man stood silhouetted in the gap. 'What the devil was that?' he called. There was shouting too from the direction of the guardhouse. The torches appeared, bobbing through the dark. Cowering behind the trunk of the tree, Blake stared down at the tell-tale gash, bone-white in the gloom, where the branch had torn away. In daylight it would be obvious that it had been sawn half through; at night, with foliage tossing all around it, there was a chance the clue might be missed. Clinging to the trunk, he held his breath.

The beams swung to and fro as the soldiers advanced. Reflected light gleamed from the barrels of the revolvers they held.

One of the beams halted; the other swung across, converging on the foot of the oak. The soldiers approached the fence, playing the beams up, down, left and right. 'It's all right,' one of them yelled over the uproar in the wood. 'Just the damned wind! Bloody great branch has torn away from one of the trees.'

The soldiers returned to the guardhouse. The workshop door closed. Darkness flooded the site once more. Blake breathed again.

He climbed back up to what he thought of as his own branch. Feeling for the looped rope, he unwound the whole length and allowed it to drop from the outer extremity, where he had firmly knotted one end earlier.

Thinking of his damaged palms, he had tied double knots at eighteen-inch intervals all the way down before he left the hayfield. With these to help his descent, he hoped to avoid – or at least minimize – rope burns when he let himself down to swing out over the fence.

It would be as well just the same, he thought, face down along the branch, to test it now, before the action started. He lowered himself until his feet could grip one of the knots. Then, with great care, he transferred his hands – and his weight – from the branch to the rope.

It wasn't too difficult with the help of the knots. Certainly the grazed palms still gave him hell, but soon he was clinging to the lower end a few feet above the top of the fence. Just to check that the plan was feasible, he started to shift his weight, swinging the rope backwards and for-wards, confirming that the lost branch would allow him enough back-swing to work up the proper momentum.

Yes, up and over, back among the roaring branches, forward again with the dull gleam of the wire beneath his feet. A long way off, he could hear an aero engine in the night sky. Some lucky pilot – perhaps from the field at Paderborn? – learning to fly at night.

It could have been nothing but the thought of flight, the concept of being alone, in control of his own destiny, safe in a machine above the world – but suddenly, agonizingly, Blake was seized by a terrible panic. The sound of machinery was all at once unbearably loud. Nausea clawed at his stomach. His legs and arms trembled and an icy chill gripped his back.

He wasn't at the controls of an aeroplane, where he belonged. He was swinging at the end of a rope far behind the lines in enemy territory, preparing to plunge himself into an adventure as mad as it was dangerous. The mission was no longer academic, a chess game in his head. Those were real soldiers on the other side of the wire fence, real enemies with real guns; men who would shoot to kill if they even saw him. The whole thing was impossible, a joke. He must climb back at once to the safety of his branch.

He saw again the scout car turn over, the burst of flame. Saw his friend run past to save the burning driver, saw the landscape stilled as he felt the searing heat and stopped dead . . .

He didn't climb back up the rope. He let go and dropped ten feet to the ground.

Shuddering in every limb, he stumbled to his feet and turned his back to run. He ran blindly away, away from the factory, blindly through the howling trees.

14

'We lost twenty-three machines yesterday in the Somme sector alone,' the major-general said accusingly. 'Hang it all, when's your fellow going to come up with results?'

'Very soon, sir . . . we hope,' the brigadier told him.

'What do you mean, you hope? How's it going? What's his latest report?'

The brigadier cleared his throat. 'Well, sir, the fact is . . . actually we have lost touch with him.'

'Good God! What the devil happened?'

'He crash-landed his machine near the Weser valley,' the brigadier said. 'Got out from the wreck undamaged, and signalled our contact in Germany that evening as instructed. The next signal, the following day, reported that he had moved south-west. Place called Paderborn. Told the contact that he was going to spend the night there and move on to Siegsdorf the next morning. Said, apparently, that he'd come across something important that could affect the mission.'

'And?'

'I'm afraid that's the last we heard of him. Never signalled the next day. Or yesterday. Either he's been taken or forced to abandon his transmitter.'

'Good grief, man! You must replace him at once, then.'

'Think of the time that would take, sir. The contact

reports that there's reason to believe he did get to Siegsdorf. We decided to wait one more day.'

The officers were sitting on either side of a desk in a staff office on the first floor of a government annexe opposite Mudie's bookshop in Oxford Street. An RAOC corporal sat taking notes beneath a large-scale map of Germany hanging on one wall.

'And you really think the chap's worth waiting for?' the major-general demanded. 'Competent and trustworthy enough to allow him that margin?'

'To be honest,' the brigadier confessed, 'I thought meself that the young blighter was a bit on the arty-crafty side. More of a civvy really. But my adjutant – Hesketh, you know – Hesketh has a great deal of faith in him. Spent half a bloody afternoon telling me why he was the only man for the job.'

'H'm. Yes, well ...' The senior man pushed back his swivel chair, rose to his feet and walked to the window.

There was a traffic jam on the corner below. Two hundred yards away a huge slant of rubble blocked the street where a Zeppelin bomb had destroyed half a department store. Two horse-drawn omnibuses going in different directions were locked together wheel to wheel, and a scarlet Royal Mail van, running up on to the pavement in an attempt to bypass the block, had crashed into a pillar box. A ragged urchin carrying a pile of newspapers dropped from the step of one bus and dodged, whistling, between the wheels to cross the street. He ran into an alley between two houses with boarded-up windows and vanished – for ever.

Standing with his back to the room and his hands clasped behind him, the major-general sighed.

Had the arty-crafty young man with the title Patrice

Blake disappeared as finally – and as completely – as the boy with the newspapers? Or were there more leaves inside that particular book yet to be filled before the covers were closed?

It is not wars and deaths and diseases and natural catastrophes that age and sadden us, the major-general reflected, but the way people on omnibuses look and feel, and run into alleys between bomb-damaged houses.

Then he thought of all the young men, perhaps just as arty and crafty as this beggar Blake, who would fall screaming from the sky tomorrow or die above the earth with bullets in their backs, and he shook his head.

Abruptly he swung around to face into the room. 'Very well,' he said to the brigadier. 'Twenty-four hours.'

15

Shame was not the emotion uppermost in Blake's mind: it was the only emotion there.

He had awoken at dawn lying beneath the familiar haystack, with no recollection of his flight beyond that initial panic-stricken dash away from the factory and out of the wood. He must have run blindly past the gates and on down the road to the harvested field, allowing his subconscious to convey him to the one safe haven he had found in this hostile country.

Waking up was itself a nightmare. Awareness at first filtered slowly through the clouds of a half-remembered dream, registered an agreeable sensation of exhaustion relieved, coupled with a stiff neck and a pain in his back, and then confirmed to him his own identity. He opened his eyes, to see beads of dew glistening on the rough cloth of his greatcoat and brightness in the sky above white mist blanketing the far side of the field.

It was the realization that the palms of his hands hurt that jolted him into the horror of his situation. Oh, Jesus. He had failed, let the side down, betrayed the trust placed in him. He had quit under fire – not even under fire – funking it at the last moment when everything was in place and ready to go. As the Yanks said, he had chickened out. Now, with agonizing clarity, he saw again the wire fence, the knotted rope and the soldiers' torches. He heard the insistent hum of machinery and the shrilling bell.

Never send to know for whom the bell tolls; it tolls for thee.

It tolled for cowardice, desertion and dereliction of duty; it tolled for the loss of self-respect and the compulsion to run.

Blake was overwhelmed by guilt and the dreadful knowledge that he could neither control nor master his abject, craven fear. The knowledge hit him with the impact of a blow to the stomach.

He turned over and vomited into the straw.

Before nine o'clock that morning Blake was back in Siegsdorf. He had stumbled through more fields, passed village women washing sheets on flat stones by a stream, held his breath as a squadron of cavalry – Uhlans with tall boots and spiked helmets – cantered across the country road. Now he was approaching the central square along the town's main street.

Between the burgomaster's office, the town hall and the railway station, there was a covered market with a few stalls of fruit and vegetables visible through the stone arches. Queues had already formed outside the shops that were open and there was a crowd milling around the entrance to a food office where ration tickets were issued. Blake skirted a shuttered hotel and paused outside a cheap restaurant in a row of crooked, gabled, half-timbered houses.

His mind was ablaze with a single thought: his honour, his faith in himself must be avenged, restored.

He must return to the factory and do it again – right this time. Whatever the cost.

Exhaustion, provoked by lack of sleep, hunger, stress

and the insidious effect of the head cold that was now, undeniably, taking hold of him had produced the aberration responsible for his weakness. Without these defects, he rationalized, the operation would have gone ahead as planned.

A second attempt would be – must be – successful. Certainly there was danger; it was normal to be afraid. Admittedly, there was a cowardly streak in him – lack of moral fibre, the army disdainfully called it – but such things, for God's sake, could be overcome.

Had he been in good form, the failure, the inexcusable would never have happened. To regain that form, he must eat properly, rest, and convince himself that the blackout was a bad dream.

The first step, then, had been the determination to return to Siegsdorf. Shame anyway rendered the neighbourhood of the factory insupportable. If there were police checks while he was in town, the hell with it – he would brazen them out.

The bravado was, of course, superficial, a psychological ploy enabling him to live with himself and his humiliation. It was hunger as much as anything else that drove him back. But it served to carry him through the first agonizing hours of self-hate and defeat.

He stood outside the restaurant, eyeing the police picketing the station a hundred yards away. He couldn't see inside: the morning was chilly and the windows were steamed up. He had small change now, so he would go in anyway, whether the place was deserted or full. He was moving towards the door when his eye was caught by a series of marks on the steamy window.

A passing child on the way to school, he supposed, had scrawled capital letters in the condensation, the way

some people drew pictures, funny faces. He read 'DNAL'
. . . and a little below, 'TNOC'.

He shrugged. The letters meant nothing, conveyed
nothing to him . . . until he realized that the condensation
was on the inside of the heated room, not outside in the
cold. So they had been written from the inside . . .

Astonishingly a small circular space was rubbed clear
on the far side of the window, and in it there appeared
what seemed to be a hand with a beckoning finger.

And written from the inside, the letters would spell
out 'LAND' and 'CONT'. His Morse call-sign and the
cut-out's response.

He stood there dumbfounded. Those two groups of
letters had been scrawled to convey a message outside
the restaurant. But could it possibly, conceivably be
meant for him? *Was* it an incredible coincidence? Or
had the cut-out another agent in the area, with identical
call-signs?

The pulses in Blake's wrists were hammering. His
breath caught in his throat. There was only one way
to find out. He glanced again at that ghostly, beckoning
finger. Movingly slightly, it was still crooked.

He swallowed, turned to his right, walked five
paces. He climbed three steps and pushed open the
restaurant door. A bell clanged overhead. He strode
inside.

The place was overcrowded, overheated, humid. He
smelled sausage meat, sauerkraut, the acrid odour of
bad coffee. There were five small tables ranged beneath
the window. Advancing, he looked for the circular space
in the condensation.

It was beside, and slightly behind, the middle table.
There were two chairs, but only one was occupied.

He paused fractionally in mid-stride, and then continued at the same pace. There must be some mistake: the customer at the table was a young woman.

He looked beyond. Not possible either. The stout, middle-aged German sitting there beneath a pig's-bristle haircut was wearing thick woollen gloves as he gulped steaming coffee from a bowl. Even without the gloves, he was too far forward to have traced the letters or rubbed the steamy window clear.

Blake bit his lip. Was it possible that those same letters had quite a different meaning, by coincidence a risqué meaning to Germans on the home front? Was there a chance that the young woman was in fact a prostitute seeking trade?

In *Siegsdorf-am-Lippe*? At nine o'clock in the morning? With a disreputable down-and-out like himself?

Pack it in, man! he told himself.

The girl was well dressed, wearing some kind of uniform, quite pretty. She had thin hands and slender, elegant wrists. She looked out of place among the workers and small shopkeepers in that cheap restaurant.

Blake was level with her table, staring carefully straight ahead, when she spoke. 'Gunter! How nice to see you – and what a surprise!' in quite a loud voice. And then, very quietly indeed: 'Do please sit down.'

Blake stopped dead. The second sentence had been murmured in flawless French. '*Asseyez-vous, je vous en prie.*'

He dropped into the vacant chair, the sweat starting on his forehead.

'You must be famished,' the girl said in German. 'After all that travelling. Let me order something for you at once.' She raised the beckoning hand to call over a slatternly woman carrying a tray of used cups and saucers.

'Thank you,' Blake stammered as the waitress approached. 'I . . . I'll have the sauerkraut with black bread, a knackwurst on the side and a glass of beer.'

'And a large schnapps,' the girl added.

The woman nodded and went away.

Blake stared across the table, waiting for a lead. She had curling auburn hair, tucked under a close-fitting velour hat. The uniform was greenish-grey, with a high-buttoned jacket and a skirt that must have reached almost to her ankles.

'It's quieter here than Detmold or Paderborn, don't you think?' she said conversationally. 'And much less noisy than Dortmund, especially near the railway station.'

'It has its advantages,' he said, looking straight at her. Her eyes were very wide, halfway between jade green and hazel. There was some kind of military badge or cockade attached to the ribbon at one side of her hat.

For him, things had begun to fall into place. Apart from the obvious hint that she was in some mysterious way familiar with his recent movements, it was the lapse into French – clearly a signal – that did it.

He remembered that this particular area of Germany had once been colonized by French Protestant refugees after Louis XIV had revoked the Edict of Nantes in 1685. He recalled too that, during his initial briefing, the cartographer had told him that he was going to 'one of the few Hun regions with something of a French cultural tradition'. The chap had also said he might be able to exploit his ancestry. That settled it. A family with a French connection 'not altogether hostile', as he had put it – what ground could be more fertile for the recruitment of secret agents! The girl *must* be associated in some way with his lost cut-out . . .

The waitress set food and drink before him. He gulped

the schnapps and started greedily forking bread and sausage into his mouth.

The girl allowed him to get halfway through the sauerkraut before she said sympathetically: 'You've had a hard time of it, haven't you?'

Blake looked up from his plate. He raised his glass and swallowed some beer. 'How do you know?'

'I have been looking for you ever since you lost the transmitter,' she said.

'You mean . . . ? You're telling me that you yourself . . . ?' He was still staring. '*You* are the cut-out? You're in this part of the country already, so why the damned Morse at all, then? Why didn't they just instruct us to meet?'

'It is important – or was important – that there was no possible connection between us. As a permanent operative, you understand, I have other work to do also. But once our means of contact was removed, London decided an exception would have to be made, and I was ordered to make myself known to you.'

'Yes, but, I mean, how did you know where I was? How did you find me? How, for God's sake, did you know I would be passing this particular restaurant at this particular time today, that I would actually come in?' He shook his head. 'Come to that, how the devil did you know that I was me anyway?'

'I did have a photograph,' she smiled. 'And if one is in the know, you don't look so *very* German – even with the scar.'

'I still don't understand . . .'

'All I knew was that you were coming to Siegsdorf. I'd no idea what for: we never discuss the details of missions with agents . . .'

'Yes, they told me on no account to refer to it. They call it security.'

'. . . so I thought the best thing, after the police had taken your transmitter, was simply to come here myself and wait for you.'

'How did you know that was what happened? That the police had it?'

She touched the buttoned jacket. An agreeable curve thrust it out above the tight waist. 'This is the uniform of an auxiliary nursing service attached to the air command. I am based at the aerodrome outside Paderborn. It is not difficult to hear the echoes of what goes on – especially when it concerns a mysterious flying machine arriving from the north.'

'People talk. I know. So you learned . . . ?'

'I heard about your escape from the hotel in Paderborn,' the girl said. 'I assumed you would eventually come here. So I came too, hoping I would be able to help.'

Blake had finished his meal. He pushed away his plate. 'You must be a very good – what do they call it? – a very discreet tail,' he said.

'It was not necessary actually to follow you. You saw the hotel down the road, the one all boarded up? . . . Exactly. So. Well, it is closed for the duration of the war. But I have a key because it belongs to my aunt and uncle. All I had to do was keep a watch from behind the shutters there. I saw you arrive at the station yesterday – from Dortmund, that was smart! I saw you again later, visiting shops. And then you left, walking along the road to Salzkotten.' The girl raised one hand, signalling that she wanted the bill.

After the waitress had taken the money, she continued, still keeping her voice well down below the hubbub of voices in the crowded restaurant: 'There is only one place on that road that could possibly interest you: the Krupp subsidiary where they make spare parts for aeroplanes. I assume you went there?' She looked at Blake enquiringly.

He nodded but made no comment.

'As you did not return until this morning,' the girl said, 'I wondered if perhaps your mission had succeeded, and you might not need my help after all. I thought it wise, just the same, to make contact. So I hurried here to leave my little . . . message . . . in the hope that you might stop and see it.'

'Weren't you taking a bit of a risk there? That I might not have stopped. Or gone straight to the station?'

'Not really. If you had been up all night you would need a meal . . . and this is the only eating place open in town. What shall I tell London: that you have succeeded?'

'No,' Blake said shortly. 'There was . . . a hitch.'

'What happened?'

'Something went wrong. It's a question, well, of getting inside that factory. I had to postpone the attempt, try it again another day.'

'Naturally, I shall help all I can. What exactly do you have to do?'

'Like yourself, I have been told not to discuss the details.'

'I understand.' She pushed back her chair. 'You need to rest. I think it is time we left this place.'

They left together and she led him, via a narrow alley, to the rear entrance of the closed hotel.

Her name was Kristin. 'Kristin Dony,' she told him. 'Probably a corruption of Donnée or Dounet, sometime after my family fled here in the eighteenth century.' Her parents were dead, and the aunt who owned the hotel was in Berlin, working as some kind of clerk at the Ministry of the Interior.

Blake lay on a dust sheet covering a feather bed, luxuriating in the sheer comfort of a surface that accepted his tired body without an angle or a lump or a rigid plane. Kristin had gone to find ointment, bandages and disinfectant for his damaged hands – and also to make her report to London.

'In Morse?' Blake had exclaimed. 'All the way from here?'

'No, no.' She laughed. 'By wireless and then telephone. Through Switzerland. What shall I tell them?'

'Tell them that I have arrived at . . . the target.' He thought for a moment. 'Yes, tell them that there was an . . . unforeseen difficulty . . . but that I hope to leave tomorrow with . . . what is required.'

'Very well,' she said. 'Forgive me, but that sounds, well, a little vague. Will they understand exactly what you mean?'

'Oh, yes,' he said. 'They will understand all right.'

Content at last to find that he was no longer totally alone, he turned over and drifted into a dreamless sleep.

He awoke to the sound of horses' hooves clip-clopping over the cobbles, a noisy altercation between two men somewhere below and the rumble of iron-rimmed wheels along the street. In the distance, a lorry engine with one cylinder missing revved up and died, revved up and died.

Kristin was sitting by the shuttered window. She had taken off her jacket and he saw indeed that there was a generous bosom beneath the cream silk blouse tucked into her skirt. Spread out on an occasional table in front of her he saw ham, tomatoes, what looked like a jar of pickled herrings – and a bottle of Sekt, the German champagne.

'I was too late to get more bread,' she said. 'Today's ration had all gone.'

'It looks like a feast!' Blake said, pushing himself up on to one elbow. 'Did you get through?'

'Oh, yes. Message received and understood. Instructions for you were restricted to a single word: "Urgent".'

He smiled. 'As if I didn't know!'

'Part of my work,' Kristin said, 'involves the rehabilitation of returned prisoners of war and the resettlement of troops invalided out of the army. But although at the moment you could pass for either of these, I think it best that we are not seen together – at least until after dark. In case you don't agree, I have brought you a razor.'

'May you be blessed,' he said, fingering the irritation on his unshaven jaw.

'The wisest thing to do, I believe, is to stay here under cover until you think it time to return to the factory. Before that, we can eat and, so far as is possible, amuse ourselves. Does the idea meet with your approval?'

'Nothing,' Blake said truthfully, 'would give me greater pleasure.'

16

Afterwards, Blake could never remember exactly the order in which things happened, that gloomy day in Siegsdorf.

Outside the town, he supposed, the sun never pierced the clouds enough to dispel the early morning mist. Certainly, each time he peered through a gap between the shutters, he saw nothing but a uniform grey overhead. And sometime in the afternoon it must have begun to rain, for when the masked street lamps were tipped into flame by the long pole of the lighter on his bicycle, the flagged pavement and cobbles below glistened damply in the glaring gaslight.

They ate early, and when the Sekt was finished, Kristin produced a flask of schnapps which added a comfortable glow to the inner warmth produced by the sparkling wine. A little before ten o'clock they left – via the rear entrance and the alley as before – because he wanted to arrive at the factory well before the pre-midnight break and arrange the new rope she had procured for him.

In between, however – somehow, in their room in that deserted hotel – the first step was taken in the direction of what he was to remember as one of the most exciting adventures of his life . . .

It must have started, he thought later, when she was changing the bandages she had bound around his hands.

He had already shaved and bathed as well as he could in the cold water of the bathroom. He sat on the bed in a drowsy haze, fortified by the alcohol, determined this time to succeed and to hell with the risks. But underlying this euphoric bravado, scarcely recognizable but throbbing deep within him, was a craving for reassurance and moral support and human warmth. To sustain him on the high he had worked himself up to, he needed appreciation and approval.

What more reassuring, then, than a woman's arms around him; what could be warmer – and indeed more supportive – than a woman's body?

Yes, there was no doubt about it: the hands must have taken, as it were, the first step. His fingers after all were free. He had a very definite remembrance of the initial, electric thrill he felt when the padded tips first brushed against her flesh . . . just above the wrist, he thought.

Did he clutch? Did he stroke? Was that breath-stopping exhilaration the result of an exploration of his own . . . or was Kristin's response less a reaction to any move of his than a spontaneous expression of hidden desire? Of complicity in the face of a shared danger? Of tenderness even?

The tips of her own fingers were cool on his forehead, cooler tracing the line of his jaw . . . then suddenly hot and hard as one hand clenched on either side of his chin, hollowing his cheeks and forcing open his mouth as she leaned down to kiss him.

That was the start of the dizzy period, what he thought of afterwards as the ecstasy.

Her tongue, warm and wet and muscular, speared through as his lips flew open, probing his mouth, teeth, gums, the inner recesses of his cheeks. Dazedly, he allowed his own tongue to be sucked into her mouth.

She was lying on the bed beside him, her arms crossed over his back to grasp his shoulders. Her breathing, fast and shallow, jetted hotly against his cheek. Through two layers of clothes, Blake could feel the heat of her belly against his hardness.

With trembling fingers, he unbuttoned the silk blouse. Beneath thin shoulder straps, the straight line of her bust bodice bulged out over the bosom whose fullness he had already admired. The breasts themselves – she must have whisked off the flimsy garment with her own hands – were a splendour of creamy flesh, swelling from her chest in ripe curves. He cradled their heavy warmth in his bandaged hands as she bent over him on hands and knees. Big nipples, hard and hot, flowered from the puckered brown circles at their tips. Some of the buttons at the side of her long skirt had come undone.

Between the waistband and these hanging delights, Kristin's body was tightly constricted by a whalebone corset inset with panels of yellow leather. Yellow, he supposed, because of the cream-coloured blouse. He reached both hands behind her waist to loosen the severe lacing, but she shook her head and reached back to remove them. 'No, no,' she whispered. 'It takes much too long to put it back on again. Unfasten the rest of my skirt.'

Except in a brothel, to a young man of Blake's background it was almost unthinkable at that time to be naked in bed with an unmarried woman. Equally rare to be able at close quarters to stare at, and revel in, the sight of female nudity. The mess, of course, was full of lascivious tales involving prurient housemaids creeping upstairs after dark to initiate the young master, and farmers' daughters in hay lofts. But nothing like this ever seemed to happen to anyone you knew, and still less to yourself. In the bedroom of the closed hotel in Siegsdorf, Patrice Blake found out for the first time what the Bible meant when it referred to 'knowing' a woman.

Kristin stood silhouetted against the street lighting which crept through the slats between the shutters. Wearing nothing but the corset, knee-length stockings and buttoned black boots with cuban heels which just covered her ankles, she seemed to him the most voluptuous, the most supremely sensual sight he had ever seen in his life.

'And now,' she said hoarsely, 'I think it is time for you to move over on that bed and make room for me, for we have things to say to each other that don't actually need words.'

Blake's heart was thumping in his chest and his mouth was dry, but not from fear this time. Not fear, at any rate, of death and pain and physical harm. A touch perhaps of apprehension at the mystery of woman, but he was much too excited to notice that.

Kristin walked over to the bed and plunged the four fingers of one hand between two of the buttons fastening his fly. Yanking open the front of his corduroys, she pulled them roughly down to his ankles. The fingers reached for him, wrapped firmly around the aching proof of his desire.

Blake thought his heart would stop.

She was straddling him, bare knees clamped to his ribs up near his armpits. Then, slowly, she lowered those padded hips and all at once he was gasping as he was engulfed in the scalding heat of her body.

Later, when the schnapps was finished, she lay on her back and took him into her again, thrusting fiercely up against him as he penetrated, breasts heaving and small cries choked in her throat. All his life he would remember the warmth of those breasts against his naked chest, the graze of damp pubic hair against his belly and the infinite suppleness of the corseted body clamped to his. When finally it was time, it felt to him like a fall from grace.

'There will be a lot of activity at the factory tonight,' Kristin said. 'They sent up three of the new Dr-1 three-winged machines on motor trailers this afternoon. I think the Fokker people are trying out some kind of modification to the original design.'

'Good Lord,' Blake said, 'how do you know that?'

'They were talking about it at the aerodrome yesterday, before I came over here.'

'Why didn't you tell me before?'

'I am afraid it slipped my mind. Why, does it matter?'

'If they're going to work on them all night, presumably in the open air, it might make all the difference – one way or the other, good or bad.'

'My dear, I'm sorry.' She tucked a hand in his arm. They had walked in silence leaving the town, until the last houses were behind them. The place was deserted, with most of the windows already dark, which made it all the wiser, Blake thought, not to run the slightest risk of attracting attention.

He was still a little dizzy from their lovemaking, not quite sure, as the alcoholic euphoria faded, whether or not to believe the evidence provided by his own memory, the tingling still in his fingers, the ache in his loins.

Kristin had been much more matter-of-fact, companionable, almost domesticated about the whole thing – but certainly a little less romantic. Perhaps it was not the first time she had plunged into such an adventure. He put the thought from his mind. They were approaching the brow of the hill beyond which the wood and the factory lay.

They were aware of the sulphurous glow some time before they breasted the rise.

'Great Scott!' he exclaimed as the view opened up before them. 'You were right about the activity, old thing!'

Yellow arc lights flooded the area between the guard-house and the first workshops with glaring brilliance, etching the small, snub-nosed triplanes against the night. Crowding the six-wheeled military trailers, uniformed riggers of the Imperial Army Air Service mingled with factory technicians working on the new aeroplanes. One of them, with its polished aluminium engine cowling removed, was being fitted with parts handed up from a trolley wheeled from one of the workshops. An officer in boots and riding breeches lounged, smoking a cigarette in a holder, against the door of an open Mercedes staff car, with one foot raised to the wide running-board.

Blake and Kristin stopped, half hidden by the branches of a hawthorn growing in a hedgerow. 'No chance tonight, I'm afraid, of sneaking past unnoticed,' he said in a low voice.

'You mean we'll have to skirt the whole site? Through the fields?'

'Don't worry,' he said bitterly. 'I'm familiar with the route.'

17

Light reflected from the far side of the factory helped them to make a rapid, virtually noiseless passage through the wood.

As soon as they arrived at the fence he saw that the broken branch had been removed. And the rope, of course, had gone. 'I'd half expected to find a sentry posted here,' he murmured.

'Did you leave a saw here?' Kristin asked, gazing up at the scarred trunk of the oak.

'Er . . . yes. Yes, I'm afraid I did.' Blake smarted again from the humiliation of the previous night's defeat.

'A good thing,' she said. 'They probably put it down to theft.'

'Theft? But that's what I was . . .'

'Theft by local people, by villagers. It's hard to keep warm in wartime winters, and there's no coal for non-combatants. Plenty of folks secretly lay in a stock of wood during the summer months, when there's less chance of being caught.'

He nodded, thinking of the mythical Frau Schneider, invented to explain his purchase of the saw. 'And the rope?'

'*You* know it was used to lower you down,' Kristin said. 'Anyone seeing it together with a half-sawn branch and an abandoned saw would assume it was there to climb *up*.'

'I suppose you're right,' he said doubtfully. 'In any case, I'd better push on with the replacement. I want to be over there before the break. If there is a break on a night as busy as this.' He began unwinding the new rope from his waist.

'You know our German love of routine,' Kristin said. 'There will be a break.'

'It must be something very new they are fitting,' he said, preparing to climb. 'They're not going to send up every aeroplane individually – every machine operating on the Western Front, I mean – not if it's a regular modification that could be incorporated during assembly on a production line.'

He was interested to know if she had any idea of the object of his mission. So far, although she had several times made casual references to it, he had maintained a complete discretion, revealing only that 'plans' were involved. If anything went wrong, after all, and she was caught . . . well, the Germans had brutal methods of persuasion, and what she didn't know she couldn't tell.

All she said now, however, was: 'I expect you are right.'

Stripping off the greatcoat, he stowed the workshop diagram and the tools he would need into the pockets of his corduroys. He climbed to what he thought of as his branch, edged out along it, and made the new rope fast. Then, carefully, he lowered himself until he was hanging as before just above the fence.

Kristin was perched on a thick bough ten or twelve feet up – a position from which she could give him a push each time he swung back into the gap where the other branch had been.

He was feeling confident, almost jubilant. The fact of having an accomplice, someone actually there whom he could not possibly demean himself to let down, had erased his terror – not so much his fear of the mission itself as his horror at the thought of his own weakness. For now, at any rate, that was in the past tense.

Flexing his body from the hips, bandaged hands hot around two knots, Blake began swinging the rope. When the pendulum of which he himself was the weight had sufficient momentum, he felt the first hard shove in the back as he sailed within Kristin's reach. The arc of his swing progressively increased.

Out over the fence . . . back, and shove . . . out again towards the silhouetted bulk of the admin block . . . in beneath the oak . . . out and up once more after the succeeding push . . . But the problem was that the further the swing took him, the higher he was from the ground at the end of its impetus. He had to decide between a long drop near the block and a shorter fall only halfway across the strip separating fence and factory.

There wasn't really a choice. He had to risk the long drop. He let go of the rope at the instant gravity imposed a fractional pause before the back-swing.

He fell heavily – between fifteen and twenty feet, he thought later – shoulder-rolled and staggered up with all the breath knocked from his body. Panting, he lurched the few yards to the wall of the building. Kristin would already be scaling the tree to recover the rope. Hopefully, she would be waiting with it when he returned, ready to cast it over and help him climb the fence.

Now, though, he was faced with the most difficult question of all. Which way in?

It was probable that the loading bay pass doors on his side of the workshops would be unlocked since there was so much activity outside. He had no means of telling, on the other hand, how many engineers might still be working inside. The yellow floodlights ruled out the gap between the buildings, the covered walkway and, of course, anything on the far side. There remained the two-storey block and the glass workshop roofs below it. Again, there was really no choice.

A patrol had passed just before he climbed the oak. In what was left of the half-hour before the next was due, he would have to use the arched window embrasures, in the dark, to scale the façade and struggle up to the roof or force an entry to the upper floor. After that there were three possible options: steal downstairs to the canteen level and use the walkway to gain the first workshop; re-emerge from the building – if there was a window above the gap – and use the walkway roof to reach the wall and then the roof of the shop; or leap down from the roof of the block to the workshop roof. The drop here was quite small, but the space to be crossed was at least ten feet.

One way or the other, it had to be the façade.

Beneath the nearest embrasure, he reached up and grabbed the sill. It wasn't too difficult to haul himself up – except for the painful pressure on his hands. Gritting his teeth, he raised himself upright and felt for the projections he had memorized on his initial examination of the site. The architect had made the two rows of embrasures integral with the façade as a whole. Blake had reached the summit of the arch and was feeling for the sill of the window above when light sprang suddenly below his feet from the shuttered windows of the ground floor.

The canteen lights had been switched on. There *was* going to be a break – and it would be at any minute. He would have to hurry. His feet scraped noisily on the stonework as he scrambled to the higher level. Once on this sill – after he had canted the first heel up, the second seemed to require an interminable time and effort – he had the choice of an immediate entry, or another climb, from the top of this arch to the roof parapet. No particular difficulty there. It was only five or six feet. And he would have welcomed the chance to patrol the workshop roofs, looking down into the interior to see how the workforce was disposed. But the transfer from this roof to those could be difficult, hazardous, and he couldn't really afford the time now. The essential was to get inside.

He examined the second-floor window. This one was not shuttered, but it was closed and locked. In the instant that he felt for the tiny diamond cutter secreted in his pocket, the factory bell rang.

The hell with cutting out a circle and removing it attached to the sticky tape so that he could get his hand in. He thumped one bandaged fist against the glass, hoping that the smash of falling shards would be drowned as the bell continued to ring.

He thrust in an arm, manipulated the catch, pushed up the window and stepped inside. There was a lot of noise from below now, as workers crowded into the canteen.

Moving warily in the dark – he assumed he was in an office – he skirted desks, chairs, what was probably a steel filing cabinet, and moved towards the thread of light showing beneath a door. Very slowly, he eased it open. He saw a small landing, a stairway spiralling down into the brilliance below.

When he could hear no more traffic passing from the workshops to the canteen, he crept downstairs. In a niche by the double doors leading to the walkway, brown overall tunics hung from a rail. He took one, shrugged into it, pushed open the doors and went through into the first of the workshops.

Judging by the array of dials, small electrical windings, transformers and wired clips strewn over the benches, this was some kind of assembly shop for gauges and meters. Completed instruments – white figures on black faces in a six-inch circular shell – stood racked by the door to the loading bay, ready to be packaged.

The next twinned building – they were separated only by two doors and a short length of passageway – was clearly the one making most of the noise. He saw belt-driven lathes, overhead pulleys, banks of machinery whose purpose eluded him. The shop, deserted like the first, was heavy with the thin reek of machine oil.

He opened the door to the third. Immediately the one at the far end of the passage was flung open. Fear surged through him, savage as an electric shock.

A fat woman in a white coat, with braided hair coiled around her head, backed into the corridor pulling a trolley loaded with black bread and sausages under glass domes. She scarcely gave Blake, frozen by the second door, a glance.

'You'll have to get on with it if you want to eat,' she said crossly. 'I don't know what those admin folks are coming to – all these extra workers and no damned notice!'

Blake swallowed, holding open the second door for her. 'I . . . I'll be along in just a minute,' he said huskily.

'Well, look sharp about it,' she snorted, 'or you'll go hungry!'

The trolley rattled away among the machinery.

Blake heaved a sigh of relief. His forehead was dewed with sweat. Thank God, he thought, that there *were* supernumeraries around, unknown to the canteen staff!

The third workshop was his target. Here there were smaller lathes, trays of rods and couplings, several trains of gears on the benches. Something electrical hummed quietly in a corner.

He stole a quick glance at his plan. Yes, they had got it right. The two offices were there – behind him now – one on either side of the entrance. He moved swiftly to the loading bay. The door on this side of the platform, the pass door at any rate, was locked. But there was a key in the lock. Security during the break, he supposed, if the work was top secret. He turned the key and eased back the catch. A nearby escape route could be vital.

In the designer's drawing office he took out the large-scale plan, the one on rice-paper. That was the first disappointment. What he saw bore no relation whatever to the elements on his diagram. Banks of steel drawers stood where the filing cabinets should have been. Three inclined boards with green-shaded, counterbalanced lamps occupied the space where he expected a desk. Blake swore beneath his breath. Everything looked shiny and new: clearly the place had recently been refitted. He would have to go through it from top to bottom to find what he was looking for.

Voices.

He crouched down below the windows surrounding the room.

A door banged open. Two men walked into the workshop from the direction of the canteen – a factory overseer with a badge on the pocket of his white overalls and a uniformed under-officer in the Army Air Service. They were talking animatedly.

'. . . gear is fine for the Eindekkers and triplanes,' the under-officer was saying, 'but they are talking now of three- or even four-bladed propellers. They'll have to go back to the drawing board if they want . . .'

The door of the office opened.

Blake looked frenziedly right and left. There was no place to go, nowhere to hide, not a cupboard, a niche, the kneehole of a desk. He was crazy to have risked coming here while a double night shift was at work.

'I mean, you have to think of the tolerance,' the soldier said as they came in. 'Look at the 110hp Oberursel rotary! With a mechanism as crude as those guns, and a dwell on the cams of less than half a milli . . .'

He stopped in mid-sentence, his eyes fixed on Blake, cowering in one corner. 'One of yours?' he asked.

'I've never seen him before in my life,' the overseer said blankly. 'Who the devil are you? And what the hell do you think you're doing in here?'

Blake blanched. 'I'm s-s-sorry,' he stammered wildly. 'I must have lost m-m-my . . .'

The under-officer had a pistol in his hand. 'If there is any explaining to do,' he said evenly, 'it will be done in front of the Herr Rittmeister, in the guard-house. You will precede us through the adjoining workshops – and I may tell you that this Walther is loaded and the trigger mechanism is extremely light.'

He gestured towards the open door.

This cannot be happening to me, Blake thought. This is a bad dream; I shall wake up soon . . . Dear God, let me wake up *now*!

He moved towards the door, turned into the aisle between factory benches. A cold chill rippled down his spine as he felt the gun barrel prod him between the shoulder-blades.

'A common thief, do you suppose?' the under-officer asked.

'Out here, at this time of night? With all this activity around?' the overseer's voice was derisive. 'More likely a spy, I reckon. There's a lot of secret work done here, you know.'

'Well, we know what to do with spies,' the man from the Army Air Service said. He prodded again, harder. 'Come on, get a move on. Through that door.'

Desperation, stemming from sheer panic, fuelled Blake's action. Double swing doors sealed each end of the passage leading to the next workshop. The blind instinct of self-preservation took over as he passed through.

He was after all young, strong, lithe and quite athletic. He had learned, in a brief unarmed-combat course, about the effect of surprise on a man with a gun who came too close. And he had noticed that this particular man with a gun was left-handed.

Instead of pulling the doors towards him, he pushed his way through . . . and then exploded into movement.

He kicked violently back with his left leg, crashing the left-hand door against the menacing barrel of the pistol.

Canted slightly upward towards the nape of his neck, the barrel jerked instantly vertical under the shock. And the man's arm, bent double by the impact, was unable to suppress in that hundredth of a second the message already flashed from brain to forefinger. Taken totally unawares, he pressed the trigger and shot himself through the underside of the jaw, blowing off the top of his head.

Blake, who had thrown himself on to all fours as a continuation of his backward kick, whirled around to meet the attack of the overseer. Shouldering open the second door, the man came at him with a heavy steel wrench.

Still balanced on one knee, Blake raised an arm to ward off the assault and took a murderous blow on his left biceps, just below the shoulder. The numbing force of the stroke sent him crashing back into a sitting position, and he spun around on his seat before uncoiling himself to spring to his feet and meet the next attack with the only weapon he had.

This, one of the household tools he had been told might help in his burgling, was a metal rasp or file. The blade, triangular in section, tapered to a point, and there was a spike at the other end over which a wooden handle could be fitted if necessary. It was not necessary here.

Blake reversed the file swiftly in his hand, lunging inside the next blow which whistled over his shoulder. Before his attacker could draw back his arm again, he jabbed the tool forcefully upward into the man's face. The hardened steel spike plunged in beneath his left eyebrow with a horrifying squelch.

The overseer's mouth dropped open and a curious sound bubbled from his throat. For an instant he hung there, an obscene, deformed unicorn, with the rasp projecting from the socket. Then he crumpled slowly and collapsed to the floor. From the dreadful gash where his eye had been, fluid dribbled down over his unshaven cheek.

Blake too stood immobile for a single heartbeat, staring at the sprawling bodies. He was panting and his frame trembled all over. A fan of brains pricked out with splinters of bone slid down the wall just outside one of the doors. The metallic tang of fresh blood penetrated the cordite fumes, and there was a stench rising from below, where one of the men had evacuated himself as he died.

Cramming a hand over his mouth to stifle nausea, Blake ran back into the workshop. The corpse of the soldier had wedged one of the doors open, but he could not bring himself to move it and seal off the passageway.

His mind was in a whirl. He had envisaged a number of different scenes in which he played the role of burglar . . . discovered as he located the plans, surprised before he succeeded, taken prisoner, narrowly escaping . . . but it had never occurred to him that he might be the means of killing a man, let alone two.

Nor had he found the damned plans.

The sound of the shot had sounded terrifyingly loud. Could it have been heard outside, in the guardhouse, through two workshops, over the babble of voices in the canteen?

Perhaps not. There had been no outcry, no pounding of feet. But there could be no more than minutes left before the factory bell rang and workers crowded back into the shops.

What could he do? Chance a lightning survey – and the risk of capture? Admit defeat and abandon the mission, leaving himself a failure with a murderer's price-tag on his head? Get out now, at once, and return another night for a third attempt?

Don't be a BF, he told himself fiercely. Think.

The overseer and the under-officer had been complaining about the Fokker linkage when they arrived. They had spoken of modifications for different types of aeroplane. They had been talking technicalities, as if that work was actually in train, and they had come into the drawing office. In the middle of a break?

Wasn't it reasonable to assume that something urgent had brought them? That they had, in fact, come into that office to look at the blueprints?

And that the blueprints therefore must be readily accessible?

Blake hefted the Walther automatic from hand to hand – he must have snatched it up without realizing when he ran from the passageway. It was worth a try.

He raced back into the office. For the second time, a quick glance around.

There! A tall wooden cabinet, glistening with varnish. Wide, very shallow drawers. Off to one side of the drawing boards with their T-squares. He ran across. The drawers were individually locked.

The overseer should have keys . . . but he quailed at the thought of searching a body. Very well: use the second domestic utensil. A kitchen knife with the blade snapped off very short. He reached into his pocket.

With the stumpy blade inserted, he levered up and pulled down. Wood split with a splintering crash.

He found them in the third drawer down – plans, elevations, working drawings with all dimensions, the original blueprint: all from the Fokker works at Schwerin. Clearly, as he had thought, a contracted-out job here in Siegsdorf.

There were four sheets in all, each approximately eighteen inches by twenty-four. He slid them out, laid them on a desk. There was a reference number stencilled on the working drawings. Feverishly, he pulled open the drawers of filing cabinets, then a table, and found it finally on a card in a box file on the desk.

The number identified on which benches in which parts of the workshop different stages of the gear assembly were completed. The actual manufacturing process, the stamping and forging of individual elements, took place in the fourth building, but the fine machining was done here.

Blake took an eighteen-inch cardboard cylinder from a rack near the door, folded the sheets once, rolled them tightly and stuffed them into the tube. He hurried from the office.

Benches were identified by letters and figures suspended above them. He ran to the two marked as final assembly.

The completed train, not very large, looked a little like the outside connecting-rod system of an express locomotive. He was unable to relate it in any way to an aero engine – rotary, radial or in-line. Or, for that matter, to a Vickers or Lewis gun.

If possible, they had said in London, bring us back a sample in three dimensions. If possible! With the weight of that metal stowed about your person you wouldn't stagger ten yards without attracting attention!

Separate parts then? He wouldn't know which to take. He picked up a shining, beautifully machined helicoidal gear wheel from a tray. This looked something like part of a miniature car differential. Perhaps that was important? He dropped the part into his pocket.

There were graphs and tabulated sheets secured by bulldog clips hanging from brass nails above the bench. Both seemed to be concerned with the plotting of engine revolutions – divided by two, of course, since there were two blades to a propeller – against rates of fire and the muzzle speed of rounds from a machine-gun over given distances. He tore off one of each and managed to squeeze them into the cardboard tube.

Just samples, he thought with a crooked grin.

Abruptly, loud as a scream in the night, the bell shrilled somewhere in the rafters beneath the inclined glass roof of the workshop.

Blake froze, hands trembling and heart thumping . . . then ran.

He dashed for the loading bay, flung open the pass door

he had unlocked and hurled himself across the platform outside. He was about to drop when he realized the open door would throw light across the dark strip, pointing an unerring finger at his escape route.

Sobbing for breath, he ran back and pulled the door closed. This time, as he was preparing to jump, he heard the first outcry from inside the shop. The first arrivals from the canteen must have found the bodies.

He raced over the uneven ground.

'*Here!*' He heard Kristin's urgent voice. '*To your right!*'

Veering towards her, he reached the fence. A sudden tiny flick of a torch showed him the rope draped over the wire. 'Seize it and climb,' she hissed. 'The other end is fast around a tree.'

He grabbed the rope, hauled it tight, and 'walked' himself up the stiff chain-link surface. At the top, he perched for an instant and then dropped into freedom. She was already unfastening the other end.

There was now a hubbub of shouts from within the factory. Torchlight swept around the corner of the canteen block from the guardhouse. Several different voices shouted orders.

'I heard a shot,' the girl said.

'There was trouble. I had to act on the spur of the moment,' Blake said tightly.

'You are carrying a gun yourself!'

'I had to,' he said again. 'After the shot.' He wasn't prepared to explain in detail: the horror was still too close.

'Did you get what you wanted?'

'Yes,' Blake said. He had pushed the cardboard cylinder down inside his trousers, along the inside of his lame leg. Once again he was not going to elaborate. For a time, as they pushed through bushes and undergrowth, Kristin was silent. Then she said: 'We must get out of this area fast. Deeper into the wood and then as soon as possible across the road and into the fields. It will not take them long to work out which way you came and went – not with the floods in front and last night's evidence behind.'

'And the door I left unlocked over the loading bay,' he agreed.

By the time they had gathered up the rope, the rackety, air-cooled engine of a scout car had started up on the far side of the buildings. The brilliance of a searchlight silvered the outlines of roof and wall. When they were a hundred yards into the trees, he glanced over his shoulder. There were lights now all over the strip on the far side of the wire fence.

Minutes later they heard the scout car circling the outside of the site.

Between the densely growing trunks of trees, torch beams – perhaps a dozen of them – bobbed right and left, occasionally showing up a trailing branch, a canopy of leaves.

They were almost on the far side of the wood. Stars pricked the darkness between the interlaced boughs overhead. Blake had the sense of the land dropping away beyond the trees. He stopped, panting, to lean momentarily against the hollowed trunk of an oak. 'Are you all right?' the girl said. 'You seem to be – forgive me – but you seem to be, well, limping rather more than usual.'

'I'll be all right,' he said. 'Thanks.'

And indeed once he had regained his breath he was moving much faster, overtaking her as they came out into the open and careered down a slope of meadow towards a sunken lane.

The wood crowned a hilltop and now, towards the north, he was aware of the countryside rolling down towards two or three dimly glimmering points of radiance which marked the village of Salzkotten.

Above the lane, they had difficulty forcing their way through a hedgerow choked with brambles. Perhaps this was why they were taken so much by surprise by the long beam of light sweeping around a corner uphill . . . and the appearance immediately after of the scout car, coasting down the slope illuminated by its searchlight.

They were halfway across the narrow road when the beam trapped them.

Brakes squealed. The engine burst into life again and a voice yelled: 'Halt! Stay where you are or we fire!'

Blake thrust Kristin down violently into a ditch on the far side and flung himself prone among the long grasses. The voice shouted again.

Quite calmly, Blake levelled the long-barrelled Walther and shot out the searchlight. Glass tinkled, the aching glare dimmed, faded to a momentary red glow, vanished. Gunshots blazed out over the low sides of the car. He sensed the stirring of air as a bullet hummed through the grasses close to his head. Twigs and fragments of leaf fell on to his wrist. Aiming for the muzzle flashes, he fired two more shots.

The windscreen of the scout erupted. A choked cry from the passenger side.

Blake knew that the army-issue Walther '08 automatic had an eight-round magazine. The under-officer had fired once; he had himself now loosed off three. In a last-chance manoeuvre to make the second man in the scout car believe that he had armed colleagues, he stretched his arm wide, left and right, firing the last four as rapidly as possible in an effort to simulate a volley from several gunners.

The ploy was successful.

With a harsh grinding of gears, the car shot into reverse, wheeled crazily around to thump its rear end into the bank, and then zigzagged back up the hill in the darkness with tyres screaming.

Kristin dragged herself, squelching, from the ditch. She was soaked in stagnant water from the waist down. 'Well, you can certainly move fast enough when it's necessary,' she said breathlessly.

'Needs must,' Blake said. 'Although the devil driving that particular vehicle seemed a trifle less than satanic!'

'We must run for the village now,' she told him, 'before he comes back with reinforcements. On the other side of the hedgerow, of course.'

'Why the village? Wouldn't we be safer if we . . . ?'

'There's a school on the outskirts. A girls' school. Mainly for boarders. There are bicycles in a shed. Riding silently, we could be miles away by daylight.'

'Yes, but . . . I mean, where would we be . . . ?'

'We would be heading for Paderborn,' she interrupted.

'*Paderborn!* Why on earth . . . ?'

'There's an aerodrome there,' Kristin said. 'Remember?'

18

The airfield at Paderborn was not particularly well guarded. It was surrounded by a three-strand wire fence to stop cows and sheep straying in and interrupting the training programme. There were two sentries in front of the guardhouse at the entrance. But that was all.

Although both infantry and especially artillery commanders were conscious of the value of aerial observation, there was still a general feeling among the High Command that the air services were a bit of a luxury, the playthings of cranks, newfangled toys that had little to do with real soldiering.

Gunners could enthuse over the corrections to their aim supplied by aerial reports; officers planning ground attacks could welcome detailed information charting enemy troop movements 'on the other side of the hill'. But the Allied General Staff as a whole preferred blindly to follow the outdated precepts of Douglas Haig. And the Germans, of course, at the Kaiser's express command, placed all their faith in the machine-gun.

The British and French won back lost ground after an artillery bombardment by massed charges of infantry armed with rifles and bayonets; the Germans cut them down in thousands with cunning deployment of machine-gun 'nests'.

Most of the early – usually posthumous – VCs were

won by men who wiped out single-handedly one of these sandbagged emplacements with a well-directed grenade.

Even at battlefield level, where aerial reconnaissance was an accepted asset and the ability to shoot down your opponent's machines a necessity, the idea of an attack with 'ground support' from above had yet to be formulated. Certainly the aeroplanes had machine-guns, but they were inaccurate, the planes themselves were vulnerable – even to rifle fire – and bombs, if carried, rarely weighed more than twenty-five pounds. These again lacked accuracy, since there was no bomb-sight and in most cases they were released approximately over the target by hauling up a simple toggle lever.

There was then no foreseeable need to protect airfields. Most front-line examples were improvised from stretches of open grassland or large fields; offices, living quarters and mess were wooden huts; and the machines were garaged in canvas hangars. Many of them, close to the area of trench warfare, could be abandoned almost immediately if menaced by an attack; some, further behind the lines, were not even protected against aerial attack themselves.

Blake, having flown over the Western Front, knew all this. He was well aware of the transitory quality, the near-amateurishness, of most sites distinguished by the name aerodrome. He remembered with an inward smile a standard requirement of one English training squadron: that a pilot must be able to land and take off from a ploughed field. Yet he was surprised at the ease with which he and Kristin Dony penetrated Paderborn, not only the landing field but the command area and a concrete apron between the hangars and the headquarters block. It was a long way from the front, but what the hell

– they were training pilots to use prototype machines with new armament!

For a people known for their rigid discipline and attachment to routine, it seemed more than a little casual.

With the bicycles they had stolen from the girls' school – a barking dog had been the only interruption – they had traversed the twelve miles between Salzkotten and the outskirts of Paderborn via a maze of footpaths and country lanes which Blake could never have found, even with a map. Before dawn, they had abandoned the cycles below the railway embankment from which he had first seen the airfield. Then, on the far side of a narrow brick pedestrian tunnel, Kristin had led him to a platelayers' hut just outside the wire perimeter fence. Here, at first light, they had attempted to make themselves look a little more presentable.

Pedalling had practically dried out her drenched skirt, but she had to put up her hair and comb it, and then clean up as best she could the bramble scratches and the ravages of their escape through the wood.

Blake was still wearing the buttoned brown overall tunic he had taken from the canteen building at the factory. He was dishevelled, unshaven again and generally unkempt. His left upper arm, where he had taken the blow from the overseer's wrench, was swollen and exceedingly painful. The palms of his hands throbbed too, but the bandages were now filthy and had to be discarded. It was just possible, nevertheless, that he might pass – from a distance – for a mechanic or non-uniformed technician.

That was no less unlikely than Kristin's madcap scheme of hiding him at the base until he found an opportunity to steal one of the Eindekkers stationed there. At that moment, crazy though the idea was, he was too mentally exhausted to think of a believable alternative.

It was six-thirty when they left the hut, ducked under the wire and walked along a rough path trodden among the long grass, towards the nearest hangar. The bulk of the great canvas structure, she had explained, would hide their approach until they were less than fifty yards from the sick quarters where she had her office.

Yet that fifty yards seemed the longest Blake had ever walked in his life. It had been agreed that Kristin should go ahead as though there was no connection between them. And now here he was, an enemy alien, hundreds of miles inside German territory, a murderer in the eyes of the authorities, blithely approaching, on foot, the headquarters of what might be a secret military site without the slightest written justification of who he was or what he was doing. And no verbal excuse that he could think of that would bear the most cursory examination.

There was already a certain amount of activity on the far side of the hangar. A two-seater Albatros had been wheeled out into the open air, and several men in blue overalls were busy about the exposed engine block. Mechanics further away pushed a squat, saddle-tanked refuelling trolley towards an oversize biplane he thought might be a captured Ilya Mourometz bomber from the EVK – Flotilla of Flying Ships – on the Russian front. Beyond the headquarters block, a small squad of soldiers were marching and countermarching under the orders of a hoarse *Feldwebel*.

None of the men on duty appeared to notice Blake. With the hairs prickling on the nape of his neck, he approached the sick-bay hut. The last door but one on the right, she had said. It will be unlocked.

She herself had already vanished through the hut's main entrance. He stepped up to the door, turned the handle, went inside.

A small, bare room, with a table, two upright chairs and a framed print of the castle at Charlottenburg on one wall. The door clicked shut behind him. He swung around and, on the spur of the moment, tried the handle again. The door was now locked. Behind the table there was an inner door. He walked across and tried that. It, too, was locked.

Before he had time to register this, the second door was flung open.

Blake saw glistening boots, an impeccable uniform with a holstered revolver, a tall young officer with clean-cut features and short, fair hair.

'*Hauptmann* Erich Schneider,' he announced with a click of the heels. 'Foreign Intelligence. We have been expecting you, *Mr* Gerhardt Ehrlich. A sales representative, no? From Hamburg.' A thin smile. 'Well, no, perhaps not.'

Stupefied with astonishment, Blake blurted out the first thing that came to his mind. 'Schneider?' he repeated foolishly. 'From Paderborn? What a coincidence! I think I invented your mother! On the road to Belecke.'

The officer frowned. 'I do not understand. I am from Dresden, in Saxony. You, on the other hand, come from somewhere I imagine to be a good deal west and south of Hamburg.'

'Me, I understand only too well.' Blake's voice was bitter. He paused. Kristin, wearing a clean, freshly pressed uniform, was passing along the corridor behind Schneider. '*Bonjour, Mademoiselle Dony, et bons trahisons!*' he called. 'Good day and happy betrayals.'

The tap of her footsteps ceased. She reappeared behind the German. Her face was flushed.

'The oldest trick in the world,' Blake said before she could speak. 'And, of course, the oldest profession.'

The girl's colour darkened. 'I may be a Protestant of Huguenot origin,' she said, 'but my people have lived in this country for over two hundred years. I am German, and my duty lies with my country.'

'A pity you have not yet learned such attributes of the good German as decency, honour and loyalty to an ideal.' Avoiding her eyes, Blake spoke directly to Schneider. 'What fools we are,' he said, 'to trust them. Any of them.'

'It has not perhaps occurred to you,' Kristin said stiffly, 'that burglary and false pretences – to say nothing of killing people – could be considered by some as falling a trifle short of the very ideals you refer to. You should perhaps consider a saying I believe to be current in your country: that all is fair in love and war.' She smiled. 'Sometimes both.'

19

'I think it only fair to tell you,' Schneider said, 'that once we were persuaded the pilot of the wrecked Sopwith had escaped, a very strict control on all wireless telegraphy was instituted in the immediate area. It was thus that my engineers were able to localize the traitor who was to act as go-between linking you with your headquarters at the time of your very first contact.'

'Efficient,' Blake said drily. 'As one would expect.'

They sat one on either side of the table in the room he had first entered. He had been searched, and the helicoidal gear wheel, along with the empty Walther, the skeleton keys, the broken kitchen knife and his papers lay on the polished wood between them. An armed soldier stood in front of each door.

'It was under what we have, alas, to call "hardened interrogation" that the spy – who had been furnishing information to your masters for some time – was persuaded to reveal such details of your mission as he knew. It was then a simple matter to replace him with Fräulein Dony, one of our most experienced agents.'

'And the . . . the man you call the traitor?'

'He is no longer with us.'

'I see.' Blake's mouth was dry.

'Having first lost and then regained contact with you,' Schneider said, 'Fräulein Dony asked for further instructions. Rather than bring you in at once, she was told to encourage you in the furtherance of your mission. For although we now knew who you were, where you were, and even why you had taken such trouble to penetrate this far into the Fatherland, there was one thing we did not know. And rather to our surprise Fräulein Dony did not know either. Accepting her as your cut-out, you nevertheless managed to keep from her the precise nature of the plans you wished to steal from the Krupp affiliate at Siegsdorf.'

Blake said nothing.

'We arranged therefore that she could help you to enter the factory. But although you told her subsequently that you had succeeded in your quest, you had still failed to reveal exactly what that was. Not wishing to provoke suspicion on your part, she refrained from pressing the matter, believing that the stolen plans would in any case be on your person. To our surprise, however – and hers – no trace of them has been found.'

The *Hauptmann* paused. Once again Blake made no comment.

'I have to ask you now,' Schneider said evenly, 'what plans, what papers you abstracted from which workshop at the Siegsdorf factory?'

'Under internationally agreed conditions,' Blake said at last, 'I must ask to be treated as a prisoner of war. As such, I am obliged to reveal no more than my name, number, rank and, in certain cases, regiment. They are as follows: Number 1092818 Blake, Patrice; Lieutenant, the Honourable Artillery Company; at present seconded to the Royal Flying Corps.'

The German laughed. 'Those conditions apply to belligerents taken in battle,' he said. 'Men wearing uniform. It is accepted that enemies in civilian dress, captured behind the lines, may be treated as spies – the penalty for which, as you well know, is death. A similar sentence, of course, is demanded for murder. Now, to avoid . . . unpleasantness . . . before your execution, tell me at once: where are the plans you stole from Siegsdorf?'

'I must have lost them,' Blake said blandly. 'Or dropped them on the way.'

Schneider sighed. 'A pity,' he said. 'For I admire your courage. But in that case I advise you to remember where you dropped them rather quickly; otherwise I shall be obliged to hand you over to a specialized section of the Feldgendarmerie, whose methods, although in a sense sophisticated, nevertheless lack a certain refinement.'

He prodded the gearwheel on the table with a long finger, turning it around. He cleared his throat. 'You must understand my position, Lieutenant Blake,' he said. 'People are checking at this moment from which tray in the factory this was stolen. Within hours, perhaps minutes, we shall know which plans are missing. It is only a matter of time therefore – and not much of that – before we are in full possession of the secret you strive so hard to conceal. But you must know that I am answerable to very senior officers indeed. And they, for reasons of their own, insist on knowing *now* which of the many devices manufactured at Siegsdorf your High Command is so anxious to study.'

Blake swallowed. A pulse in his throat was fluttering like a bird. 'I have nothing further to add,' he said huskily.

'Very well. So be it.' The German swung around in his chair and barked a command.

The inner door opened and a *Feldwebel* from the military police saluted. 'The prisoner is to be taken at once to Unit Twelve,' Schneider said. 'The under-officer in charge is familiar with the . . . problem. He knows what questions to ask. Just remind him that the matter is urgent.'

'*Jawohl, Herr Hauptmann.*' Two men with drawn pistols appeared behind the *Feldwebel* and stamped to attention. He looked Blake in the eye and beckoned. '*Komm!*'

Blake rose to his feet. 'It was nice meeting you,' he said to Schneider.

Unit Twelve, presumably a block used for 'hardened interrogation', appeared to be on the far side of the aerodrome. The closed van in which Blake and his three-man escort were transported there was halted in front of the third of four hangars beyond the headquarters block. Through one of the small, barred windows Blake saw that the driver had stopped to allow a group of mechanics to wheel two of the new Fokker monoplanes out through the opened hangar flaps.

He had broken out in a cold sweat. Moisture trickled between his shoulder-blades. He was familiar with the sensation. He knew, reeling with giddiness in the prison van, precisely what was causing the condition in him. The situation was certainly claustrophobic. There was no immediate escape. But claustrophobic was too polite a word for the underlying cause. It was due to sheer funk.

The first of the monoplanes had been wheeled clear. Someone was swinging the propeller. The mechanics seemed to have difficulty manoeuvring the second. The van waited, engine idling, bouncing very slightly on its long cantilever springs.

The thought of the interrogation to which he would be submitted in a few short minutes now clawed at Blake's vitals . . . Fists smashing brutally into his flesh, wire whips across his back, his head held down in a bucket of water or his fingernails ripped off . . . Saliva ran salt on either side of his tongue. He choked back scalding vomit that rose in his throat.

Why in God's name hadn't he told the man what he wanted to know? He would tell the interrogators . . . yes, before they began their filthy work, he would . . .

Then the sudden stark realization. Even if he did, he was still a spy. There would still be the firing squad.

All the blood in his body seemed to drain down to his feet. He knew that his face must have gone very white. Wooden benches ran along each side of the van. The two guards sat opposite him, the *Feldwebel* on a tip-up seat that folded down from the partition separating them from the cab. The three Germans appeared suddenly very large, swelling in his vision, which was going black at the edges.

He knew he was going to faint.

Stupidly he felt it necessary to excuse himself . . . Christ, he was going to soil his trousers! He struggled to his feet.

The second monoplane was wheeled clear. The van driver shouted some obscenity, which was replied to from the ground.

'I'm s-s-sorry,' Blake gagged as one of the soldiers started to rise from his seat. 'I'm afraid I . . . I can't help . . .'

The driver trod hard on the throttle pedal and let in the clutch with a savage jerk. The van bucketed forward as the solid tyres bit into tarmac.

Blake was hurled against the single door in the rear of the van.

The door burst open and he pitched out on to the apron.

The van had accelerated another forty or fifty yards before the hammering on his partition caused the driver to screech to a halt. One of the guards was already outside and running back.

Blake struggled up from his hands and knees. Every symptom of panic – perhaps it was the sudden rush of fresh air? – every symptom had vanished, leaving him in a one-dimensional world conditioned by a single imperative: *run like hell!*

Fear lent him wings. A phrase from a trashy novel he had read flashed into his head. He was on his feet and racing as he had never raced before towards the Eindekkers, the mechanics open-mouthed at the shouting behind. A shot rang out.

Blake dashed for the overalled group. They wouldn't shoot once he was among the men. A second slug whistled past his head and then he was scattering the workers, shouldering them violently aside, hitting out with his fists as he hared towards the first of the monoplanes.

The engine was idling, the propeller ticking over; two men held the wingtips and two more shoved, wheeling the machine towards the grassy outfield. A young man in a leather flying jacket swung his helmet from one hand as he followed them.

The instinct for self-preservation had sharpened Blake's reactions, speeded up his thinking, sent the adrenalin storming through his frame to accelerate muscular effort.

He launched himself at the pilot, sent him sprawling with a backhander and ran for the aeroplane.

It was a strange-looking machine, slightly old-fashioned visually. Square-tipped wings sprouted from the aluminium cowling just forward of the cockpit; the long, square-section fabric tail terminated in a rudder shaped like a comma. A spider's web of bracing wires ran up to the wings from the complex steel tube undercarriage.

Blake reached it as the mechanics stopped pushing, alerted by the pandemonium behind him. Sensing his intention, the one on his side of the fuselage ran for the cockpit and started to clamber in; the near wingtip man let go of the fabric-covered spars and raced to cut Blake off.

He knocked the man flat with a looping, roundhouse right as he ran, then seized the cockpit jumper bodily from behind, dragged him clear with a superhuman effort and flung him too to the ground.

He leaped for the padded cockpit rim, hauled himself up and dropped into the pilot's seat.

More by luck than instinct or knowledge, his hand found the throttle control and he pushed, hard.

The noise of the clattering rotary rose to a roar. The ticking propeller spun to a silver disc. The Fokker shuddered on its disc wheels.

Slowly at first, and then with increasing speed, it shrugged off the two remaining mechanics, yawed slightly and ran out on to the grass.

Blake glanced over his shoulder. A scout car with a machine-gun mounted above the windshield was speeding along the perimeter track. Behind him, they were swinging the propeller of the second Eindekker. Within minutes, perhaps seconds, there would be pursuit . . . and pursuit equipped with synchronized, twin Spandau 7.92mm machine-guns. Firing forward through the arc of the propeller.

He would be chased by the very machinery he had been sent to investigate!

The same guns, with their single telescopic sight, lay along the cowling in front of him. But there was going to be no foolhardy attempt at a dogfight here – not with a machine he had never even seen before, with controls that were totally unfamiliar, even with an opponent who was probably only a trainee.

No nonsense either about turning into the wind. He was determined to race straight across the field the way he was facing now, taking off crosswind to save time . . . and keep away from the scout car with its gun.

He would check the manipulation of rudder and ailerons once he was in the air; all he was interested in now was lift.

The Eindekker gathered speed, bumping over the uneven ground. Blake's scarred hands grasped the two polished wood handles at the top of the control column. When he judged the aeroplane to be approaching fifty miles per hour, he began delicately easing the stick fractionally back and then forward again, feeling for the first slight reaction of the aerofoil surfaces.

The wire fence, and the hedge beyond it on the far side of the field, seemed alarmingly close – and to be approaching alarmingly fast. But the little machine was steady and it was responsive. Blake still had two hundred yards in hand when he coaxed her off the ground – the stick light now in his hands – over the fence and the embankment and the slate roofs beyond.

He wasn't even going to attempt a turn until he was at what the altimeter told him was the equivalent of two hundred feet. Nor was he going to aim at more than two hundred and fifty throughout the whole journey. Why waste time climbing when there could be a lethal pursuer closing up behind?

And, after all, he had only twelve miles to fly.

Back to Siegsdorf, to the factory, to the wood behind it . . . and the hollow tree in which he had hidden the cardboard tube containing the stolen plans.

20

Why had he done it? What could have prompted him to stow away the cardboard cylinder inside a hollow tree during their escape from the factory? With the object of his mission safely in his hands, why would he deliberately have placed it out of his own reach?

Because he feared capture, but was convinced he would be able to escape and recover the plans later? That seemed unlikely. And in any case he had no recollection of thinking that.

There was, of course, a more prosaic reason: the eighteen-inch cylinder, stuffed inside his trousers, had completely stiffened his lame leg and slowed him down dangerously as they forced their way through the undergrowth. But was that in itself sufficient for him to take such a risk? Blake thought not.

Certainly, at the time, he had had not the least suspicion that the girl was not his cut-out. With hindsight he could see that there had been pointers – little things that maybe should have at least alerted him or prompted him to ask more questions. The fact that she herself on several occasions did ask, contrary to routine, about his specific orders. The fact that she knew in advance that three triplanes would be at the factory that night – an unusually detailed piece of information for a nursing auxiliary to have. Above all that she knew just a little too much about his own movements. 'I heard about your escape from the hotel in Paderborn,' she had said.

In the time available, she could not possibly have heard that as gossip in the aerodrome mess: she could only have heard it from police or security quarters.

It was, of course, he thought bitterly, the sex which had blinded him to what should have been obvious . . . or at least worth closer attention. Because of it he had trusted her without further questioning.

And yet . . . and yet . . . *something* had prompted him to get shot of the incriminating cylinder while he was still with her. Perhaps, subconsciously, he had registered those pointers; maybe, in times of stress, the subconscious was brighter than the conscious?

At the moment, skimming the rooftops of Paderborn, he was thankful that he *had* done it, however difficult it might be to profit from that fact. And thankful too – be honest! – to the subconscious decision, the split-second determination when the opportunity arose, to grab an aeroplane in an attempt to get it back.

That was his second piece of luck. The first had been that unexpected opening of the prison van door. The third, he supposed, was the result of that dreadful night after his cowardly run from the factory.

The field of stubble where he had slept by the haystack. The harvest was in; the surface was flat enough and wide enough to land a small aeroplane.

If, of course, he survived the landing!

He was getting used to the unfamiliar Fokker controls. The rudder was stiff and the plane slow to react because of its small surface; the ailerons were stiffer when he moved the stick sideways. But otherwise he had so far discovered no vices. Apart from the inherent characteristic of all rotary engines: the fact that they tend to run only at idle or full speed, fine control being a luxury granted to few. A 'blip switch' fitted to the control column, familiar to Blake from British machines powered by rotaries, could cut the ignition to several or all of the cylinders, temporarily reducing power in approach.

Between the hand-cranked starting magneto and the fuel filler pipe there was a small switch panel with different settings marked. He assumed this was similar to one he had seen on a French Nieuport, which allowed the pilot to select different combinations of the cylinders to fire and/or cut out. But he wasn't going to experiment that far! Getting her down in one piece was what mattered now.

Whether he wished, or would be able, to take off again depended on what happened after that. And on the actions of the man piloting the second Eindekker.

He glanced back over the tapered tail. Yes, there he was, a miniature silhouette against the rising sun perhaps a couple of miles away. He appeared to be climbing steeply. Gaining height perhaps so that he could increase speed in a dive and catch Blake up. He wasn't to know how short the flight was to be!

Siegsdorf, huddled around a curve in the River Lippe, was visible ahead. Railway lines curving away below gleamed in the early morning sunshine. He banked warily over the station and the familiar square, flew over a river bridge, and headed for Salzkotten.

In front of the Fokker windscreen, an inverted steel V rose from the engine cowling. From the summit of this, four bracing wires stretched out on either side to steady the single wing, already located by a similar number slanting up from the undercarriage below. The wind sang an alto chord through the wires as he flipped the switch to cut ignition and began to lose height

... one hundred and eighty feet ... one fifty ... a hundred ...

Between the legs of the metal V Blake looked over the perforated housing of a Spandau machine-gun at fields misted by the spinning propeller. He saw the roofs and church spire of Salzkotten, half hidden among trees. He saw the hilltop factory and the woods behind. Then the village sank from sight below the wood as he dropped lower still.

He was approaching the stubble field at a height of fifty feet, thirty ... He was coming in much too fast. He blipped the switch again. The propeller feathered. Too fast, too fast – and no chance of a circuit: he would be lucky as it was to stop taxiing and get clear of the machine before the pursuer landed behind him. Or simply circled and started to shoot.

The ochre surface of the field flashed towards him. He remembered once hearing a pilot say that the average Fokker had the same glide angle as a piano.

Very well, he would *drop* the bitch down! A hedge shot past beneath the wing. He juggled with the stick. There was nothing more he could do now.

The Eindekker hit the ground with a rending crash, bounced what seemed like twenty feet into the air, thumped down once more, then wheeled into a crazy half-circle, dragging one wing like a wounded bird as undercarriage spars collapsed. It shot across the field, scoring deep furrows in the stubbled earth, and finally came to rest against the haystack with the engine stalled and one blade of the propeller snapped.

So much for the take-off! Blake thought, vaulting over the cockpit rim and running for the trees at the far end of the field.

The second Eindekker was planing in to land. They

must have told him Blake was unarmed and instructed him to take the runaway prisoner.

Throttled back severely, the monoplane made an impeccable three-pointer, lost speed, swung around and taxied toward the haystack. The pilot jumped out as the engine died. There was a pistol in his hand.

Blake heard the man shout as he ran. A single shot rang out, cracking back as an echo from a bank below the wood. He didn't even bother to start zigzagging: as something of a gunnery expert, he knew that firing a service revolver at a moving target more than fifty yards away was a waste of time and ammunition.

He scrambled, panting, up the bank. This could be a textbook exercise from the unarmed-combat course. But what he needed, first, was a suitable tree, and secondly a dense enough package of trunks and branches and undergrowth to hide him when he climbed into it. He had to force his way two hundred yards into the wood before he found the right place.

Even then it was a matter of split-second timing. The pilot had been gaining on him, and Blake could hear the thrashing of leaves a little too close for comfort as he dragged himself up on to the horizontal branch he had been looking for.

The pilot – an older, tougher man than the one Blake had floored with his backhander – ran out into the miniature clearing beneath the tree, looking right and left. He was marginally too far out for the drop Blake had planned, but there was nothing to be done about that now.

As the man started forward again, Blake launched himself out and down. His two feet crashed into him just below the shoulders, felling him to the carpet of pine needles below the tree. Before the man could get his breath back, before he realized what had happened, the edge of Blake's left hand had chopped him savagely across the side of the neck.

The pilot gagged, trying to heave himself up from his prone position. But Blake was already straddling the small of his back. With his right, he reached for the pistol, which had flown out of the man's hand, seized it by the barrel and brought the butt down once, twice, three times on the back of his head.

The German groaned, twitched once, then lay still.

Blake was sweating. He had a choice now. Recover the plans at once and deal with the problems of the pilot, the plane and his possible escape later. Or vice versa. It depended on how long the man was going to be unconscious. And over this he had no control – and no knowledge of the probabilities either.

Better, then, to go for the plans first.

It took him twenty minutes to complete his traverse of the wood, cross the Salzkotten road and retrace his steps through the wood behind the factory. If the hollow oak had not been on the far fringe, it would have taken him twice as long. Holding his breath, he plunged one hand into the fissured trunk.

The tube was still there. It was damp and a little less stiff – either from nocturnal dew or a shower – but the papers inside seemed undamaged except for a slight smudging on one of the working drawings. He re-rolled them and thrust them back inside.

Now he would have to steel himself for the difficult part. The landing of two Fokkers in a cornfield less than half a mile from the factory would most certainly have brought a patrol down from the guardhouse to find out what the hell was going on. They would expect an explanation, from one if not two pilots.

Blake aimed to provide that . . . if luck continued to be with him.

The man he had knocked out still lay on the ground beneath the tree. Feeling for a wrist and kneeling close so that he could manoeuvre one ear close to the slack mouth, Blake discovered that there was a pulse beating. The breath was stertorous and shallow, but fairly even. Very well, he could safely leave him for the time necessary. But first there were things to do.

He had never before realized how difficult it would be to remove the clothes from – or to dress – a human body that was a dead weight. The task, a disagreeable one, took him well over ten minutes. By which time the chorus of voices from the stubbled field had become frighteningly audible.

Finally, however, Blake was dressed in a German army uniform with a fleece-lined leather flying coat over his shoulders. The unconscious pilot lay in Blake's corduroys, army tunic and buttoned brown overalls.

Blake drew a deep breath. His plan, such as it was, depended on the fact that the factory guard would have seen neither him nor the pilot before. Any identification therefore would rely solely on the clothes that each wore.

Stifling the apprehension he felt, Blake picked up the German's pistol, stuffed it in the left-hand pocket of the flying coat, and hurried back through the wood.

He jumped down the bank and ran towards the group of soldiers – about a dozen of them – gathered around the undamaged Eindekker.

An officer came towards him. 'What the devil . . . ?' he began.

'He got away,' Blake panted. 'Lost him in the damned

wood behind the factory. Elusive bastard. He runs like the wind.'

'*Who* got away? What are you doing? What was *he* doing? Why are you here?'

The officer was scarcely coherent. He didn't know how to deal with situations that were not in the book.

'Escaped prisoner from Paderborn,' Blake said shortly. 'An *Englander* spy. Got away from a prison van, snaffled one of these, by God' – he jerked his head towards the Fokker – 'and took off! I was told to follow him, bring him back dead or alive.' He shrugged. 'Unfortunately he was too quick for me. Not my line, anyway: I'm not a policeman; I drive aeroplanes.'

'What do you wish us to do, *Herr Major*?' The officer had suddenly noticed the badges of rank on Blake's sleeve and epaulette. He had not, in fact, taken them in before himself. Now he allowed an authoritative note to creep into his voice.

'Throw a cordon around these woods,' he snapped. 'Block the road between here and Salzkotten. Contact your headquarters at once and double the guard on the factory. You are looking for a youngish man, about my height, dressed in workman's trousers, an army tunic and a brown factory overseer's coat. He may be armed.'

The young officer saluted. '*Jawohl, Herr Major*.' He raised a hand to summon an NCO.

'But first,' Blake pursued, 'tell your men to turn this machine around, wheel it to the far end of the field and help me ready it for take-off. I must get back at once to Paderborn and make my report.' He sighed. 'Unfortunately a negative one. I wish you better luck.'

'Yes, sir. Thank you, sir.' The German saluted again, rapped out a few terse commands to the NCO and detailed six men to manhandle the Eindekker. Four more returned to the factory at the double.

It wouldn't take them long to locate the pilot, especially if he had come to in the meantime. Perhaps rather longer before they believed his story. After all, the regional alert would by now have specified a runaway, dressed thus, who spoke perfect German but had no papers – and the man's papers were in Blake's pocket.

By the time the story was straightened out, anyway, Blake himself hoped to be over the hills and far away.

He had no idea how much fuel there was in the Eindekker's tank. There was no gauge. It didn't matter too much anyway: other than leaving the Detmold–Siegsdorf area as quickly as possible, he had no specific goal in mind. Only when he was well clear and the immediate heat was off could he begin to think of how to get himself and the precious plans back to England.

For the moment he was content to let the monoplane ferry him as far as it could – or for as long as he thought it safe to stay in the air. After that the real trouble would begin! For all the alternative suggestions mulled over with his superiors at home had been predicated on a continuing contact with his cut-out. Now that he was deprived of that advice and knowledge of the country, at least one of the possible escape routes – through Switzerland with the help of existing operatives – was definitively cut.

For the first time, he permitted himself to think objectively of Kristin's treachery and betrayal. Now that the first sick horror had passed, he found that he was less disgusted at her behaviour – after all, in a sense she was only doing, morally, much the same as he was – as he was appalled at his own stupidity. How could he have been so naive, so easily hoodwinked?

He wondered if she was continuing to send bogus reports on his progress, or lack of it, to London. By now, in any case, they would know exactly what he was after. It would, of course, be useful to the German intelligence services to have a double agent in place with the means to send false information and possibly find out more about Allied agents working in the Fatherland. But she wasn't going to last long if telephone contact with Switzerland was involved: even with all the call-signs correct, the voice would give her away at once.

Blake put the girl from his mind. He had been airborne for ten minutes. The take-off had been difficult. The soldiers hadn't understood that each cylinder of a rotary must be primed with neat petrol while the engine is turned over by hand, before it will fire. And when at last this had been correctly done, not one of them had the least idea how to swing a propeller. Finally – even if his own logbook did record only five out of ten for this exercise! – Blake had to improvise chocks and swing it himself, with the officer, duly briefed, installed in the cockpit.

Once he was back at the controls, there was no more than a momentary trauma to overcome, as he took in the slight downhill slant of the field and breathed a short prayer that the Fokker would come unstuck before the blackthorns marking its lower limit.

Fortunately he was facing into the wind and – as he had found out before – the little machine needed only a very short run. He was fifteen feet above the hedge when he cleared the far end of the stubble.

Waving a farewell arm at the soldiers below, he banked the Eindekker and set a course for Paderborn. He kept low, which was reasonable over a distance that short, so that he would be out of sight as soon as possible. When he had covered half the twelve miles, he vectored sharply right and began to climb.

He levelled out at ten thousand feet, by which time the sun was high in the sky and the misty countryside below had dwindled to a familiar map-like patchwork. At that height the air was still solid enough to make breathing euphoric rather than laborious. He was glad nevertheless to have the fleece-lined flying jacket.

He was back at last where he belonged, feet on the rudder bar, hands on a control column and the wide world empty around him. He began to sing.

Blake was in fact getting used to what had become his alternations of fear and elation, bravado and funk. If only he could be granted the power of selection . . . or at least the possibility of knowing which he would be at the mercy of in a given situation.

He was heading at the moment practically due west, edging a little southwards, when the pall of smoke rising over the industrialized sections of the Ruhr drifted uncomfortably close. Clearly the crucible of German war production would be guarded more heavily than the open country to the east.

So far as an eventual escape was concerned, Switzerland was some two hundred and twenty miles due south. The battlefields of the Western Front were about the same distance ahead. Between the two, he reckoned the front-line chaos would give him a better chance of crossing secretly into Allied territory, and thus a quick return to base, than an attempt to force the heavily policed Swiss frontier. Better still would be neutral Holland, but that was north of the Ruhr and doubtless even more strictly guarded.

He was not, in any case, expecting the monoplane to take him the whole way, whichever direction he chose.

Even if the tank had been full when it left Paderborn. He dare not risk staying in the air too long: a general alert would report that a rogue Eindekker was on the loose somewhere up there, and it would need only one keen observer to recognize the plane for them to know which way he was going. Which would mean scouts sent up to intercept him from aerodromes on his route.

If only, he thought, the machine *could* take him safely the thirty-odd miles to Holland ... This, he realized seconds after the thought had come to him, was the second 'if only' since take-off which would have no chance whatever of a satisfactory or encouraging follow-up.

Between the two legs of the bracing wire pivot, he saw them perhaps three miles ahead: four specks against the pale western sky that rapidly resolved themselves into aeroplanes with black crosses on wings and fuselage. Two Halberstadt reconnaissance two-seaters with a pair of Albatros D-Va scouts as fighter escort.

They were climbing steeply and they were coming his way.

21

Blake had not been expecting – and certainly had no appetite for – a dogfight. Nor had he anticipated, this far into Germany, that the aviation authorities would cotton on to his route so quickly or put up opposition ahead of him so fast.

There seemed, however, no alternative. The nearest cloud bank was ten miles away, uncomfortably far to the north. There was another directly ahead, but it was twice as far and the four German machines were in the way – and climbing rapidly. They would be at his altitude before he had covered a quarter of the distance.

He bit his lip. His mount was newer, faster and almost certainly more manoeuvrable than the Albatros scouts or the Halberstadts. But he was totally unfamiliar with its aerobatic characteristics, he had only just got used to the controls and his aggregate flying time in this Eindekker and the previous one was considerably less than an hour. And in any case it was four against one – two of the four benefiting from auxiliary guns fired from the rear cockpit.

Down below – the Fokker tilting fractionally to starboard – industrial smoke partially concealed a huge complex of factory chimneys, railway lines, gasometers and blast furnaces belching flame. Staring down over the padded cockpit rim Blake saw steelworks and marshalling yards stretching away to a dull grey gleam that must be the Rhine. He reckoned that he must be some way south of Essen. The interceptors had probably been put up from one of the aerodromes on the outskirts of Düsseldorf.

He swore. If he was right, he was less than thirty miles from the Dutch frontier. A hell of a time, and a hell of a place, he thought distractedly, to be faced with seasoned adversaries equipped, between them, with something like six or eight deadly machine-guns.

The two-seater Halberstadts must have taken off before the scouts – or been alerted from a nearer aerodrome. They were almost at his level, and the Albatros fighters still a mile behind and several hundred feet lower.

Very well. He would have to do what he could to disable or frighten away the slower observation planes before the escort arrived.

He reached forward and up for an experimental tug at the toggles below the twin Spandau magazine covers.

For an instant the racketing roar of the 110hp Oberursel rotary was drowned by the explosive blast hammered from the guns. The wood and fabric fuselage shuddered under the recoil of the two short bursts. Blake nodded grimly. At least he wasn't flying into a trap unarmed.

The leading Halberstadt was less than two hundred yards away. Abruptly, the pilot dipped the nose of the machine to pass twenty or thirty feet below Blake, at a slight angle. This, Blake knew, was to let the gunner in the rear cockpit have an unobstructed upward shot at the blind spot below his tail. After which the plane would zoom back up to his level, half roll and turn to come in for a frontal attack on one flank or the other.

He tipped the Eindekker on to one wing, screamed into a near-vertical dive, half rolled himself and crossed the Halberstadt's flight path fifty feet lower down. This left him free to climb steeply and fire at the belly of the second observation machine. The pilot saw him coming and veered sharply away, but Blake was happy to see a line of holes stitched across the rear fuselage and through the tailplane and rudder as the Spandaus spat fire from the blunt nose of the Fokker.

He was now directly in line with the second Albatros. Attack being the best means of defence – and surprise theoretically the best weapon of all – he decided on the spur of the moment to play the amateur card. Pulling the nose of the monoplane sharply up a hundred yards in front of the scout, he banked steeply and then dropped the machine into a near-vertical dive.

As he had hoped, the German, believing he was dealing with a beginner and not yet concentrated into a true battle awareness, howled down after him with both guns blazing.

Blake steepened his dive still more. The Albatros followed, gaining now as the range closed.

The Fokker was shuddering in every spar. Slipstream loaded with a mist of castor oil tore at Blake's goggled face. Elongated tears appeared in the wing fabric and something thumped heavily back in the tail. A stray bullet nicked one of the bracing wires and it snapped with a noise like a plucked violin string.

Blake was betting on the German pilot's eagerness for an easy kill – and on an aviation intelligence report he had read, which stated: 'Virtually all Albatros DVs suffer structural failures in steep dives, due to a flutter in the lower wing.'

The bet was well placed. The hail of machine-gun fire ceased. The biplane hurtled past . . . but it wasn't diving; it was dropping. He saw the pilot wrestling with the controls. The lower starboard wing had buckled, tearing free of the V-shaped strut linking it to the wing above. As Blake watched, it broke away and floated off on its own. The crippled machine cartwheeled twice, sank tail down into an uncontrollable spin, somersaulted out of that and finally spiralled out of sight.

With sweat streaming from his brow to course through the hot oil stinging his face, Blake hauled on the control column as forcefully as he dared to coax his plane out of its dive. Once more the entire airframe juddered. Something was flapping out of sight behind. It was two thousand feet before he finally levelled out. With the height lost evading the Halberstadt, he saw that the altimeter now registered no more than four thousand nine hundred.

The remaining Albatros and the two observation planes were circling down more warily, waiting to drop on him out of the sun.

That would not do at all. Blake had to get back upstairs if he was going to come out of this in one piece. Gritting his teeth, he heaved the stick back again as far as it would come under maximum power, shooting up into the sky like a cork from a bottle as he kicked hard on the rudder bar.

The Albatros sailed past him with guns spitting as he rose.

He hung the Eindekker on its propeller above the Halberstadts, treated this as the zenith of a loop, then completed the circle to swoop down on the slower two-seater he had already damaged. With his face pressed to the rubberized fabric of the telescopic gunsight eyepiece, he opened fire with both guns.

He saw the observer, frantically swinging his weapon around on its ring mount, slump suddenly back against the cockpit rim, saw the pilot jerk forward to slide down the instrument panel, saw flame blossom from behind the exposed engine block.

The Halberstadt erupted into a seething fireball. Black debris shot out into the sky, and the carcass dropped from sight trailing a long plume of oily smoke.

Blake was trembling. He hated to see them die. But there were still two more determined to get him. He jerked the toggles again as the Albatros swam into view broadside on – a perfect kill for synchronized guns.

The engine continued its clattering roar but the Spandaus remained silent. He tugged fiercely again . . . but the scout had wheeled away. And the guns were mute.

Blake cursed. Both magazines were exhausted. They must have been partly used on one of the target runs at Paderborn. And there were no spares to be seen. He thrust the stick forward and dived again.

He hadn't noticed before, but the encounter had taken them quite a long way south, and no further towards the cloud bank in the west. The only believable cover that he could see was a blanket of industrial smoke lying over a mining area ten miles ahead and several thousand feet below him. It was, again, due south; not too far, he estimated, from Cologne.

This time, the Fokker was vibrating badly during the dive. The flapping behind had become an ugly thump. Although the second Albatros pilot was unwilling to risk structural failure in a dive this steep, the remaining Halberstadt was gamely following Blake down, shooting as he came.

Once you got used to it, Blake thought, the Eindekker really was a treat to fly, vibrations and all.

No sooner had the thought formulated itself than the

machine dropped its nose further still and threw itself into a spin.

He swore again. What the hell? He wrestled with the stick, the rudder bar. What the devil was the matter now? Why wouldn't she . . . ?

The pounding behind was reaching a climax. Over his shoulder he saw with horror that the port elevator had broken away from the tailplane. It was flapping wildly in the slipstream, held in place only by its control cables. Holes appeared in the rudder and the rear part of the fuselage as the Halberstadt circled overhead with the rear gunner firing down from his cockpit ring.

Five hundred feet above the smoke layer, the monoplane was becoming uncontrollable. Blake set his teeth, compensating for the loss of control surface with reverse rudder and skilful juggling of the ailerons. Grey wisps loaded with sulphurous fumes and the choking odour of coal gas were already whipping through the screaming stays by the time he finally halted the sickening corkscrew fall and levelled out in a shallow, stumbling descent. It was obvious, however, that the flight was over: he had scarcely any directional control, he could not climb and – just to hammer in the last nail! – the engine coughed, spat and choked into silence. The fuel tank was empty. He had to put down.

Blindly, with the propeller spinning to a standstill, he sank through the dark cloud.

It was only about two hundred feet thick. Below it, the Eindekker staggered out above a smoky wasteland of colliery wheels, chimneys and gantries carrying serpentine coils of metal piping. A little way to the west was the broad pale ribbon of the Rhine. In such a landscape, it was the only hope.

The Halberstadt emerged from a cloud a mile away to

the east. It was followed by the Albatros. They banked at once and headed for the Fokker.

Blake coaxed the machine towards the river, losing height as slowly as he dared while keeping as far ahead of the pursuers as he could. The swirling water leaped towards him.

He pancaked the Eindekker between a complex of ancient wharves and a tug towing a string of barges loaded with coal. It dropped twenty feet into the stream with a shattering crash and a huge surge of white foam, sinking at once in a cloud of steam.

Grasping his precious cardboard tube, Blake was already standing on the wing. He jumped as the doomed plane gurgled away beneath him, and struck out one-handed towards the tug, holding the plans above his head.

As he had hoped, the tug veered towards him. A seaman leaned out over the low stern, proffering a boat-hook. Blake grabbed it and was hauled aboard.

'What the devil was going on up there?' the grizzled skipper asked when Blake, relieved of his sodden sheepskin, wrapped in a blanket and fortified with schnapps, stood beside him on the tiny bridge.

'An exercise,' Blake said. 'Practising for the Western Front. But some dolt of a rigger had made a mistake: without knowing it, one of my colleagues up there was firing live ammunition.'

'Good God!' the skipper said. 'What will they think of next?'

'What indeed!'

'You were lucky you weren't killed.'

'That is perfectly true,' Blake said fervently. He looked up into the sky. The two planes, having circled the river banks once or twice, had flown away. Warehouses and cranes slid towards them on either side. A police launch creamed past in the opposite direction. 'The only thing is,' he added, 'I have to make my report pretty damn quick. Could you possibly put me ashore at Cologne? You wouldn't even need to tie up: just come close enough to a quay for me to jump.'

The skipper took his pipe from his mouth and spat into the river. 'You're a bit late for that, friend,' he said. 'We're heading upstream. Cologne is ten kilometres astern! I'll land you at Koblenz, though, if that would suit.' He re-lit the pipe, shielding the match flame from the breeze with cupped hands. 'In a couple of hours.'

'Perfect. And many thanks,' Blake said. 'Er . . . I'm not from this part of the country. It's a big town, Koblenz?'

The skipper chuckled. 'Big enough,' he said.

22

The brigadier and the major-general sat drinking lobster soup at the counter of Scott's restaurant in Coventry Street. Between the two white soup plates with their blue rims stood a recently opened bottle of Chablis.

'Thirty-seven yesterday,' the senior man said. 'Poor young blighters are falling out of the sky quicker than we can ship out bloody replacements. And some of those are being posted with less than a couple of weeks' training.' He shook his head. 'Life expectation of a lad like that can be a matter of hours in the sky rather than weeks or even days.'

'Yes, sir. I know. But if we can . . .'

'To say nothing,' the major-general pursued, 'of the difficulty of finding the machines they're going to fly – and probably die – in. Trenchard's really got the wind up, I can tell you.'

'If only we knew,' the brigadier said, 'for sure. I mean to say, the last signal we got from S-12 was optimistic. The last but one, I should say. Our man had actually got into the factory. And out again. But apparently without the stuff. He was to go back the following night.'

The major-general grunted. 'That got you an extension of your twenty-four hours,' he said. 'Now you're trying to wriggle out of that. What exactly did the *very* last signal say?'

The brigadier cleared his throat. He crooked a finger to summon the barman and indicated that he should pour the wine. 'It was a little odd,' he said. 'The staging contact in Switzerland – the chap who receives S-12's messages and passes them on by telephone – he said our man had got in the second time successfuly. But he didn't say – or, rather, S-12 didn't say – whether or not he had the plans.'

'Well, I must say that's a bit rum,' the major-general exclaimed. 'It's only the aim of the whole damned operation, after all! Chap gets down to the far end of the field unopposed, then doesn't say whether or not he scored a try!'

'Exactly. It leaves us in what I call a tricky situation. Do we assume yes, and wait patiently for more news? Or do we, as they say, make other arrangements?'

The major-general grunted again, then drank some wine. 'This soup's uncommonly good,' he observed. 'What is there off-ration that it's safe to eat?'

'The turbot, sir,' the barman intervened. 'Poached, with Hollandaise sauce. Arrived from Grimsby early this morning. Very popular with our regulars, sir, the turbot.'

'Very well. Two turbots then.'

The street doors swung open, letting in a gust of cool air, the rumble of wheels and the sound of motor traffic circling Piccadilly Circus two hundred yards away. Three naval officers entered and installed themselves at the far end of the bar. They were followed by a man and a woman in civilian clothes who were given a table in an alcove.

The major-general and his companion turned around on their stools, their haughty gaze sweeping over dark panelling and brasswork and crimson leather chairs – and then over the new arrivals – as if outraged by the intrusion of strangers into their private domain.

'Anyway,' the major-general said, turning back to his fish.

'Thing is,' the brigadier told him, 'there's actually something else deuced tricky here, sir. I can't exactly say it's another signal from S-12. But it's *about* him. Fellow in Switzerland was a shade puzzled. These Morse experts, you see, get to *know* their contacts in a way. The same way musicians can tell the difference between one pianist and another playing the same piece. Matter of rhythm and touch; way the key's handled, impact, spacing of dots and dashes. Almost like a signature.'

'So I have been told. And so?'

'Well, our Swiss wallah thought – he wasn't sure, mind, but he *thought* – that there was something rum about the last couple of transmissions. Almost as though another operator was sending the stuff. Correct call-signs and all, but *different*. Also the abbreviations, what we call the cablese, were as you might say in a different vein. As if there was another kind of intelligence at work.' The brigadier paused. He drank some wine and held up his glass for more.

'Fellow wondered at first whether S-12 was off colour or something of that sort,' he continued. 'Then, of course, he thought maybe the Hun had bagged the chap and he was transmitting under duress. Naturally we told him to check.'

The major-general was forking flakes of turbot into his mouth. 'Jolly good,' he enthused. 'We were right to take the chap's advice. What is this S-12 caper anyway?'

'Just a matter of identification,' the brigadier said. 'You know: no names, no bloody pack drill! S stands for Saxony; the number signifies that we are dealing with the twelfth agent on the list. Elderly fellow, actually. Lived there forty years.'

'What happened when your Swiss man checked?'

'Couldn't regain contact. No go. No signal at the proper time. Then – this was the queerest thing of all – a call at the wrong time, late in the evening. But before our contact could put in a special code question we have, asking for a coded confirmation that everything was all right and above board . . . before that, S-12 *himself* started to ask questions.' The brigadier shook his head. 'Most unusual. Out of court. Said our man was scot-free and heading south, *but that he wanted urgent confirmation of exactly what plans he was to filch*. I mean, I ask you!'

'What did your Swiss end say?'

'Didn't have a chance to say anything. Before he could ask why, the line was cut. Completely dead.'

'You mean your telephone line with the Swiss?'

'No, no. The wireless transmission, the Morse. Simply ceased. And nothing since, neither at the right time nor any other. The Swiss keeps trying, but the blasted airwaves remain silent. Call-sign's never answered; not a bloody sausage.'

Nodding his head slowly, the major-general laid down his fork. 'Very rum, as you say,' he commented. 'Very rum indeed.'

'I stopped Fräulein Dony sending at that moment,' *Hauptmann* Schneider said, 'because at that moment we received confirmation from the factory of what was missing. There was no need to wait for an answer we already knew. Besides, there was a risk that this kind of question might make the *Englanders* suspicious if we persisted. And it could be useful in the future, keeping the young woman in place as a supposed agent of theirs.'

Schneider was making his report at Hohenstein to Rudolph von Sonderstern. Through the pines beyond the long windows, sunlight glinted on the fast-moving water of the river below.

'So it is Fokker's interrupter gear they were after,' the *Kommandant* mused. 'Pity. But I suppose they were going to come up with something similar themselves before long anyway.' He smiled. 'At least it wasn't the rapid-fire mechanism or the new sighting machine for the delivery of bombs. It is a relief to know that they are apparently unaware of those.'

'With respect, *Herr General-Major*,' Schneider ventured, 'the unfortunate fact that the spy succeeded in stealing the plans for the Fokker gear does not necessarily mean that he will safely return with them to England. We have every hope that he will be recaptured and the papers recovered.'

'H'm. And how far, young man, or more properly how near, has this optimistic prophecy, this forecast, come to realization?'

'We know approximately where he is; we know in which direction he is heading. With an efficient collaboration between our own operatives and the police of the Cologne region, it should be possible very soon to block him ahead and catch up with him from behind.'

'As efficient as the way in which he was imprisoned at Paderborn? As the manner in which he was permitted – twice – to steal aeroplanes of the Imperial Army Air Service, and use one of them to destroy two more in the air?'

Schneider coloured. 'It must be admitted, *Herr General-Major*,' he said, 'that we are dealing with a resourceful man. And with an expert pilot. If we . . .'

'Do we too not have resourceful men, rather more of them, at our disposal? And pilots equally expert?'

'Yes, sir. Of course. It is more a matter of where they are deployed, and whether that deployment can be effected at the right time, when it concerns a quarry completely autonomous, able to speak the language perfectly and apparently equipped with plenty of money.'

The *Hauptmann* paused, staring through a window at the tree-covered hillside. The sun had vanished behind a cloud and the upper branches of the pines were tossing. Von Sonderstern, ramrod-straight in an oak chair like a throne, waited for him to continue.

Schneider, standing at attention, was at a disadvantage. 'It has to be remembered, sir,' he said awkwardly, 'that he *was* efficiently delivered to us, originally, by our female agent. His subsequent escape – and the fact that a machine was standing nearby with the engine running – were totally unforeseen.'

'In matters of national security,' Sonderstern said severely, 'the unforeseen is to be expected.'

'Yes, *Herr General-Major*. The door to the prison van should, of course, have been locked. The *Feldwebel* in charge of the escort swears that it was, that he effected this himself. It is possible that he was mistaken, is lying or even that the sudden start, the fault of the driver, threw the prisoner with such force against the door that it burst open the lock. Both men, in any case, have been disciplined.'

Schneider swallowed. He was dying to raise one hand and extend a finger to ease his tight collar away from his neck. 'With regard to the pilot who followed the stolen aeroplane,' he said, 'I feel, sir, that I should point out this was not a man trained to deal with escaped prisoners or deal with professional spies. The fact that he was mastered by the fugitive, relieved of his clothes and left unconscious while the man apparently retrieved the stolen drawings from some hiding place was unfortunate . . .'

'Most unfortunate. Go on.'

'. . . as was the fact that the soldiers who arrived had seen neither of them before, and thus were persuaded easily that that – er – one was the other. After that, it was after all a matter of aerial combat. And, as in such matters, it was skill and experience that counted. The fugitive certainly destroyed one machine, but the other was lost due to a structural failure – a defect common to the type. And the stolen aeroplane was in fact shot down by the remaining pilots.'

'Yes. Into the Rhine. And the pilot?'

'The aviators reported that he swam free. It is thought that he may have been picked up by a river craft heading upstream. But the fact that we are aware of this; the fact that . . .'

'The fact this, the fact that!' the *Kommandant* snapped. 'You deliver me nothing but what you call *facts*, young man. But every one is a *fact* connected with something that is in some way or another a failure. The next time I see you, I expect every "fact" that you present me with to concern a success. Is that clearly understood?'

'*Jawohl, Herr General-Major,*' Schneider said miserably.

Blake stood in the shadow of a buttress projecting from the wall of the Ehrenbreitstein citadel, a fortress commanding the confluence of the Rhine and the Moselle at Koblenz.

The sun, low down in the western sky, silhouetted the roofs of the city and the seventeenth-century belfries of the Liebfrauenkirche on the far side of the Rhine. The river traffic – barges laden with sand, cement, timber; a steamer transporting crated machinery; a police launch – was dense. He thought he would wait until it was almost dark before he crossed the Pfaffendorfer bridge and passed beneath the trees of the Rheinanlagen waterfront promenade on his way to the old town. It was already two hours since the tugboat skipper had put him ashore – and one hour fifty minutes since he had seen the vessel stopped in midstream and boarded by military police.

They had left five minutes later, but it was clear that

the surviving pilots had witnessed his escape from the crippled Eindekker before it sank, and reported it as soon as they returned to base. The hunt was on and the pursuers were closing in.

For the moment Blake was content to lose himself if possible in the narrow lanes of the old town. He was dressed in the uniform – not quite dry – of a German army major. Reluctantly, he had abandoned the sodden sheepskin flying jacket. In his pocket were the papers of one Bruno Früchtnicht, born in Bad Kreuznach in 1892, and what remained of the identity of Gerhardt Ehrlich, native of Hamburg, although the production of either, assuming the Kaiser's security services were efficient, would lead to a prison cell.

The stolen interrupter gear drawings, smudged a little more but still quite legible, had been removed from the cardboard tube, folded and lodged beneath his shirt just above the waistband of his uniform trousers.

The Belgian frontier, and behind it the wooded plateaux of the Ardennes, lay some fifty miles due west. Once on the far side, which was after all the French-speaking part of the country, he hoped he might be able to get help from the occupied population.

For the moment though, the problem was how to traverse those fifty miles of heavily policed, manhunt-alerted and indisputably hostile country. He would start after dark. Until then, failing a military check in the warren of the old town, he must hope that the officer's uniform would act as protective colouring.

The tugboat skipper had joked that Koblenz was 'large enough'. He hoped fervently that it was large enough to conceal the movements of a hunted man with papers that could save hundreds of lives plastered to his back . . .

23

Blake was making his way cautiously through the old town, between the market-place and the Entenpfuhl, less than three hundred yards from the Moselle. He had slunk into a narrow lane twisting away from the curving street which followed the line of the original medieval city wall, hoping to reach the river. With luck, he reasoned, there would be skiffs or rowing boats somewhere along the waterfront; if his luck held, he would be able to free one from its moorings and drift across to the far bank. After that, he could turn west and take one of the lesser roads leading to the Belgian frontier.

The lane was unlit. But the market-place behind, less crowded since the night had fallen, was nevertheless still busy enough to be a danger to a hunted man. Longshoremen and soldiers on leave mingled with drab housewives eddying around the stalls not yet stripped of the little they had to sell. Beneath the raftered roof, the long shadows of merchants packing up to go home danced in the wavering illumination of naphtha flares. A thin drizzle had begun to fall, veneering the cobbled square with reflected light.

Blake trod as quietly as he could between the ancient houses. The stench of rotting fruit and vegetables faded behind him. His shadow dwindled and died. The worn granite setts beneath his feet no longer gleamed. He turned a sharp corner and walked into total darkness.

All at once he was aware of the night sounds of the city: the hoot of a tugboat cutting through distant voices, an accordion behind one of the shuttered façades. A long way to the west, he could hear the puffing of a locomotive and the clatter of buffers in a goods yard.

He trod in a deep puddle and stumbled, cursing the water which splashed up to soak the lower part of his leg.

Footsteps from a recessed entry ahead. The sudden unexpected command: 'Halt!' A loud click and an instantaneous dazzle of white light. Frozen between two paces, he was caught in the blinding beam of a torch.

There were three of them. Throwing up an arm to shield his eyes, he had an impression of bulky figures, a gleam from buttons and boots.

'Military police,' the man with the torch announced. The beam played over Blake's still dishevelled form, his damp and rumpled uniform. '*Ach, so!* Our apologies, *Herr Major*, but we have our orders. If the *Herr Major* permits, it will be necessary to examine his papers.'

Blake was in a quandary. To say he didn't have them, that he had lost them, would be courting disaster. To pretend that he had left them in barracks or at his hotel would be equally useless: he had no idea what regiments were quartered in Koblenz and he knew the name of no hotels. Dare he on the other hand show the papers that went with the uniform, the identification of the pilot whose aeroplane he had stolen near the factory? Or would the security forces have been efficient enough, after his crash landing in the Rhine, to alert the authorities this far away that a major of that name was a fugitive with a price on his head?

'Your papers, please!' The voice of the MP was becoming more peremptory.

'I am sorry,' Blake said, having decided there was only one thing to do. 'I was temporarily blinded. You took me by surprise.' He fumbled out the papers, handed them over.

One of the men had moved around behind him. Another had stepped in very close: warm breath redolent of cigar smoke and beer fanned his cheek. The torch beam played over the water-damaged, slightly buckled pages. The MP turned back, flicked forward again, leaned down to scrutinize one particular leaf.

'So,' he said, straightening up. 'Major Bruno Frücht-nicht, eh?'

'That is so.'

'Attached to the Imperial Army Air Service?'

'Correct.'

'Born in Bad Kreuznach . . .'

'Exactly,'

'. . . in what year precisely?'

'In '92,' Blake said, dry-mouthed.

'Yes. It so happens that I am from Bad Kreuznach myself,' the MP said. 'Perhaps the *Herr Major* would be so kind as to tell us the name of the island served by the Alte Nahebrücke? And also, as further proof of his fondness for our mutual birthplace, the name of the street in which the Römerhalle can be found?'

Blake swallowed. He had, of course, no idea. Heidelberg is less than fifty miles from Bad Kreuznach, but he had never visited the spa during his year at the German university. He said nothing. There was nothing to say.

'Very well.' The MP was suddenly brisk. 'This accords exactly with our instructions, our alert. If the *Herr Major*,' he said with a sneer, 'permits, I think it would be well if he accompanied us.'

'He will not be needing this.' The man behind plunged

one hand into Blake's sagging uniform pocket and produced the Walther he had stolen.

Fleetingly, Blake had thought of using it, but against three professionals, at close quarters, such a move would have been suicidal. He allowed himself to be bustled ahead along the lane, with one MP still behind and one gripping an arm on either side. There didn't seem to be any point in trying to make conversation. None of the MPs had anything to say. He had the impression that the one behind had drawn a gun.

The lane turned again, at almost a right angle. They must be heading straight for the Moselle side of the tongue of land on which the old town was built. Some way ahead, there was light. A wide square with gas lamps which thrust the façades at the lane's exit into sharp relief.

Blake examined the options open to him. They were pitifully few. Shooting was a non-starter, since he had no gun. Running for cover was out of the question. A sudden attack with fists and feet – on three heavyweights, one of whom certainly was armed – was also ruled out. He himself, on the other hand, was fit, agile and relatively strong.

From the façade of the last house in the lane, a wrought-iron bracket, perhaps once the support for a shop sign or an innkeeper's notice, projected ten or twelve feet above the ground. Immediately above the leaded panes of the bow window, there was a semicircular balcony protected by a stone balustrade. They were almost level with the house. The bracket was silhouetted against the lights of the square.

Abruptly, Blake shook off the restraining grips, took half a dozen lightning steps forward and sprang high into the air.

His outstretched hands, smarting still from the raw

palms, clenched around two of the curved bracket supports . . . and held.

Jackknifing from the hips and knees, he arched his body forward and up until one heel lodged on a narrow ledge at the foot of the balustrade. A moment later, with a titanic heave and a painful wrench of shoulders and waist, he had projected himself upwards and scrambled over the balustrade on to the balcony.

Panting, he heard cursing from below. A shot. And then another. Chips of stonework stung his cheek . . . but by then he was jerking apart the half-closed shutters giving on to the balcony.

The French windows beyond were ajar. Blake pulled them open and rose half upright to stumble through into a lighted room.

'Good God!' he heard a woman exclaim. 'Usually they pass by Madam in reception to make an appointment or at least check that one is not actually busy with a client. But if it's that urgent . . . well, the bed's been made and it's just behind you!'

He stared. She was sitting in front of a dressing-table with pink mirrors – a busty woman of about forty wearing a semi-transparent black nightdress and a feather boa which just managed not to conceal generous slopes of breast. A painted smile beneath blonde curls faded as she saw Blake's stricken face. 'What is it?' she said urgently. 'The police?'

'Military.'

'Quick, then. They're no friends of mine. Get into that wardrobe and pull the door closed. I'll tell them you've run through.' The smile, genuine this time, revealed a gold tooth at one side of a wide mouth. The woman flung open an inner door, ran to the French windows and uttered a very convincing scream. 'Help! Help!' she yelled. 'A man! . . . He just burst into my room . . . He ran through, towards the fire escape!'

Blake was just registering the fact that he had blundered into a brothel. Inside the wardrobe, half stifled by sequins and hanging satin, choking on the scent of cheap perfume, he heard the babble of voices below the balcony.

'All right. I'm coming up . . . Bader, give me a hand up, then run round to the back as quick as you damned well can . . .'

A scramble of boots on stone, a gasp of breath and then what sounded like a heavy fall. The same voice, the MP with the torch, panting now, much nearer: 'Schwerin, circle the block. Contact Bader behind. There's an alley . . . Yes, madam. Which way did he go?'

The woman, running from the French windows to the door, said breathlessly: 'This way . . . almost knocked me over. I think the fire escape . . .'

'Where? Quick.'

'End of the corridor. Turn right. There's an emergency door . . .'

The last sentence was lost in the diminishing clump of heavy feet.

The wardrobe door jerked open. For an instant she stood there, undecided, then hurried across and opened the windows wider. 'Could you get down again, the way you came in?'

'I suppose so. If I had to.' Blake emerged from the wardrobe.

'You do have to. Now. They'd never expect you to return the way you came in.'

'That makes sense,' Blake said. 'The escaped prisoner doubling back towards the jail.' He moved in the direction of the balcony.

The woman caught his arm. 'Listen. Which way are you heading?'

'West. Towards Belgium.'

'I thought so. Look, if you want, young man, I can help you a little in that direction. I'm leaving here in half an hour. Visiting a client out on the Mayen road. I could take you that far.'

'Well, really, that is most ... I don't know how to ...'

'Don't waste time on words.' She turned a small tap to extinguish the flame of the gaslight above the dressing-table. 'Listen. Do you know the Altmeier Ufer?'

'I'm afraid not.'

'It runs along the riverside. Turn left below and it's a couple of hundred metres. When you get there, turn left again, and you'll see a bridge not far ahead. There's a wall with buttresses. Wait there behind one of those and I'll pick you up in forty minutes.'

'Yes, but how do I ... ?'

'Do you know what a hansom cab is?'

Blake smiled in the darkness. 'I think so. One of those curious horse-drawn carriages the *Englanders* use in London?'

'That's right. You sit hidden behind two flaps, with the cabbie behind you and above.' She moved closer to him. He was suddenly very much physically aware of her – the ample breasts, the big, warm body. Her breath stirred the hairs of his moustache. The sweetness of cachous, perhaps with a hint of schnapps?

'There's no fuel for motor cabs,' she said. 'Everything is back to horses. The man we use has this imported hansom. His stand is by the old flower market, just beyond the church. You'll recognize the cab at once. It's the only one – and he can be trusted.'

Soft fingers touched Blake's face. 'Go now,' the woman said. 'But I'd be telling a lie if I denied that I'd be happier if you stayed a while – a good-looking young fellow like you!' She pushed him gently towards the open French windows.

Blake transferred himself with some difficulty from the balustrade to the iron bracket. It was raining harder now and the stonework was greasy, the metal dripping and hard to grip. He lowered himself carefully until he was hanging at the full stretch of his arms, then dropped the few feet to the wet roadway.

Above him, he heard the click of closing shutters. Light suddenly gleamed again behind the slits. Somewhere over the roofs, he thought he heard the MPs shouting, but it could have been merchants in the market-place crying their wares.

Turning up the collar of his jacket, he hunched his shoulders against the rain and walked swiftly towards the river.

Her name was Birgit. He sat beside her in the cab with his thigh pressed against hers. Because of the rain, a tarpaulin screen had been rigged over the gate-like flaps and up as far as their chins. Apart from a routine '*Guten Abend, mein Herr*' when Blake stepped out from behind the buttress to flag him down, the cabbie had made no comment.

The two large wheels of the hansom rattled over the cobbles as the horse trotted briskly across the Balduinbrücke. There was very little traffic on the far side of the Moselle: an occasional four-wheeler, a solitary Mercedes-Benz landaulette with brass oil lamps flaring, a convoy of lorries crammed with soldiers on the way into town.

Birgit was discretion personified. She made no attempt whatever to question him. It was enough that he was a fugitive from the law; she had no wish to learn the details. There was a warmth about her, a certain human quality that was almost maternal, which, despite her profession, led him to trust her implicitly.

They had left the wide western avenue and taken a suburban by-road twisting past scattered patches of woodland when he blurted out: 'Birgit, I can't tell you . . . there is no way I can convey my appreciation for the help, the kindness . . .'

'Ssssshhh!' Leaning against him, she laid a finger across his lips. 'If I can be of assistance to someone in trouble, that is good enough for me. Someone helped me once – got me out of a hell of a scrape and a probable year inside – and I've never forgotten.'

A few minutes later he heard her laughing softly over the clip-clop of the horse's hooves.

'I've no wish to be nosey,' she said in answer to his query, 'but I imagine they . . . the people after you . . . will be looking for a man wearing the uniform of an army major?'

'Only too true,' Blake said.

'Well, I just had an idea.' She laughed again, almost a giggle, he thought. 'The client I'm going to see – not a man I'm fond of, to tell the truth – he's an *Ober-Leutnant*. And he's about the same build as you.'

'You mean . . . ?'

'He is lodged in a requisitioned pavilion, a self-contained apartment in a wooden building in the garden of a large house. After I have been there . . . a certain time . . . he will doubtless remove his uniform. Customarily, it is hung over the back of a chair just inside the door of his salon. The salon is at the end of a short hallway.'

Blake was staring at her through the dark. Her profile, turned straight ahead, was visible as a darker blur against the night outside.

'If I was to keep him *very* occupied,' Birgit said, 'and if I was to arrange that the outer door was left unlocked . . .'

She left the sentence unfinished. The cab was jolting over potholes in the road. Rain pock-marked puddles glistening with light reflected from a house nearby.

'There are . . . no servants?' Blake asked huskily.

'None.'

'And you really think that I . . . ?'

'Listen,' she said for the third time. 'It would not, I am convinced, be difficult for a young, athletic man – a man who can jump up on to first-floor balconies – to open two doors without noise, creep silently ten metres down a carpeted hallway and lift a jacket and maybe trousers from a chair without disturbing a man agreeably occupied beneath a large and heavy woman!'

Blake laughed in his turn. '*Liebchen*,' he crowed, 'I love you.'

'As to that, I am hoping perhaps that you can prove it. Sometime.' He felt what he took to be a visiting card thrust into his hand. 'If ever you should happen to be this way again,' she said.

'It would be a pleasure,' Blake said. And meant it.

'*Gott in Himmel!*' Rudolph von Sonderstern smashed his fist so hard against the refectory table in the great hall at Hohenstein that the decanter and glasses rattled on their silver tray at the far end. 'The dolts had their hands on him,' he bellowed. 'The man was actually under arrest – and they let him get away *again*!'

24

Blake had no idea exactly when or where he crossed the border between Germany and Belgium. Certainly, when he was convinced that he was near, he had forsaken footpaths and tracks and taken to the woods. Perhaps the imaginary line was not continuously patrolled. Perhaps he had just been lucky.

With the sky thatched over by leaves, it had been a matter of chance maintaining a constant westerly direction in the gloom. No birds sang in the depths of the woodland. No wind stirred the branches far overhead. From time to time he was startled by a scurrying rustle as some forest creature fled before his advance. But for most of the day the swish and crackle of his own progress through the thick undergrowth – anxious though he was to avoid it – became the sole accompaniment to his escape.

It was almost dusk when he found himself at the edge of a small clearing, led there by the familiar thunk of chopping wood and the sound of distant voices. Crouched down behind a screen of bushes, he stared out from beneath the trees. He saw a grassy slope with a timber chalet on the far side. Behind the shack were neatly stacked wood piles, what looked like a fenced-in farmyard, and a horse grazing beyond a fifty-yard patch of cultivation. From a tall brick chimney at one end of the chalet, blue smoke spiralled lazily up into the darkening sky.

The woodcutter, almost invisible against the dark mass of the forest, swung his axe beside a felled pine. There was a second man beside him, loading logs as they were chopped into an ancient farm cart. As Blake watched, a woman wearing an apron came to the door of the chalet and called out something to the workers. Her voice rose shrilly over the clucking of hens. Perhaps supper was already on the table.

The woman was wearing nondescript clothes – a long skirt, a cotton smock and a scarf tied around her head. The men could have been labourers from anywhere in Europe.

It was only when he heard their shouted reply that he realized they were talking in Flemish.

That was odd, as this was the Walloon or French-speaking part of Belgium. What the hell. He breathed a deep sigh of relief – he had made it, at least the first stage of his journey to the west: he was on the right side of the German frontier!

He felt an impulse to show himself, to run across the grass and ask their help. He was physically exhausted and faint from hunger. The Belgians were reputed to be violently hostile to the occupiers ... and then he remembered that he was himself in the uniform of an occupier.

He grinned to himself. It had been ludicrously easy, snitching the jacket and breeches of the *Ober-Leutnant* of whom Birgit was 'not very fond'. He hoped she would not in any way be blamed for the loss, that it would be put down to a passing sneak-thief. And that, after all, was what Blake was.

The cabbie had been instructed to wait 'as usual'.

Blake made a pretence, after kissing the woman good-bye, of continuing along the road. Later he circled the property from behind, finding the officer's billet exactly as described. There were lights behind the shutters of the big house, but thankfully no dogs. Probably eaten, he thought, if the rationing situation in Germany was as severe as he had been told.

The outer door of the wooden pavilion was heavy and inclined to creak. He had eased it open inch by inch, pushing hard upwards on the handle to relieve the pressure on the hinges. The loudest noise he heard during the five minutes it took was the hammering of his own heart.

He could feel the sweat running down into his eyes as he slid himself through the narrow gap he had made. The hallway was carpeted, warm, with a hint of cigar smoke and the fumes of brandy. From beyond a door at the far end, he heard a murmur of voices.

Holding his breath, Blake stole towards the door.

It was ajar. Through the crack, he spied a dimly lit room with pink-shaded lamps on wall brackets. A wide, low, rumpled bed, flanked by a night table loaded with bottles and glasses, was occupied by two naked bodies. Blake saw the hairy, widespread legs of a man lying prone on his back, the swelling, rounded globes of the backside of a woman moving above him, a heavy breast in jiggling profile. The words of the couple, moaned through gasping breath, were unintelligible.

As Birgit had promised, a chair, with the uniform neatly draped over its back, was within easy reach of the doorway. He had only to push the door open another foot to grasp the smooth field-grey material. Warily, he lifted the trousers. A metal buckle on a loose leather belt swung out and hit the curved back of the chair.

Blake froze, his hand in mid-air, the garment halfway raised from the jacket. The single, sharp metallic sound had seemed to him as loud, as obtrusive, as a shot or a shout.

He was aware that the woman had redoubled her exertions, that the panting on the bed had suddenly become more urgent. But there was no direct reaction to his mistake.

Thankfully, he released the breath he had been holding. With infinite caution he completed the first part of his theft, laying the trousers beside him on the carpet. He reached in for the jacket.

This was more difficult. Knobs terminating the posts which supported the chair back had to be disengaged from the shoulders and the upper part of the sleeves. He rose upright and inserted one of his own shoulders into the gap between the door and the lintel. The added height made the task easier. The slight whisper of material as the jacket pulled free was masked by the creak of the bed.

There remained a polished cross-over uniform belt not unlike a British Sam Browne. It was looped over the nearest knob – and there was a holstered revolver attached to it. This was a prize too good to be missed. Feeling now the total unreality of the situation – the naked couple slaving away on that bed, himself as absurd as an adulterer in a French farce – Blake found within himself the mindless courage that goes with recklessness. Boldly, he stepped half into the room and unhooked the heavy belt with a single swift movement.

A pair of highly polished boots stood on the far side of the chair, but to venture in far enough to reach for those would be tempting fate. He would have to be content with the scuffed pair he had taken off the Eindekker pilot.

Silently, with a heartfelt mental thank you to Birgit,

he withdrew from the doorway, picked up the uniform and crept out of the pavilion.

For a moment, imbued with this same sense of the ridiculous – almost as though he was taking part in some juvenile university jape – he had thought of leaving the uniform he was wearing in place of the one he had stolen. He had not seen the officer's face, but he could imagine his expression when he discovered that during his exertions he had been promoted in rank from an *Ober-Leutnant* to a Major!

But no, that would never do. It might implicate the woman. It would certainly tip off the pursuers, if the officer reported the theft, that their quarry was a leopard who constantly changed his spots. As it was, there could be no conceivable connection between the *Englander* spy who had escaped from the police in Koblenz and a banal pilferer who had robbed an officer some miles to the west.

A mile away from the pavilion, he walked into a small copse and changed into the new uniform. It was a little tight across the chest and the breeches tended to bag at the knee. But it would do at a distance, especially when the belt was buckled on.

The purloined clothes were a trifle damp, but the rain had stopped now, and anyway there was nothing he could do about it. He stuffed the discarded garments beneath a low-growing bush, scattered fallen leaves over them as best as he could in the dark, and returned to the road.

He continued to walk.

During the next twelve hours a fictional story about a commandeered motor car which had broken down, and a driver who had gone to look for a garage mechanic, gained him lifts from a doctor on a night call, a carter with a two-horse wagon piled high with turnips and a military transport returning to Liège with a load of fresh uniforms for troops about to be moved up into the line.

Cold fear tightened his chest during the fifteen-mile journey in the transport. He had no idea of the state of the war, the badges on his uniform meant nothing to him and he hadn't the least idea of the kind of replies he ought to give to questions of a military nature. But he needed to move west fast: the offer was too tempting to refuse.

In the event it didn't matter. The driver, a private soldier, and his NCO mate were regulars. Questioning an officer was unthinkable, and they were not going to enter into conversation unless they were spoken to first. He left them with a single word of thanks and a crisp salute at a small town called Blankenheim.

They would have taken him right through into Belgium, but he had no way of knowing whether the frontier was operated in a normal fashion, with examination of papers and questions from MPs, or whether military traffic was waved straight through into occupied territory. It was certainly not a question an officer would ask of other ranks. Equally, it was a risk he dare not take blind.

Blankenheim was between ten and twelve miles from the border. More than half that distance was through the densely wooded hills of the Ardennes.

It was only when he had left the road, subsequently renouncing footpaths and forest tracks, that Blake felt the tension of the past few days ease sufficiently to allow him time for reflection.

Paramount among three questions clamouring for response was the problem of his connection – or lack of it – with London. What was the last they had heard of him? How much truth, if any, had there been in Kristin's last transmission supposedly on his behalf? Would they know he had the plans – or would the Germans, once they knew what he had been after, have instructed her to deny this? Did London even know that he was still alive? Or might she have reported that he had been taken prisoner to account for the lack of definite news?

Forcing his way – still westwards, he hoped – through the interminable underbrush carpeting the forest floor, Blake realized that, basically, every response depended on the answer to Question Number Two. Had the German intelligence services kept her in place as a double agent, monitoring messages from the unsuspecting British and supplying false information in return? Or had they considered her usefulness, in this particular case, at an end once he had laid his hands on the Fokker drawings?

There was no way on earth that he could contact London himself, not without a cut-out, not at any rate until he reached the British side of the battlefield – and even then there would be enormous problems.

The answer to Question Two, he reasoned, would itself depend on Kristin's relation with the contact in Switzerland. If it was purely by Morse, there would be no obstacle to her continuing indefinitely. If on the other hand the liaison involved occasional telephone contact, the substitution would be revealed the moment a call was required. Or received. And whether or not the Germans knew, yes or no, if telephone communications came into it depended in its turn on how much information they had squeezed out of the original cut-out before he was executed.

It was at this point in his deliberations that Blake came across the woodcutters' glade in the forest.

Only after he had decided not to show himself – a

dog had begun barking in the yard beside the chalet – was he able to resume his analysis.

Skirting the property half a mile away in the woods, he had to admit to himself finally that, in reality, his three questions boiled down to one. Because both of the first two were intimately related to the enigma that was the third: Kristin.

It was possible, of course, that he was over-complicating things on account of his personal involvement, finding reasons to obscure his humiliation, masking the hurt stemming from his wounded pride. It was equally possible, probable even, that he was quite simply mistaken. Betrayal is a hard pill to swallow.

But the question had posed itself insistently a dozen times, a hundred times, since he had fled from the aerodrome at Paderborn. Was it a real option, or an attempt by his subconscious to rationalize an emotional defeat? He could hear the words now. She had reminded him, once the intelligence officer had made his entrance, that all was fair in love or war. Then she had added, with an ambiguity that was to torture him later: 'Sometimes both'.

The question was this. He *knew* the rear door of the prison van had been locked. He had *heard* it locked. Yet it had flown open at once when he lurched against it.

Kristin had been on the concrete apron outside the hangar when he was led out to the van. He had seen her finishing a conversation with a group of officers and start to walk his way when he was pushed inside by the MPs.

Was it possible, was it conceivable, that it was she, in some way, who had surreptitiously unlocked that door?

The most infuriating thing of all was that this was the one question to which he would never, ever know the answer.

25

The biggest, perhaps the most unwelcome, surprise Blake received throughout his German odyssey was delivered over a lunch table the following day, at a small restaurant in Malmédy.

He had passed the night uncomfortably in a barn on the westward fringe of the forest, walked out into a lush green pastureland beneath a cloudless sky the following morning and found a barber's shop in the first village he approached.

Ravenously hungry, he had then wolfed acorn coffee and an unappetizing sausage before he set out to walk south along the network of minor roads webbing the region.

Malmédy was eleven miles away. In normal times it would have been considered a pretty town – still on the wooded Ardennes plateau, a huddle of steep gabled roofs and tall houses with slatted shutters gashed by narrow, winding streets. Beneath the wrought-iron balconies overlooking a sloping central square, illuminated fountains played among the flower-beds on summer evenings, and there was a conical pavilion straight out of a Lehár operetta housing gold-braided uniforms and brass instruments. In the town hall visitors could be supplied with illustrated leaflets suggesting woodland rambles and explaining why it was forbidden to shoot deer.

None of these luxuries was available in time of war. There was a German garrison on the outskirts of town. German soldiers thronged the silent streets. The Belgian inhabitants were sullen and subdued. Most of the shops were shuttered, because there was nothing to sell and very little to eat. The brass instruments had been confiscated, along with metal parts stripped from every factory and workshop in the region, to be sent to the Fatherland to help satisfy the insatiable demands of an armaments industry invariably short of shell cases.

There were no flowers in Malmédy's square now: the only spot of colour flared from a single pot of geraniums, scarlet blooms on a fifth-floor balcony facing south near the town hall. But the woman who lived there, it was whispered, had been known to consort with German officers.

As a German officer himself, Blake felt reasonably free to wander. He was unlikely to attract attention; he had noticed men from half a dozen different formations already: infantrymen, sappers, ordnance officers, gunners, even an occasional aviator. Passing the town hall, he saw that the entrance doors were closed and locked, with a steel-helmeted sentry posted on either side. A side door was plastered with papers: casualty lists, orders from the local *Kommandant*, the official daily war communiqués – not only that of the German army, he discovered with surprise, but also copies of those issued by the French and English General Staffs. In a war that was largely static, he supposed, neither side was likely to publish exaggerated claims.

In a shallow glass case attached to the wall, a map of northern France displayed, with the use of a thin red ribbon and coloured pins, the current position of the front line. Oh, jolly good! Blake thought with a wry inward smile. From Malmédy to the nearest points on the front it was no more than a hundred miles, a hundred and twenty-five if you wanted the nearest British sector, in the region of Péronne.

That, of course, was as the crow flies. Most crows Blake had observed seemed to fly in circles, but never mind – for an enemy alien wanted for spying, a non-crow obliged to keep to the minor roads and show himself as little as possible, it was clear that those distances would be greatly increased.

The round hundred miles would take him to the French sector on the River Aisne, north of Reims. The hell with it: what was an extra twenty-five when distances of that order were involved and no aeroplane was at hand! Péronne was nearer home anyway. Apart from which it could prove deucedly hard to get his story believed by the French. Especially in a highly contested area morbidly alert for German spies and dangerously near Paris. There was an additional benefit to be gained from a route leading west-south-west from Malmédy, a plus that could well cancel out the extra mileage: apart from Dinant, there was not a single large town to be passed on the way.

It was just after midday. Suffused, illogically enough, with a sudden confidence, he walked into a small restaurant with a sign in the window stating that it was out of bounds to Other Ranks. He sat down at a table. One of the advantages of being an occupier – especially to one with no papers – was that officers were not required to produce ration tickets. He ordered beer with a dish of stewed pork.

Soon the restaurant began to fill up, mostly with Germans, some of them in civilian clothes but mainly junior officers. The food was terrible, but Blake was too hungry to care. He was scouring the plate with a crust of dry bread when he heard the voice behind him. '*Patsy!*

Good God, but it can't be. Yet it *is*: Patsy Blake by all that's holy! What in *hell* are you doing here?'

At the sound of that first explosive word, Blake had started like a man who has received an electric shock. One hundredth of a second later he registered the fact that the speaker had exclaimed *in English*. And with that came the horrific realization that whoever it was did actually know him, knew his real name . . .

He swivelled violently around in his chair – an instinctive, involuntary movement as rapidly executed as the abrupt halt when he was faced with danger. He hadn't even had time for the fleeting thought – brazen it out; say, 'Sir, you must be mistaken!' 'Who do you think you are?' – before he had recognized the speaker.

A young man of his own age, darkly handsome, with bright blue eyes. Hermann Gruener. They had been classmates at Heidelberg.

Gruener smiled. 'Forgive the language slip,' he said in a low voice. He was sitting alone at the next table. 'It was surprised out of me. You must admit, Patsy, that this *is* a surprise!'

Blake swallowed. He had been called Patsy at Heidelberg, not because of anything effeminate about him, but because of the American usage – a patsy was someone who always took the blame for everything. In Blake's case it might have been because he wished, as a foreigner, to ingratiate himself with his fellow students when he first arrived at the university: in all of their more exuberant rags and rebellions against authority, he was invariably the first to own up, and the name had stuck. Hermann Gruener had been his closest collaborator.

'Out with it, Patsy,' he was saying now. 'Own up again! What the devil *are* you doing here? In that uniform?'

Blake spoke for the first time. Gruener was wearing

225

the uniform of a *Hauptmann* in the Imperial Army Air Service. 'Hermann,' he said gruffly, 'I'm not . . . I don't know what to say to you.'

The German smiled again. 'You had better say something, old friend,' he advised. 'It is fairly obvious that you are not here selling tickets for a Salvation Army fête. Nor, I would imagine, have you adopted a German uniform as part of a satirical sketch designed to amuse the troops on the other side of the line.'

Blake shook his head wordlessly. He was totally at a loss.

'In which case,' Gruener pursued, 'friends that we are, this leaves me in a most awkward position. It is clear, you see, that you must be engaged on some mission which is, to say the least, hostile to my country. Perhaps you could – for old times' sake, shall we say? – tell me something about it?'

Blake shook his head again. 'There is nothing I can tell you, Hermann,' he said wretchedly.

He was aware, beneath the banter, how much his old friend's loyalties must be strained – between duty to an abstract and fellow-feeling for a human being, between simple affection and adherence to an ideal. He was himself agonizingly conscious of the wadded drawings burning below his shoulder-blades, plans which would allow young men he did not know more easily to shoot down and kill young men like Hermann, whom he did know.

He sighed. There was nothing either of them could do about the situation.

'In that case,' Gruener was saying, 'I have no alternative but to ask you to consider yourself under arrest.' He cleared his throat, producing a holstered revolver and laying it unobtrusively on the table in front of him. He looked around the crowded room. 'I could call on a dozen, two dozen men to help me if you were to resist. There isn't a hope in hell of your getting away, as you must know. But rather than have you hustled out publicly, I would prefer that we walk out of here quietly together, saving you the embarrassment – provided that I have your assurance that you accept formally that this arrest has in principle been made. And your word of honour that you will make no attempt to escape during the short walk we have to make to my divisional headquarters.'

'Very well,' Blake said. 'And thank you.'

Gruener inclined his head. He was looking distressed. 'First, however,' he said, 'I have to make a telephone call. May I have your parole that, to avoid any kind of disturbance, you will remain quietly here at this table, making no attempt to leave, during my absence?'

'You have it,' Blake said.

'Word of honour?'

'My word as an officer and English gentleman.'

'There is a suspicion,' Hermann Gruener said after his telephone call, 'that I may have as my prisoner a certain foreigner who flew an aeroplane an unbelievable distance so that he could rob a factory in Rhineland-Westphalia of plans that have a military significance. I don't suppose, Patsy, that you would care to comment on that?'

'I'm afraid not,' Blake said.

They were walking, in apparently nonchalant fashion, to Gruener's headquarters – it was in fact over a mile, on the outskirts of the town – two young German officers engaged in what seemed a friendly conversation. Blake had surrendered his pistol and had it returned to him minus the magazine.

'There is an additional complication,' the German

continued, 'which makes the matter a good deal more serious. It appears that two members of the factory personnel were killed. To say nothing of assaults on aviation staff and the theft of not one but *two* machines, the property of the Army Air Service. I need hardly tell you of the penalties this foreigner faces . . . should he be positively identified.'

Blake said nothing.

'Apart from this matter of espionage,' Gruener said, 'perhaps you could tell me what uniform you customarily wear – when you are not visiting countries abroad, that is. Or is a cloak and dagger your normal attire?'

Again, Blake remained silent.

Gruener shot him a sideways glance. 'Good God,' he said. 'That scar! You were never involved with duelling when we were together. Don't say you went back to Heidelberg for a second year?'

Blake shook his head, unable to resist a smile. 'Not a sabre,' he said. 'An FE-2b trainer. A circuit and too hard a bump.'

'Ah! So. Then we are in fact basically in the same . . . business . . . even if it is on opposite sides of the fence, no? Somehow that makes me feel better.'

Blake nodded but said nothing. They turned a corner of the road and he saw, as the land fell away to a shallow valley, a hutted camp with sentries posted by the wire gates and a number of motor transports ranged in a gravelled space outside a guardhouse. A small grass airfield was attached to the site.

'My orders,' Gruener said, 'are to fly you back to Paderborn, where those with detailed knowledge of the case can interrogate you.' He walked for some minutes in silence, then added inconsequentially, with a wave at the field: 'It was here that our first pilot to be killed on active service crashed to his death in August 1914, only a few days after war was declared. *Ober-Leutnant* Reinhold Jahnow. He was older than us. He had pilot's licence No. 80, a veteran of the Balkan campaign in 1912. He was a good instructor and a good man.'

The sentries swung wide the gates as they approached, then sprang to attention, clicked their heels and saluted. Blake remembered just in time to imitate Gruener's languid, typically Air Service, non-*junker* response.

Ten minutes later they were sitting facing one another across a wide table in one of the smaller huts on the fringe of the field. Outside the window the sun gleamed on the freshly painted lozenge camouflage adorning the top wings of two Fokker biplanes and a Halberstadt.

The room appeared at one time to have been used as a drawing office. Shallow drawers crammed an outsize filing cabinet, and two adjustable inclined boards stood on tall wooden stands against one wall. Apart from the fact that Gruener's living quarters were visible through a half-open door, Blake was irresistibly reminded both of the factory workshop and of the room in the Heston headquarters where he had received his first briefing. There was even an aero engine coughing to life somewhere outside.

The similarity was reinforced – acutely – by Gruener's first question.

'I accept that I cannot expect any kind of admission,' he said. 'Which would in any case leave me in a most invidious position. My position, as it is, I find most distressing. I am sorry I met you. But, having done so, I cannot un-meet you, any more than I can banish from my mind what I have been told. What I do not *know*, however, cannot oblige me to take any particular course of action. The question I am going to put to you is thus entirely hypothetical, academic even.' He undid the three top buttons of his uniform tunic and eased his collar from his neck.

'You have told me nothing. I therefore make no assumptions,' he said awkwardly. 'But *were* you to be someone in, shall we say, the shoes of the foreigner sought by the authorities, and *had* you in fact stolen some plans, what would you think such a person would have done with them?'

Before Blake could reply he added, 'I ask only for an opinion, not for facts. Look, Patsy, I do not wish to embarrass both of us by having you submit to a body search. Other people in other places can do that if they consider it necessary. Nor do I relish the thought of sending a friend to what would almost certainly turn out to be a firing squad. Anything, any hint therefore, which might influence my . . . thinking . . . and therefore any action I might take . . . Oh, shit, man: throw me a rope! What would this man do . . . have done?'

Blake repressed a grin. Gruener was certainly leaning over backwards! 'In such a case,' he said carefully, 'I would think your man – if he happened to be in the position I am in – I think he would already have got rid of the plans.'

'I see. How would he have done that?'

'I imagine he would have passed them on to an agent in Switzerland, via a contact unknown to his original cut-out. Rolled up in a cardboard tube he would doubtless have found in the office from which the plans were . . . removed.'

'A cardboard tube. I see,' Gruener said again. 'Would your hypothetical thief, do you suppose, swear if interrogated that this was what he had done?'

'He would.'

'On his honour?'

'On his honour,' Blake lied firmly, once more acutely conscious of the wad of paper clamped to his back. He was not prepared to break his word when it came to his own behaviour, but he was if it was a question of success or failure for the mission. He felt suddenly very small, nevertheless. Gruener was sticking out his neck, not having him handcuffed in a cell awaiting the arrival of the Feldgendarmerie. And here he was, betraying his confidence as surely as his had been betrayed by Kristin. On the other hand, Kristin had not been an old friend to start with. But it was she who said 'All's fair . . .'

'Very well!' Gruener slapped the desk with his open hand, his boyish features suddenly illuminated with the raffish, devil-may-care expression which had so characterized his behaviour when they were students together. 'Patsy, I'm going to give you a chance.'

'A chance?'

'Yes. Your theoretical man, if he had already delivered his booty, would presumably have only one more thing to do: get the hell over to the Allied side of the line as quickly as possible. Am I right?'

'I would think so.'

'Right. Now I'll tell you what: we never duelled during our university days; but, given our respective services, we could very well have been duelling today – in our respective machines, over the Western Front. You agree?'

'Yes, but . . . ?' Blake frowned. What was coming next?

'Circumstances have decreed otherwise, but I intend to offer you the chance of another kind of duel, one in which you have exactly the same hopes of success as myself.'

'Hermann, I'm afraid I don't understand.'

'We are going to have a game of Heidelberg chess,' Gruener said.

231

26

Heidelberg chess was a joke, an extravagance invented by the rowdier spirits of the university town in the early years of the century. It was a game in which physical – especially alimentary – stamina was of more value than the ability to see and plan ahead. In this respect it was perhaps an intellectual equivalent of the duelling for which the place was famous.

On an outsize board, conventional chessmen were replaced by drinking glasses of different shapes and sizes – a tall-stemmed hock glass for the king, a champagne flute for the queen, Madeira, schnapps and whisky glasses for bishops, knights and rooks. The pawns were represented by normal wineglasses.

Each glass was then filled to the brim with the wine or spirit for which it was designed. Pawns, of course, were tanked up with ordinary table wine, white or red. Behind them, different chasing on the glasses distinguished one side from the other.

The point of the game, other than the banal one of winning or losing, was the rule that every time a piece was taken, the player who lost it was obliged to drink the contents in a single draught.

Gruener tore a sheet of paper from a huge drawing pad and hurriedly divided it into sixty-four squares with a charcoal stick. He summoned an orderly from the officers' mess and demanded two different sets of sixteen glasses, with the seven different liquor bottles required to complete the pieces. When everything was in place, the two adversaries faced one another across the wide table. Blake chose white – largely because he thought the white wine would meld better with the other drinks each time he lost a pawn – and the German red.

A further rule of this chess variant was the necessity to call out each move aloud in a special jargon tailored for the game: *Seven – red: hock to flute two . . . Nine – white: schnapps to Madeira three . . . Thirteen: red whiskies . . .*

Frequently, after a dozen or so moves, players became so helpless with drunken giggles that the contest had to be abandoned.

'The difference about this match,' Gruener said, 'is that I have, regretfully, to limit the time in which each move is made to four minutes.' He produced an alarm clock surmounted by a bell, wound it up and set the hands. 'My instructions are to be in Paderborn before dark. Clearly, therefore, I cannot delay the take-off indefinitely.'

Blake wound and started the alarm clock and moved a pawn. 'You said something about "a chance",' he observed, intrigued but still puzzled by his captor's train of thought. 'Now you are talking about a match. Are you offering some kind of prize for the victor?'

'Certainly.'

'Namely?'

Gruener advanced one of his own pawns. He gestured towards the sector of airfield visible through the window. An Albatros reconnaissance two-seater, with a polished aluminium nose and a bolster tank attached to the top wing centre section, was being wheeled out by a group of mechanics. 'That is the machine allocated to me,' he said. 'The match is to decide who pilots it.'

Swift as a released bird, a sudden ray of hope transfixed Blake. 'Hermann,' he said, 'are you telling me . . . ?'

'In a two-seater, naturally it is the pilot who determines the flight plan, the route to be followed,' Gruener said. 'Your move, Patsy.'

27

The Albatros was not equipped with guns. It would have been impossible anyway to mount one firing through the propeller, for the front of the slender fuselage, with its triangular rudder and completely flat top, was obscured by the engine. This upright, four-cylinder in-line unit stood, from the crankshaft upwards, totally exposed above the aluminium nose and propeller boss. An overhead exhaust belched out hot fumes dangerously near the centre section fuel tank.

The pilot's view was further impeded by the head and shoulders of his observer, who sat in the forward cockpit.

Lowering himself into the rear seat, Blake felt as disoriented as he ever had in an unfamiliar machine. The cockpit layout seemed to him aberrant. The control column had two cylindrical, polished wood grips, one outrigged on either side of the shaft. There was no instrument panel: five of the six instruments were placed haphazardly, most of them low down below the wooden frames which held the separately formed plywood fuselage sides together. The sixth, a large, white-faced revolution counter, was attached to a tubular steel former just below the padded leather cockpit rim and a plaque bearing the legend 'ALBATROS N-986 RS/C'.

The sense of unreality was emphasized by the fact that

he was convinced that he should by rights be seating himself in the forward cockpit. He did not believe Gruener had deliberately lost the chess match: the young German was too ethical a man, too firmly attached to his own moral certainties for that. Nevertheless – even if he had been playing to win – it had to be admitted that Blake's own priorities were more urgent than his.

The reasons for suggesting the game in the first place, Blake thought, were less difficult to establish. It seemed to him that, as an honourable man, Gruener's loyalties were equally divided: between the person and the state, the theory and the practice. He couldn't, as he said, un-know that he had encountered an enemy alien, masquerading in a uniform he was not entitled to wear; he couldn't just pat him on the back and wish him luck. It would be very much against the grain, on the other hand, to deliver a friend into the care of an executioner.

Torn between such conflicting imperatives, Gruener had in fact funked the positive action. He would let fate make the decision.

As in so many affairs of honour, the matter would be decided by a duel.

'The silver cylinder just below the bulkhead,' Gruener was calling from the forward cockpit, 'the one with the push-pull plunger and the word "prime" above it.'

'What? ... Oh. Yes, right-ho.' Startled out of his reverie, Blake saw that there was a mechanic at each of the Albatros's wingtips. A third stood ready to swing the propeller. There was a red label with white lettering gummed to the iron former. He read: 'Start: full rich mixture – pump throttle three times'.

He checked switches and dials that he recognized, and obeyed the instruction.

The engine wheezed as the propeller was turned four

times. Blake wondered if the power unit was a Mercedes or an Argus. The propeller was expertly, briskly swung. He saw a puff of blue smoke. The blades revolved. The engine chattered to life with a satisfying roar. Gingerly, he manipulated the throttle.

The chocks were whisked away. Guided by the wingtip men, the Albatros trundled out towards the wind-sock at the far end of the field, rudder wagging and ailerons dipping as Blake experimented with the controls. When they were level with the perimeter fence, he turned the machine into the wind.

Gruener looked over his shoulder and nodded. The mechanics stood aside. Blake took off.

It wasn't as difficult as he expected. The engine was powerful and the aeroplane extremely light. The breeze had freshened since the morning, blowing quite hard from the west – and that was the direction he wanted to go.

Hopping at first like a magpie traversing the rough ground, the machine settled into a blustering run as Blake urged the throttle open. He felt the first hint of lift when they were less than halfway across the field, easing the stick gently back into his stomach as the speed increased.

At a little over fifty miles per hour the Albatros left the ground, soaring over the hutted camp and the grey roofs on the outskirts of town. Woods streamed past below the wings, then fields, a farm with browsing cattle, the slow loops of a river. Blake continued steeply climbing, no banks, no turns, the compass setting due west, until the altimeter registered five thousand feet.

The controls were heavy, but the machine responded quickly once they were actuated. What really got on his nerves was the noise. Apart from the racket of the naked engine, the entire framework of the machine vibrated and clattered and shook with a force that seemed to him quite deafening. Plywood panelling attached to the longerons and formers was acoustically a great deal less satisfactory than the doped fabric to which he was accustomed!

Yet again, Blake's mind was buzzing with unanswered questions. How much fuel did the Albatros carry? How many miles to the gallon did she fly? What was going to happen when the tank ran dry? Would the plane be reported missing if it failed to follow the original flight plan? Above all, what was he going to do with Gruener if he managed a safe landing?

The first question almost answered itself. Unless a refuelling stop had been planned, there must be enough fuel to take them from Malmédy to Paderborn, presumably with a little in reserve. That was a distance of approximately 135 miles. And this coincidentally – he had looked at a map – was precisely the distance to the nearest part of the front line, the British sector somewhere between Lens and Arras. Was there enough nevertheless to get them safely across the whole battlefield and avoid the possibility of being shot down – either by Allied scouts or the overzealous gunners?

One thing had been made very clear to him. Gruener himself would answer none of those questions. There had been no problems leaving the aerodrome: the *Herr Hauptmann* had been expected to take off with another officer. But when Blake had stammered, as they were about to climb into the Albatros: 'Look, Hermann, are you absolutely *sure* . . . ?' the German had at once held up a restraining hand.

'I offered you a chance,' he said. 'You won the match fair and square. So now you are the pilot. And as I said, the pilot decides everything. Everything.' And he had turned his back and clambered up into the forward cockpit.

Message received and understood. Fate had swung the pendulum Blake's way. It was up to him to take that chance. Gruener would do nothing to hinder him . . . but then again he certainly wasn't going to help.

Blake shook his head, thinking back over the game. He had played very carefully, trying as much as anything to protect the pieces filled with spirits rather than wine, so that he would not have to mix his drinks too much. Gruener had been more reckless, sacrificing two bishops (schnapps) and a knight (whisky) rather quickly. Perhaps it was the effect of these that had allowed Blake, after a Dragon Variation, to check in nine moves and mate in thirteen?

He smiled – they were flying over a lake – as another thought crossed his mind. If they had to force-land and found themselves still on the German side of the line . . . what then? Wouldn't that place the ball very neatly back into Gruener's court?

Whatever the problems, whatever the risks, Blake felt, a ride in an aeroplane was a thousand times better than the idea of walking that 135-mile route, relying on lifts or hoping to steal a car or bicycle. A passenger train behind the lines in subjugated Belgium – even 135 miles behind – was a miracle too far-fetched even to be considered.

The sky was swept clear of clouds in the west. The earth below was partly obscured now by an overall haze. Immediately in front of them, only half a dozen diameters above the horizon, the sinking sun blazed an angry red.

Shaking in every joint, the noisy biplane forged ahead. Blake wondered, staring past Gruener's hunched shoulders and leather-helmeted head, what the man was thinking. Much the same things, shot through with additional information, as he was himself probably.

What was he planning to do when they came down? It would, of course, depend on which side of the line it was ... but had he any specific action in mind, or was he going to play it by ear?

Most importantly, now that he had sobered up, did he regret his quixotic move?

It was some time since they had left the wooded plateaux of the Ardennes. A large town, spined with the bright streaks of railway lines, sprawled across the flat landscape stretching away beneath them. That would be Dinant, Blake assumed. Some way off to the north-west, smokeless factory chimneys, conical slag heaps and colliery wheels marked the shattered outskirts of Charleroi. Flying over the pale ribbon of the Meuse a few minutes earlier, he had thought they must be almost halfway there – wherever 'there' was. The needle of the fuel gauge, which was not calibrated in precise quantities, certainly trembled midway between 'full' and 'empty'.

Gruener, as a good observer should, was the first to see the single-seaters. He stabbed out an arm and pointed. Perhaps three miles ahead: four dark specks in formation, silhouetted against the glare.

Blake at once suffered the familiar chill, looked for the toggles actuating the synchronized guns ... and remembered, first, that he was in the rear cockpit with no clear view, secondly that the Albatros was in any case unarmed. An instant afterwards he remembered that he was piloting a German aeroplane. And the scouts, this far away from the battlefield, would surely be German too.

The quartet, a Pfalz leading three Fokker biplanes in V formation, approached rapidly, several hundred yards to the starboard of their course. The bulbous nose of the leading machine was painted red; the fuselage of each

Fokker sported a zigzag of black stripes and a polished engine cowling.

When they were almost abreast, the Pfalz peeled away from the other three, dived in the direction of the Albatros, then executed a neat loop with the reconnaissance two-seater as the central point of the circle. The Fokkers broke formation, soared away right and left, and banked steeply to pass above, beneath and alongside the Albatros, carefree as lambs gambolling in an upland pasture. Each goggled pilot waved as his machine shot past. Gruener waved back. And finally Blake, feeling curiously shabby, almost ashamed, raised an arm in salute.

When the bellow of unsilenced engines had at last faded and the flight, re-formed, had flown away towards the east, Blake relaxed with a sigh of relief. Stupid and unnecessary, that sudden shaft of fear, he told himself. He had drink taken, as the Irish say. Perhaps he was still a little bit under the influence. Better in any case to save the chill for what must certainly come later.

It was dusk when the engine of the Albatros spluttered and choked. The needle of the fuel gauge was jammed firmly against the end-stop. Blake swore, banking the plane to look below. A land of woods and fields, of green hills and hollows and farms and streams, could be seen to be desecrated by war, smeared with a foulness as evident as the marks from a bloodied body dragged across the floor. He shook his head. Pinpoints of light from an artillery barrage flickered through the gloom below. He leaned forward to thump Gruener on the shoulder. 'I'm going to have to put her down,' he shouted above the racket of the dying engine.

The German turned around. He was smiling. Quite

clearly he was enjoying the situation. 'You're the pilot,' he replied. 'The decisions are up to you.'

With a last explosive backfire and a diminishing rumble, the engine relapsed into silence. The bright disc of the propeller thickened, became opaque, separated into distinct blades and spun to a halt.

They started to lose height at once, wind singing through the crosswires and stays with an alto wail.

Blake bit his lip. Gruener was right. With no tractive power to modify his speed or allow him to climb, his skill as a pilot was indeed at a premium.

The German, true to his character, would be eager to see just how Blake proposed to meet the challenge. His own safety, the life-or-death options the situation offered, would remain subservient to the fascination of discovering what his one-time English friend would do with the 'chance' he had been given.

Blake himself was too busy to examine those options. With the risk of a stall always present, and no engine to pull him out of it, his choice of manoeuvres was limited. Everything depended on the normal gliding angle of the Albatros.

A large wing surface and a slender fuselage, coupled with a centre of gravity that was well forward, ensured – Blake soon found out – that this was fairly shallow.

So much the better. The furthest distance they could travel would be that at the far end of a continuous straight line: keep her dead ahead – and hope there would be a space that was not too dangerous at the end of the line. First, though, it was vital that he had some idea of what lay below. Otherwise they could be dead . . . with no ahead.

He would risk one wide circle of the immediate terrain before he settled the machine into its final glide.

He dropped the nose marginally, banking just enough to minimize the risk of a spin.

From four thousand feet, the terrain was rapidly becoming obscure.

Buildings, whole or ruined it was impossible to say, loomed here and there out of the dusk. Southwards there was woodland, almost a forest. And there were, or had been, trenches: the land was scarred with haphazard, darker streaks as far as he could see in every direction. But any action there was seemed, perhaps unfortunately, some way ahead. Flashes of artillery fire pierced the gloom and the red flowers of shell bursts bloomed miles to the west.

It was clear that he would have to lose at least another thousand feet, perhaps two, before he had any definite idea of the situation he was dropping them into.

He straightened out when the altimeter registered three thousand five hundred feet, heading a few points south of the concentration of gunfire. The Albatros, which gave the impression from time to time almost of limping in its descent, shuddered as the shadowy surface of the earth swam nearer.

It was ten minutes later that the desolation slid into view beneath the biplane's lower wing. This was land, it was clear, that had been fought over – country devastated by the German advance, far behind the lines now but still webbed with the geometric complex of communication trenches, pulverized by the duels of artillery which consumed shells more rapidly than the war factories could produce them. Roads, villages, railway lines and army camps had been obliterated by the fury of battle.

Over the wind's whine through struts and stays, some changed condition – a thermal upthrust, turbulence reflected from the combat below – was now creating a shrill descant stemming from the aerofoil sections of wings and tail. Sensing an increase in the vibration shuddering the two-seater's frame, Blake again lowered the nose fractionally. The airspeed indicator had already sunk its needle below the seventy miles per hour mark.

The darkened battlefield below rushed towards them with what appeared to be increasing speed, though the tell-tale needle continued to drop back.

Blake was now worried. Not the nail-biting anxiety of the man who is afraid but the professional concern of the expert unsure if the tools are equal to the job. In the same way that the engines used by Fokker accepted very little between the idle and full throttle, so some aeroplanes allowed a minimum of flexibility between full speed and the stall. The Albatros two-seater seemed to be one of them.

He lowered the nose further still. If they were not going to fall out of the sky, a deliberate dive – with the attendant danger brought by a high landing speed – was the only option.

The wind screamed between the wires. The wings began to shake.

Elements of the devastated landscape now began to manifest themselves, assembling a village street bordered by rubble, a smashed bridge, a lopped-off factory chimney from the murk. At a thousand feet, it was clear that the battlefield itself had moved on. Looking down over the quivering cockpit rim, Blake saw a long line of lorries and horse-drawn artillery winding through a shallow valley. Rows of tents peaked along the edge of a blasted wood. The muttering rumble of gunfire was audible, but the twinkling flashes and the blossoming shell bursts were still some miles to the west.

He changed direction slightly. There was a long slant

of open ground where the barrage was less intense ten degrees southwards. The Albatros side-slipped, dropping a hundred feet sickeningly in an air pocket. He sawed the control column, treading the rudder bar in an attempt to jockey the machine back on an even keel with elevators and ailerons. Sluggishly, they rolled back into level flight.

The earth's dark surface hurtled towards them.

Abruptly, life speeded up as dramatically as a film. Flattened hedges, craters, the pulverized remains of a farm streaked past below the wings. There were trenches down there now. A myriad points of light stitched together the almost-dark. Tracer arced up towards them, rising lazily to race past. A cracking detonation, followed by three more, rocked the plane as a group of anti-aircraft shells burst into orange flame fifty yards to the left.

Blake fought the controls once more. A high-pitched whistling shrilled from a group of holes ripped by shrapnel from the upper port wing. He freed a hand to thump Gruener on the shoulder.

'Hold on!' he yelled. 'This is it . . .'

Gruener was already holding on. His gloved hands clenched the padded cockpit rim. He ducked his head as the Albatros dropped.

At the last moment Blake yanked the stick slightly back to raise the nose, allowing the machine to plummet to the invisible ground.

For a heartstopping instant life – and the Albatros – stood still. Then there was a rending crash as they hit . . . bounced . . . grounded again to slew violently sideways . . . and started to race downhill.

Seconds later Blake and Gruener were thrown heavily forward. Trapped in a huge tangle of barbed wire, the plane groaned to a halt as the smashed undercarriage collapsed, the nose ploughed into the earth and the tail rose into the air.

The two men extricated themselves from the wreck and dropped to the ground.

'Bravo, Patsy!' Gruener said. 'I couldn't have done better myself.'

It seemed like a long time later but was probably no more than ten minutes. Blake and Gruener lay on the slope of a shell hole half filled with water. A three-quarter moon, rising into the night sky, gilded the surface and cast a wan light over the plundered land.

They had taken refuge there for two reasons. First, it was necessary to find out as far as possible where they were. Not geographically, but in relation to the ebb and flow of battle, the front line, no man's land, the artillery. Secondly, because, wherever this was, the crashed Albatros and they themselves were already targets.

They had been attacked by tracer and anti-aircraft shells as they came down. Seconds after they dropped from their cockpits there had been a blaze of machine-gun fire from further up the hill and a stream of bullets thunked into the carcass of the aeroplane. Then, hearing the once-familiar whine, Blake had hurled Gruener into the crater a heartbeat before the first mortar shell burst among the nests of barbed wire. Three more followed, shaking the ground. A trickle of earth and small pebbles broke away from the edge of the hole and cascaded into the water, fragmenting the reflection of the moon.

The fifth shattering explosion was nearer the Albatros and the sixth was a direct hit. There was a high enough concentration of fumes left in the empty fuel tank to transform the wreck into a blazing fireball.

When the hot fragments of wood and metal had stopped

pelting their backs and the flames had guttered to a fiery travesty of an aircraft outline, Blake raised his head and shoulders and looked up the hillside.

In a landscape where a forty-foot rise was an impregnable position, this miniature ridge must be something like a fortress. But where was the opposing line? And which of the combatants held the sector he could see?

He looked down the slope. A little way off to one side, perhaps eighty or a hundred yards away, the gutted remnants of a tall building raised jagged walls against the sky. It looked as if it could once have been a warehouse. Behind it was something higher still – a mill? an office block? – and here there was a suggestion of a balustraded parapet balanced above a shattered façade. At the far end, above empty windows that held no reflections, a turret and dome still stood.

Further down, the moonlight revealed the splintered stumps of trees, some kind of earthworks, an unrecognizable tangle of steel that might once have been a scout car. Blake could also make out what looked suspiciously like the bodies of several horses.

'What was that noise?' Gruener asked suddenly.

'What noise?'

The German's reply was lost in a hellish thunder of explosions. All along the ridge behind them, and out of sight beyond it, dozens, hundreds, thousands of high-explosive shells erupted in an ear-shattering cacophony. The flickering flame outlining the crest blazed into the night with redoubled fury at each successive wave of detonations.

And then, as unexpectedly as it started, the artillery barrage ceased. The scream of shells was stilled.

A star shell burst in the sky, flooding the land with livid

brilliance. That was when the chatter of machine-guns started.

'There's that noise again,' Gruener mouthed in Blake's ear. 'It sounds like singing to me.'

It did sound like singing – or at least shouting of some kind. In the distance, further down the hill. It swelled to some kind of climax. Innumerable voices. And then, 'Look!' Gruener cried. 'There!'

Blake looked, straining his eyes. He caught his breath.

In the harsh, pitiless light, the splintered trees seemed to move.

The movement coalesced, resolved itself into a long, wavering line extending far beyond the desecrated wood, separating itself from the trees.

The line was advancing. The sound of voices increased to a roar . . . and all at once that line was a flood of men, hundreds and hundreds of them, shoulder to shoulder, pounding up the slope towards the ridge with bayonets at the ready.

Machine-gun fire, punctuated now by the crackle of small arms, increased in volume. Some of the men fell.

'Christ!' Blake yelled. 'We're in the middle of bloody no man's land!'

28

The big guns started to fire again at dawn – only this time it was not a single destructive barrage but an artillery duel. Eighteen-pounders and *Feldkanone*, howitzers and trench mortars made the brightening day hideous with the reverberating fury of their cannonades.

From the top floor of the gutted warehouse, Blake looked out over the hillside where he had crash-landed the Albatros. He could see neither the field guns, the mortars, nor the heavier-calibre pieces – only the thundering hell of the shell bursts along the ridge and among the splintered remnants of the wood below. Between those two lines, around the blackened spars of the aeroplane, skewered on the barbed wire, the dead lay singly or in untidy heaps. Whoever had made the attack – and, from what he could see of the uniforms and the tin hats, it had been the British – had failed to take the ridge.

He and Gruener had simply stayed face down in the shell crater and prayed, quaking with fear as the barrage crept nearer and the advancing soldiers, scythed down by machine-guns, fell all around them.

During a temporary lull they had raced, bent double, across the battlefield towards the ruined buildings. Half-way there they had stumbled into an old second-line trench leading to what must have been a command post, destroyed in a previous bombardment. Burst sandbags here, and a savaged corrugated-iron roof, surrounded the silent witnesses to death and a hasty retreat – a smashed field telephone, mud-caked boots, the remains of a machine-gun tripod, and parts of a radio transmitter. There was an overpowering stench of putrefied flesh.

Beyond the dugout the trench had been obliterated by shell fire, but they saw in the light of another star shell, half buried by the fallen earth, several tins of condensed milk and a flat metal box packed with chocolates and cigarettes, a Christmas gift to every soldier from the Princess Royal.

By the time they had crawled the rest of the way to the warehouse, the attack behind them had been beaten off and only the groans of the wounded, punctuated by an occasional sniper's shot at the stretcher parties, broke the silence of the night.

Not daring to speak aloud, they had slept uneasily, propped up against baulks of timber on the ground floor. Far above them, stars shone between rafters where the roof had gone. The smell this time was of brick dust and charred wood.

When the dawn bombardment began they had separated – partly to see if they could spy out some relatively safe route out of the battle zone, partly to investigate the possibility of holing up in the hope that the zone itself would move.

Blake had climbed a rusted zigzag fire escape to the warehouse's top-floor gallery; Gruener was looking in the other direction. He had wormed his way across to the other building and used the domed turret at the far end of the soot-grimed, red-brick façade as a lookout post. He was kneeling behind a balustrade at the edge of a balcony circling the dome when one of the artillery batteries received orders to forget the ridge and start shelling the two ruins.

The first salvo burst against the block's ground-floor entrance, below the turret, a maelstrom of flame, brown smoke and choking plaster dust. When the air had cleared, Blake saw that half the lower part of the façade had been smashed away. Through the pall of dust hazing the narrow gap between the two buildings, the wrecked interior of the block was visible: blackened joists below a vanished floor, collapsed partition walls, a sagging stairway.

Gruener was signalling him from the balcony around the dome. Before Blake could semaphore a reply from the glassless window at the top of the fire escape, a second salvo erupted below.

One, two, three, and a thunderous reverberation as a fourth shell exploded high up against the red-brick wall. British artillery, he thought: the General Staff had recently reduced the number of guns in a battery from six to four in order to increase the number of batteries by fifty per cent and – hopefully – reduce the appalling wastage of ammunition.

There was now a huge archway blasted out of the face of the building. Bricks showered from the ragged edge at the top of the arch. Blocks of masonry fell to the growing chaos of rubble below.

The third salvo fell short, three shells only among the craters on the hillside. Even so, it was near enough to shake the foundations of the warehouse. The effect of the vibrations on the block behind was more dramatic.

The entire length of the remaining façade separated itself from the steeply pitched roof, hung for an instant in mid-air, and then slid to the ground as a single unit, to collapse on the rubble with a roar three times as loud as the detonations provoking the chute. This time the tower of yellow dust took five minutes to subside.

Coughing violently, spitting dust from his dry mouth, Blake peered through the murk. Sulphurous smoke still boiled around the base of the block. As he watched, the wall on the far side leaned outwards and fell. The dust rolled upwards again, acrid and suffocating. When the rising sun began to penetrate, he saw that the roof too had gone. Only the two end walls remained. Among the twisted pipes and charred beams projecting from the inner face of these, like the casts of fossils in a prehistoric cliff, the pale traces of cupboards, stairways and fireplaces that had been torn away bore witness to the life that had once been lived there.

Astoundingly, although the dome had gone, a sector of the terrace and balustrade, perhaps a third of the whole circumference, was still perched on a brick pinnacle above the junction of two walls.

Gruener was lying on the portion that remained.

He was alive. His back was to the warehouse, but through the balusters Blake could see him stirring, trying to sit up. There was blood on the balcony tiles beneath him.

Blake stared, aghast. No more shells had fallen. Whoever was inspecting the site through invisible field-glasses must have decided that it was no longer a danger as a possible sniper's refuge or machine-gun nest. But the artillery duel continued between the wood and the ridge. At each crescendo of the opposing barrages the column of brickwork was visibly shaking. The blast-damaged end wall was liable to disintegrate and send the wounded German five floors to his death at any moment.

Craning forward through the window embrasure, Blake saw the worst thing of all.

From among the fractured pipes and twisted conduits spining the ruin, a thick electric cable still spanned the gap to link the remains of the dome with the roof of his own building.

In other words there was a chance – at odds of a hundred to one perhaps, but still a chance – that Gruener could be rescued. And he was the only person in the world who might be able to do it.

Who *might* be able to. The electric cable was heavily insulated, undamaged, stapled to the cornice of the warehouse and the brickwork below the shattered balcony. It was just conceivable that a man in good training could reach that cable, make his way hand over hand to the parapet and return with a wounded companion over his shoulder. But it would be horribly dangerous . . . even for someone who didn't suffer from vertigo, lack of moral fibre and sheer funk. For someone, in fact, like Blake himself.

The drop must be sixty or seventy feet. The weight of even one man dragging on the wire could disturb the balance of the tottering wall, pull it out of the perpendicular and send it plummeting to the rubble below.

Gruener wouldn't know about the cable. He could turn his back, let the German take his chance, and nobody would be the wiser. Or he could take this insane, suicidal gamble: he could attempt to retain Gruener's respect – and, perhaps more importantly, his own – by balancing a rescue attempt against the probable loss of his life. The choice was his. There were no outside factors to complicate it. But the quaking wall could collapse at any moment: the decision must be made *now*.

He was on Salisbury Plain again, faced with the blazing scout car and the man trapped inside it.

In a sense, he was in a position of power. Although

Gruener didn't know it yet, his life – or death – was in Blake's hands. Perhaps it was because of the obscure feeling of superiority this gave him that he decided to take the gamble, to make an attempt to get the German off his crumbling perch. In one way he had been dealt a winning hand. But did he have the guts to play it?

The cable looked sound enough. But it was halfway between his window and the end of the building. The only way of reaching it was along a six-inch-wide decorative ledge passing above the window.

Blake swallowed. He leaned out and looked down. At once the dread signs of vertigo clawed at his diaphragm and the nape of his neck. The sheer face of the warehouse plunged dizzily into the rubble. Iron pipes and strips of planking projected from the dust cloud hanging over the jumble of masonry. He was alone with his fear and his determination. He pulled himself up into a crouching position on the window-sill. If he didn't do it now, he would never do it . . .

The window glass was long gone, but the horizontal frame of the sash was still jammed across the centre. Holding on to this, he stood warily upright on the outside of the ledge with his back to the drop. He was breathing shallowly and his forehead was cold. Now he must lean against the side of the frame, climb up until his feet rested on the sash, hold the top of the frame with one hand and reach for the ledge with the other.

For a man in good physical condition, pulling himself up on to a six-inch ledge, flexing his arms until he was high enough to cock up a leg and find a purchase with his foot, was simple enough. The difficulty was to do it without seeing what lay below. Don't look down. Never look down. Don't even *think* of what lies below. How many times had his Scottish break-and-enter tutor said that? The trick was to imagine you were doing it at ground-floor level, only a few feet from mother earth.

Like most tricks it was not as easy as it looked. Blake felt a surge of anger. It wasn't fair: he had already done this; it was the escape from the hotel in Paderborn all over again!

Getting the second leg up was the nightmare. He stretched, straightening the first, spreading his arms, forcing chest, belly and cheek against the brick . . . slowly, slowly drawing up that second knee. But there was bound to be a moment, jerking the toe of his boot over the projection, when his haunches, his backside stuck dangerously far out over the abyss. He drew a quavering breath, blanked out his mind, moved smoothly, swiftly . . . and did it.

He was balanced on the balls of his feet, legs spread, knees slightly bent, his arms outstretched and his two heels projecting over the void. Above him, just within reach, was a low stone coping at the lower limit of the roof. Very carefully he reached up one hand and then the other to grasp it. It was then that he realized there was no going back: the ledge was too narrow; there was no way he could scramble back to the window without overbalancing and toppling into eternity. A small sound escaped his dry lips. It was not just because of the effort pushing himself against the wall that his calf muscles were trembling uncontrollably.

He began to move. The world had removed itself, become immeasurably distant. The thunder of the artillery, the shallow whistle of his own breath, the hoarse scrape of his uniform against the brickwork and the drone of an aeroplane on the dawn patrol remained at the outermost fringe of his consciousness. He was below the dormers in Paderborn, escaping from the policeman in the loden coat, upside down in the cockpit of the crashed Pup, facing the inferno of the scout car.

He advanced his left foot, his left hand. He slid up his right. Perhaps too quickly: in his haste he snatched. The fingers of the left hand had closed over the stone right angle and held. But somehow the right slipped, and the brusqueness of the movement cast it – and with it the right leg – away from the wall and the ledge. Like an opening gate, pivoting on fingers and toes, Blake's body swung out over the gap.

Then he was desperately swivelling his left foot, exerting pressure with the scarred fingers of the left hand, to swing himself back facing the wall again.

The stone fringe of the ledge crumbled. His left foot slipped into space.

Blake uttered a despairing cry. The entire weight of his body dropped, wrenching intolerably at his left shoulder, wrist and fingers. For a timeless moment he was prevented from falling only by the frenzied clutching of those fingers over the coping.

Then, agonizingly, he scrabbled for a foothold, found it, straightened the leg, brought up the other one to relieve the load on his screaming muscles, and at last reached up to lock his right hand once more on the coping. He was gasping for breath and his eyes were streaming. Inch by inch he started to edge in the direction of the electric cable.

But his cry of anguish had alerted Gruener. The German rolled over on his tottering perch, his features caked with blood and dust. Clearly some fragment explosively displaced in one of the salvoes must have wounded him badly. He saw Blake spread-eagled against the wall at the top of the opposite façade. 'No!' he cried hoarsely during a temporary lull in the bombardment. 'Patsy, don't be a fool. You'll never make it. There's nothing you can do, man . . . leave me and get the hell out, for God's sake!'

Blake heard him but paid no attention. He had no breath to spare for a reply. In any case he couldn't go back. And having surprised himself with a positive decision in the face of danger, he was damned if he was going to be cheated out of the sense of superiority this was giving him.

The distance from the fire escape window to the staples holding the electric cable was fourteen feet. It was the longest journey of Blake's life.

The cable stretched out into space halfway between the coping and the ledge, a little below his waist. There would be no problem grasping it, but he would have to stoop a little . . . let go of the coping to transfer his other hand . . . and then push away from the ledge with his feet to allow his body to swing free below the insulated wire.

And during each of these manoeuvres it would be impossible not to look down.

He had lost all sense of time. It seemed dreadfully cold where he was, high up on the shadowed side of the warehouse. The cable brushed against his thigh. He lowered his left hand and felt it. The insulation seemed not to be perished: a black composition, not too smooth, not shiny, about half as thick as his wrist.

He gripped it hard, transferred his other hand, tested the wire to make sure it would bear his weight. He closed his eyes and began leaning outward on the swaying cable.

He couldn't do it with his eyes shut.

He opened them. Space. The dizzy void. Abyss. At the foot of the chasm, smoke still curling from the jagged interstices, the wicked mound of masonry and metal.

He saw his own body, impossibly far above this, slanting from the wire to the ledge. And suddenly the vertigo swamped him. Nausea attacked, the way an extra-large wave bowls over a bather wading in the sea. He clung there, paralysed, unable to move in any direction.

Gruener was shouting weakly. 'Go back, Patsy! There's no way you can do it. Save yourself, for God's sake.'

Blake was breathing in spasmodic gulps. An icy sweat rolled off his whole body and his teeth were chattering. He groaned aloud. If he kicked off from the ledge and hung down at the full stretch of his arms, he would be able to look up at the sky.

The wrench on his arms this time was not so severe because he was prepared for it. To a man who is young and healthy, a hand-over-hand traverse of fifteen to twenty feet of thick cable is no insuperable problem – unless he is seventy feet up in the air, suffering from vertigo and looks down. Blake looked up. His throat was tight and dry. The sky, which had darkened to an aching blue, was streaked with altocumulus in the west. Further south, a flight of three Nieuport scouts escorted an ancient BE-2c observation plane.

Halfway along the cable, Blake swung out of the shadow and into the sunlight, and the warmth washed over him like a blessing. He reached the wall below Gruener's eyrie, grasped the crumbling edge of the parapet and dragged himself up on to the tiles. It was then, gasping with relief, that he realized the artillery duel had ceased some minutes ago.

Gruener had lost consciousness. Fragments of shrapnel, one of them bloodied, lay around him. So far as Blake could see, he had been hit on the side of the head and again across the upper part of his left arm. He was still bleeding.

Time then to plan the return journey . . . and Blake

saw that this was the worst place of all. Clamped fly-like against the warehouse wall, at least he was in contact with something solid: if he fell it was from something with visible mass. Hanging from the cable, he had some control over his position in space so long as his hands could lock over the wire. But here, on these square feet of bloodstained stone, fringed by a few degrees of curved balustrade, he was totally in the void. There was nowhere to look but down. If he stared up or out, even the shaking floor supporting him disappeared; if he permitted himself to glance below, oblivion yawned on every side. And the balcony on which he was crouched, what was left of it, was too small to contain his vision: it was impossible not to look beyond it. His guts turned over and the knot behind his solar plexus tightened.

It was as well that there was Gruener to consider. The slender column of brickwork swayed with Blake's every movement; he was no longer sure if the faint shuddering transmitted to his legs came from his own muscles or the pinnacle of fissured stone; small trickles of plaster cascaded away from the broken lip and occasional fragments separated to fall – he dare not think where.

He began unbuckling the three-piece German cross-over belt that he wore. Amending the straps and fasteners to secure a casualty over the shoulder was a routine problem only: he had done it often enough in infantry training.

The transfer from the remains of the parapet to the cable was almost a relief. Somehow the fragile brick tower looked more solid as an anchor for the wire than it had felt as a platform to support them. But for one horrendous instant as he leaned out to transfer their combined weight to the cable, Blake inadvertently did look down.

He stared into the jaws of hell. For a second he thought his heart really had stopped: there was nothing left for it to pump; it felt as if all the blood in his body had drained to the soles of his feet. He froze while the sweat from between his shoulder-blades ran in rivulets down his sides.

It was then, perhaps fortunately, that the distant field-glasses focused on something unusual taking place between the ruined block and the warehouse. Blake heard the sharp crack of a sniper's rifle and a bullet smacked against one of the balusters, stinging his cheek with stone chips. A second round whined through the air a foot too high.

The new fear submerged the old and galvanized Blake into activity. With the German draped over one shoulder, he started the painful and perilous journey back along the cable.

The extra weight punished his fatigued muscles, savaging hands that were still not fully healed. There was one more shot that passed over his head, and then no more. The marksman seemed to have been downhill among the splintered trees. Perhaps the bulk of the warehouse, now that they were lower down beneath the cable, was shielding them while he moved to another position. Speed, in any case, was now more vital than ever.

The hand-over-hand progress had become automatic: he had made it once, and he could make it again, even with the added burden of Gruener. There were other problems, now that he had succeeded – yes, he had succeeded! – in removing the wounded German from his lethal position. Problems he had not had time to consider before.

Apart from the sniper, what the devil was he going to do if he got back – no, when he got back – to the ledge?

Traversing that ledge with a dead weight on his back, even if he could reach up to the coping with both hands, would be a virtual impossibility. The bulk of the unconscious man would push him too far away from the wall to maintain a solid grasp. And the thought, in any case, begged the question of how, how in God's name, could he himself clamber from the cable to the ledge and at the same time reach upwards for the coping?

Just to make things more difficult, even if that was possible, how could he lower the two of them from the ledge to the fire escape window – a manoeuvre he had already rejected as impracticable for himself alone?

Such questions abruptly became academic. Blake's stomach turned as he and his supercargo suddenly seemed to drop downwards a little. Had he imagined it? No – they sank another few inches with a jerk while he was transferring his weight from his left hand to his right. He turned his head and stared at the brick pillar they had left. There was now something like twenty-one stone dragging at the electric cable . . . and the weight had begun to pull the rusted staples out of the rotten brickwork below the balustrade.

Blake groaned again. He dare not try to accelerate his pace: he would risk pulling the old iron spikes completely free. Yet with each careful move, those staples emerged a little more, the insulated wire dropped a fraction lower. There was now a thin stream of plaster trickling, like the sands of an hourglass, from the place where the staples entered the wall. Unless they were very near – near enough to cling on – they would be smashed against the warehouse façade, or shaken off to drop into the void, when the cable pulled free.

The end came when Blake was little more than halfway along the wire.

There had been the cracking percussions of anti-aircraft fire in the distance. One of the Nieuports had spun out of sight with black smoke streaming from its tail. And now there was the louder concussion of a field gun much nearer. The flat smack of the first round was followed instantly by the explosion of a shell against the brick pillar ten feet below the balustrade.

Blake never knew if there had been a second round. Pillar, balustrade and parapet disintegrated in a cloud of dust and brown smoke laced with flame. The electric cable, blown free of the shattered brickwork, swung down, weighted by its human load, towards the opposite wall.

Bracing for the final shock that would send them into eternity, Blake saw in the last tenth of a second, as they hurtled down towards the warehouse, that they would smash not into solid masonry but against a fourth-floor window embrasure that was immediately below the staples still securing their lifeline at that end. Clinging frantically to the cable, he brought up his legs an instant before the impact.

His heels exploded through splintered wood and the grimed glass of a pane still astonishingly in place as the window burst inwards.

The two men, strapped together, fell across the sill and pitched forward on to the gallery beyond.

29

The brigadier stared out of the window at Mudie's bookshop on the other side of Oxford Street. It was drizzling and the few civilians out in the lunch hour walked with heads bent and collars turned up. 'I mean,' said the brigadier, 'what the devil do you fancy your man's playing at, eh?'

'I wish I knew,' Major Hesketh said uncomfortably.

'It's deuced odd, and that's a fact. Your staging contact in Switzerland reports that he has doubts about the feller in Saxony – S-12, isn't it? He says that young Blake has been to the factory and is heading south, but he doesn't know whether or not he has the plans, is that right?'

'Yes, sir.'

'And now, thirty-six hours later, after a couple of days' silence, he signals that Blake does have the plans. That he was nabbed by the Hun but got away. Am I correct?'

'Yes, sir.'

'Very rum. So you're happy as a bloody sandboy, very bucked indeed to hear the good news . . . but when you ask for a little elaboration, such as how Blake plans to get home, you run up against another dead end.'

'It's certainly a puzzle,' Hesketh said. 'There's a lack of logic somewhere. Naturally we wanted more news. Perhaps we could set the wheels in motion to help Blake get back. The chap in Switzerland signalled S-12 to telephone him, but he never did. So the Swiss took a big risk and went into Germany himself, first Morsing a standard instruction for a rendezvous at the usual place and . . .'

'But the bugger never turned up?'

'I'm afraid not, sir. What with his previous doubts, it would seem a reasonable guess that S-12 *was* transmitting under duress. Or that the Hun had got him, squeezed the drill out of him and put a double in his place. But in that case why on earth would the double tell us that Blake had been successful? Surely that's the last thing a double's masters would want us to know?'

'Doesn't make sense, I agree,' the brigadier said. 'So what's next?'

'For the moment it's just wait and see, I'm afraid. We'll attend to S-12 later. For now, we can only hope to hear from Blake himself.'

The brigadier looked out of the window again. Outside the bookshop, a newsboy was crying a special edition of the *Morning Post*. A Zeppelin had dropped four 50lb bombs near Woolwich the previous night. Three people had been killed and seven injured. 'I think the rain's easing off,' the brigadier said. 'You better come and have lunch with me at Scott's, Hesketh. They keep me a couple of places every day and His Nibs has been summoned to Buck House to have lunch with the monarch. We can walk.'

'Thank you, sir. That would be . . . I shall be delighted.'

'Tell me one thing, Hesketh. You're a brainy kind of bird.'

'Sir?'

'Why exactly,' the brigadier asked, 'are sandboys – whatever they are – supposed to be so damn happy?'

* * *

Since Gruener seemed to be in a bad way, Blake did the only thing he could do: he took him to a field hospital and dressing station behind the German lines.

This was not as difficult as he expected. Soon after he had manoeuvred him to the ground floor of the warehouse, ripping off strips of clothing to staunch the bleeding and bandage the wounds as best he could, the guns started firing again. A creeping barrage this time, he saw, peering through a ruined doorway. And behind the advancing shell bursts a flood of soldiers in field-grey pouring down the hillside in a counter-attack.

Over the deafening clangour of high-explosive detonations he could hear the crackle of rifle fire, an occasional machine-gun stuttering, and above all the cacophony of human voices. Men shouting, screaming, dying; men terrified and yelling to submerge the fear; men bellowing with the lust to kill because it was the only way they knew to avoid death.

Blake knew instinctively, looking across the slope at the far side of the shallow valley and the wave of soldiers struggling there, that however animated, however ferocious the battle might seem, it would in fact be no more than a detail in the daily schedule of the front as a whole. Any ground gained by the men slaughtered amid the chaos of craters and barbed wire would be no more than a line of coloured pins on maps studied by staff officers safe in commandeered châteaux or dugouts well to the rear.

The sky was obscured by smoke drifting across the mangled hillside. When the advance had become lost in hand-to-hand combat somewhere among the trees below, a German *Feldwebel* and two men carrying a machine-gun, a tripod and two crates of ammunition entered the warehouse through a gap blown in the rear wall.

Blake assumed they had been sent to establish a nest which could cover any eventual retreat if the counter-attack was beaten off. His initial reaction was to hide ... but at once the pride suffusing him since he had successfully conquered at last his fear and his one-time cowardice took over.

He was after all wearing a German uniform. Nobody was going to ask for identification papers in the middle of a local extension of trench warfare. He walked boldly out and addressed the astonished NCO. 'I have a wounded officer here,' he said curtly. 'How can I get him as quickly as possible to the nearest field hospital?'

'In the ... the farm on the far side of the ridge, *Herr Hauptmann*,' the man stammered. 'Perhaps if you were to follow the stretcher bearers? I can spare one man to help you until you contact them.'

'Very well. He will be sent back to you as rapidly as convenient,' Blake snapped.

Gruener had lost a lot of blood but he was conscious again. Supported by Blake and the soldier, he hobbled out into the open air and the fumes of cordite. 'Bravo, Patsy!' he murmured as the first party they could halt loaded him on to the stretcher. 'Knight to king four – and I should imagine the move was well worth an Iron Cross. First class, of course!'

'Shut up and bleed!' Blake jested, moved by the tribute and at the same time exulting in his new-found confidence.

Surgeons and nurses sweating in the stench of blood and excrement and vomit and carbolic acid at the dressing station left their amputations and sewing among the maimed for long enough to patch up Gruener. He was a walking wounded, they said. The blood loss was important but the injuries themselves were superficial. They suggested that he report, seeing his uniform, to a temporary aerodrome three miles in the rear. Blake, who had suffered a gash on the forehead and lacerated shins when they crashed through the window, refused medical help.

An orderly driving a captured British Tin Lizzie took them away from the din of battle and deposed them, together with two infantry majors and an artillery *Ober-Leutnant*, at the hutted command post of the airfield. 'Let me do the talking,' Gruener said in a low voice as Blake helped him clamber down from the flat chassis of the Model-T Ford scout with its solid tyres and Lewis gun in place of a windscreen.

He limped into the HQ hut, leaving Blake to take stock of the different machinery the tides of war had washed up in this particular backwater.

A dozen aeroplanes were dispersed around the field – a level meadow now criss-crossed with muddy wheel tracks and the scars made by tail skids. Beyond the huts was a curious vehicle which looked like nothing more than a snail with an undercart. It was a 40-PS Panzerspähwagen, one of the earliest armoured cars, designed in 1903 by Paul Daimler and built in Vienna. All four of the disc wheels were driven, and the driver and his mate sat in an armour-plate cabin behind the 40hp Mercedes engine with only a small slit to see through. Behind them, the rear wheels were covered by the skirt of a cylindrical steel nacelle which was topped by a 360° revolving turret equipped with two machine-guns. The machine, Blake supposed, which would have been useful before static trench warfare established itself, was being kept in case a war of movement returned.

On the far side of the field a 75mm anti-aircraft gun mounted on a jacked-up Daimler-Benz truck sat in a sandbagged emplacement. Nearby, half hidden under a screen of brushwood, was a captured Renault light tank with one track missing.

Whichever combat squadron was based there, the pilots seemed to be equipped with Pfalz single-seaters. Three flights of these sharp-nosed biplanes were drawn up beyond the hutments. Blake also saw an Albatros D-III and an LVG reconnaissance plane.

Gruener reappeared, accompanied by half a dozen pilots in flying gear. There was a certain amount of ribaldry, some shoulders slapped, and then the pilots broke away to head for the Pfalz scouts. Gruener strolled over to Blake. His face was as pale as the bandages above it, but he was grinning. 'That's torn it,' he said. 'Pulled a bit of rank – socially, that is. Said I was a cousin of the Freiherr von Richthofen. Caught up in the battle with a brother officer I have to take back to Paderborn. But the bloody CO's a real *junker*: brought in his wireless operator, would you believe it, made contact with my flight commander in Malmédy, then damned well double-checked with some security officer called Schneider actually *in* Paderborn!'

'Awkward,' Blake said.

'You could say that twice again and still be underestimating it. We're being lent that old LVG two-seater – but the hell of it is, some of those Pfalz johnnies have been detailed to escort us. Security, the CO said. In case the *Englanders* jump us. But if you ask me someone has said something.'

Blake frowned. 'But if you said I was a brother officer . . . ?'

'Said you were a BO with urgent information about a spy in the Ardennes.'

'Hermann, you're going to get court-martialled if even a little of the true story gets out!'

Gruener shrugged. 'You won the chess game,' he said. 'Come on – they'll be waiting for us to install ourselves in the old bus.'

'What are we going to do?' Blake asked as they walked across.

Gruener held out a clenched fist. Two twigs projected an equal distance from between his knuckles. 'Take a twig,' he said. 'Any twig.'

Blake grasped one of the wood slivers and withdrew it.

'The longer straw. You win again!' Gruener said, throwing away the remaining twig. 'So, once we're in the plane, *you* decide what we do! Agreed?'

Blake sighed. 'If you say so.'

There was a machine-gun on a ring mounting projecting from the LVG's rear cockpit. The plane had an abnormally generous wing span, with two sets of twin struts on either side as well as N-shaped supports below the centre section. A scimitar pipe carried fumes from the exposed six-branched exhaust over the top wing.

The Pfalz scouts were already warming up. Half a dozen riggers stood around the two-seater, waiting for Gruener to give the signal to swing. Blake made a show of testing the Spandau on its ring, and settled down into the cockpit.

The altocumulus in the west now filled half the sky with cotton-wool tufts, silver-edged against the blue. 'We're heading west again, if I'm in the driving seat,' he said to Gruener, tapping him on the shoulder. 'But we'll have at least to make a pretence of going in the opposite direction at first. Perhaps when we climb to the altitude of the lowest cloud cover – well over five thousand, I'd say.'

'You tell me,' Gruener said over his shoulder.

He lowered an arm over the side of the cockpit and gave the NCO in charge of the ground crew a thumbs up. The propeller swung, the 200hp Benz engine wheezed, hiccuped and caught with a shattering roar. The NCO waved the chocks away, and the machine moved towards a wind-sock bellying out near the anti-aircraft gun emplacement.

Despite his wounds and the infernal headache he was suffering, Gruener took off neatly, effortlessly, and climbed at once to five thousand feet. The five-plane flight of Pfalz scouts followed and took up an escort formation – two on either side, one behind and below the blind spot in the tail. The nearest clouds were still several hundred feet above them.

Gruener turned round to raise enquiring eyebrows. Blake pointed upwards. The LVG continued to climb.

When the first wispy veils of white, shredded by the spinning propeller, streaked between the wings, Blake leaned out to look down. Total destruction of the green countryside was more evident from this height. From the ugly industrial sores of Lens, Douai and Béthune in the north to the fourteenth-century belfry of Bapaume in the south, the rural landscape was scarred by a swathe several miles wide of utter ruin – roads and fields and woods and villages all obliterated.

Immediately ahead of the six aeroplanes some thermal upthrust was piling the white clouds into a towering hammerhead. Gruener flew straight into it.

At once Blake was aware of the familiar weightlessness – the one-point universe with no left and no right, no up and no down: just the racket of the engine, the thin film of castor oil smarting on his face, the dense white waste with himself at its centre. Except that this time, although he was flying again, he was a passenger with another man at the controls.

Half rising in the cockpit, he leaned forward to thump Gruener on the shoulder. With his mouth close to the leather helmet he called: 'About turn, if you please, *Herr Hauptmann*. One hundred and eighty degrees should be sufficient – give or take five or ten.'

Obediently, Gruener banked the unwieldy biplane and they flew back – so far as Blake could tell – the way they came. It seemed much longer this time that they were wrapped in the cumulus. Blake was beginning to worry when they plunged suddenly into a blue so dazzling that he had to screw his eyes shut for a moment.

The sun, curiously, was beneath the lower port wing . . . until he realized, as so often occurred when flying blind, that the machine was standing on one wingtip in a near-vertical bank. Gruener half rolled on to an even course and they flew away towards the west. There was no sign of the Pfalz escorts.

Some minutes later, increasingly aware of a certain familiarity about the patchwork landscape appearing sporadically between puffballs of cloud, Blake leaned over the fuselage to stare below. Some way behind the lines, a small town on a hilltop caught his eye. Pinnacled above the huddle of grey roofs was a church with an onion-domed spire gilded with gold tiles that flashed in the midday sun.

'My God!' Blake shouted. 'That's Albert – in the Somme. Just south of Doullens and Hesdin. Hermann' – he thumped the pilot once more on the shoulder – 'turn about fifteen degrees to the north. There's an aerodrome there that I know. At Hesdigneul. It's the home base of 2 Squadron, RFC . . . There, on the far side of that rise, ten o'clock from the chalk quarry.'

He pointed down at a distant stretch of green, a brick-built headquarters block, canvas hangars, a dozen aeroplanes dispersed around the field. 'Put her down there,' he said urgently.

Gruener made no reply. He continued to fly straight ahead.

'We're on the Allied side of the line,' Blake shouted. 'You'll be treated well as an officer POW, I promise. Put her *down*, Hermann!'

'They'll be expecting you át home,' Gruener called over his shoulder. The LVG flew steadily on.

The aerodrome slid behind. Miles ahead, beyond a wilderness of dunes, a thin ribbon of blue marked the approaching sea.

Black and brown smoke clusters, some of them veined with scarlet, pock-marked the sky some way to their left. A similar rash, paler but more numerous, appeared lower down on the other side. 'We're an *enemy* aircraft now. Why don't you turn back and land?' Blake demanded.

As a reply, Gruener pointed upwards through the transparent observation panel in the centre of the LVG's top wing.

They came flashing down out of the sun, six Avro 504 fighters with Lewis guns on the top wing blazing. Blake had time to identify the long skids beneath the nose, the hoops under the lower wing – both to minimize capsized landings because of a narrow undercarriage – before Gruener stood the LVG almost on its tail and zoomed up into the first part of a loop. The machine staggered as the smoke from a near-miss shell burst whipped between the struts. There were ragged tears along the top wing and in the fuselage fabric behind Blake's cockpit, but he had no idea whether they were due to gunfire or shrapnel. Although he had no intention of shooting at a British aeroplane, he struggled up to embrace the ring mounting and cradle the Spandau. It might encourage attackers to sheer off if he looked as though he was firing.

Gruener rolled out at the top of the loop and banked steeply to avoid a flight of three RNAS Sopwith Pups with sea camouflage. He dived . . . and Blake saw to his astonishment below that two pusher machines had joined the fight – slow and unwieldy with the propellers spinning within their birdcage tails, but lethal enough if you came within range of the machine-gunners exposed in their blunt noses. He had time to identify them as a DH-2 and a Farnborough-built FE-2b before Gruener was wheeling away, losing height again as the Avros re-formed for a second attack.

But now, with astonishing speed, the sky became filled with black crosses.

Manhandling the Spandau to mime a spirited defence, Blake saw a bewildering variety of German scouts, a dozen at least, maybe twenty, rallying to protect – as they thought – one of their own. He saw Eindekkers, Halberstadts, Aviatiks, an Albatros D-V, a Pfalz. Many of the top wings were camouflaged, but the fuselages were painted in all the colours of the rainbow, in bars and stripes and zigzags and even chequered. They had, he realized, run into a mass patrol of one of the German 'circuses' – the elite groups of ace pilots fighting as a combined unit. He wondered which of the near-legendary killers was spinning across his sights. Were they in contact with Fritz Holn's Jasta 21? The Boelke squadron led by Karl Bölle? Was Gruener running from Voss, Udet, Immelmann? It was encouraging, although a little disorienting, to imagine they were being protected by such men! The attackers on the other hand might include allied aces like Mick Mannock, Billy Bishop or even Roland Garros . . .

Looping, diving, banking, spinning, the machines involved in the dogfight crowded the sky from the zenith to the blue horizon. A crippled Eindekker floated past like a wounded bird with one wing detached. A Pup vanished in a ball of orange flame. Two machines which had collided spiralled earthwards trailing long plumes of black smoke.

One of the most acrobatic German fighters, only peripherally in Blake's field of vision when he first saw it, was painted a startling scarlet all over. When it climbed steeply beneath the LVG after transforming the De Havilland pusher into a blazing inferno, he realized it was a triplane, similar if not identical to the prototype he had seen in Paderborn. For an instant the machine levelled out alongside and he felt a sudden chill before he remembered that there were black crosses on his aeroplane too. A white silk scarf fluttered in the slipstream behind the triplane pilot's helmeted head. He smiled, white teeth in an oil-smeared young face, and waved a cheerful hand.

Feeling, for a second time, somehow slightly shabby, Blake grinned and waved back, wondering if he was exchanging brotherly greetings with the 'Red Baron', Rittmeister Manfred von Richthofen himself.

The red fighter veered away, closing in a tight circle on the tail of an RNAS Pup. At the same time Gruener was forced to pull the nose of the two-seater violently up to avoid ramming an Avro 504 which was shooting hell out of an Albatros. Over his shoulder, Blake saw the German single-seater roll over to show a lacerated belly and drop like a stone. The pilot, his mouth a black O in his screaming face, was frenziedly beating at the flames streaming back from his savaged engine. Blake turned away. There was nothing to do but watch the man die.

Gruener was throwing the LVG all over the sky. His aim was purely evasive, whirling them away from anything with a red, white and blue tail. But if he had been hostile, looking for a kill, he would have been a pretty formidable opponent, Blake thought.

Now the tumbling, snarling, jockeying pack of fighters were closing in as the dogfight moved out over the sea *en masse*. To Blake, on the wrong side both ways, the complex manoeuvres of these hurtling combat machines resembled more and more the antics of angry bees disturbed from a nest.

Perhaps Gruener shared the feeling; maybe it was just that he was fed up being involved. At any rate he slammed the throttle fully open, set the LVG at a shallow climb, rolled, rolled again, then rolled a third time, driving the machine into the centre of the fray like a corkscrew.

Scouts whisked away on every side, reared up like startled horses ahead, plunged past the tail. Bullets thwacked into the fuselage, tore long strips of fabric from the wings. Miraculously neither Gruener nor Blake was touched. The two-seater bored into a patch of cloud, a minor continent blowing up from the distant coastline of England.

Three minutes later, at a height of six and a half thousand feet, they flew out into the sunlit second miracle.

The sky was empty. Above, behind and below, there was not a single aeroplane to be seen. It was as if the dogfight had never been, a figment of an overheated imagination. Shimmering in the brilliant light, the sea stretched away beneath them, as static as a sheet of wrinkled silk. Southwards, where the shadow of a cloud darkened the water, a steamer – a destroyer, perhaps, on coastal patrol – engraved a fan-shaped white wake into the blue. There was white against the blue too, overhead: a twist of condensation trail, furring out of shape as a wind higher up erased this one witness to combat in the air.

Blake bent forward to tap Gruener on the arm.

He spoke close to the leather helmet. '*Herr Hauptmann*,' he said, 'I have to confess that I took your gun while you were unconscious and defenceless. I have it with me here. My own too. And this time both weapons have loaded magazines in place. In the circumstances, and considering that we are over English territorial waters, I have regretfully to ask that you consider yourself formally under arrest.'

Gruener turned completely around and pushed up his goggles. He was smiling, the blue eyes bright in the white circles above his oil-streaked cheeks. 'I'll consider it,' he said.

'It's just that, well, to establish a *status quo* I should welcome – I quote – your assurance that you accept formally that this arrest has in principle been made. I know it sounds silly, but –'

'No sillier than a similar request in Malmédy. I know.'

'Hermann, you'll be in hell's own trouble if you go back. You can't disguise the help you have been to me. Not with all those witnesses.'

'And I shall be well treated as an officer prisoner of war, correct? With real coffee and English sausages. Patsy, your request has been noted.' Gruener settled the goggles back in place and turned back to his controls.

The English coast was very clear. A few degrees to

port, perhaps ten miles ahead, the white monolith of Beachy Head rose from the sea. Beside it, the sprawl of Eastbourne was draped across the green downs.

When they had covered half the distance, the aeroplane's engine choked, coughed and missed a few beats before picking up its normal rhythm. Gruener turned again. 'I'm afraid we're running out of juice,' he said. 'Either that or the motor's about to conk out with a dud magneto.'

The nose of the LVG dropped. 'I cannot risk trying to find a suitable field,' Gruener said. 'Not among those rolling downs. I'm going to have to put her down the moment we're over land.'

The aeroplane banked steeply. A few miles to the east there was a long, sandy beach at the foot of a grassy bluff. The engine misfired again, belching a puff of blue smoke from the overhead exhaust.

Gruener flew parallel to the coast, heading for the strand.

Green slopes with bungalows, a motor bus crawling along a gravelled country road, rose rapidly towards the biplane. Gruener throttled back, raised the nose slightly and dropped them beyond a line of breakwaters to make a textbook three-point landing on hard sand.

They taxied to a halt with the engine idling.

Three men with khaki puttees and tin hats appeared from a line of dunes and ran towards the plane as Blake clambered from the cockpit – two soldiers and a lance-corporal.

'Blimey!' the NCO exclaimed, stopping dead when he saw the uniform Blake wore. 'Coupla Jerries straight from the Western Front. Fucky Nell!'

'What does he say?' Gruener called from the front cockpit.

'He is invoking a goddess of war familiar to the working classes,' Blake said.

'Not Nell Gwynn?'

'Er, no . . . not exactly. Oh, I don't know though . . . perhaps!'

'What is it, Fritz?' one of the privates guffawed. 'Missed the way to Berlin, have you? Tell him, Corp: straight ahead and turn left at bloody Wipers!'

'I am a British officer,' Blake said importantly. 'I have a prisoner . . .'

'Oh, yairss!' the lance-corporal jeered. 'And I'm Lord Kitchener. Meet my friends, the Prince of Wales and Field Marshal bloody Haig.' He produced a large, rusty service revolver and pointed it at Blake. 'Talkin' of prisoners,' he said, 'there's comfortable cells back in the camp glasshouse. So both you bleeders better come with us PDQ. Nice and quiet, eh?'

Blake opened his mouth to protest, but his words were drowned by a sudden throaty roar from the LVG's engine, which had been ticking over all the time. The machine surged forwards, tail skid slewing, as the powerful slipstream scattered a cloud of sand over Blake and the soldiers. Raising an arm to shield his face from the stinging particles, Blake thought he heard a shouted remark containing the words 'love' and 'war' and 'fair'. Then the aeroplane was hopping over irregularities in the surface of the strand, spraying out fans of water as it splashed through a rivulet running into sea, gathering speed. At the far end of the beach it lifted abruptly, soared over a low cliff and climbed into the sky.

Blake nodded to himself. Par for the course. Gruener had not in fact given his word. His rigid concept of honour had allowed him to flout convention and disobey orders when it was a question of saving a friend from the firing squad, but not permitted him to sacrifice a valuable machine and deprive his country of his possible future services once that deed was done.

Blake knew very well how easy it was to fake engine trouble when there were mixture controls and ignition switches and fuel feeders to hand. He knew too that the LVG had been fuelled for a flight from the front line to Paderborn. It was less than credible therefore that it would run out of petrol on the sixty- to seventy-mile hop from the battlefield to Eastbourne.

There was, in addition to that, the matter of the straws – the second time he had been allowed to believe that chance had helped him. Gruener had thrown away the second twig before Blake could see it, but he suspected that whichever he had chosen he would have been told it was the winner.

The aeroplane, a tiny speck in the distance now, banked steeply and turned east to fly across the Channel towards France. His personal debt of honour satisfied, Hermann Gruener was going home to face the music, whatever the cost.

As the drone of the Benz engine faded and died, Blake turned towards the NCO, who was wiping sand from his eyes. 'Very well, Corporal,' he said. 'Take me to your leader.'

It was dusk before all the necessary channels had been explored and Blake had received a reply from the secret number he had memorized. But by seven o'clock he had been re-equipped with British uniform, driven to the Royal Aircraft Establishment in Farnborough in a Crossléy staff car and ushered into the presence of the civilian in charge of Experimental Research (Aviation).

The expert was a tall, thin man with horn-rimmed spectacles and receding hair. Somewhat distastefully, he removed the brown paper wrapping which had protected the Siegsdorf drawings during the days they were strapped, inside his underclothes, to Blake's back. He spread blueprints, plans and lists out on his desk, poring over the buckled paper with a large magnifying glass.

'Yes. Well. Actually,' he said at last, 'we have a fellow at Woolwich working on this kind of thing. Practically ironed out all the snags and got the system ready for our chaps when they have a scrap with the Hun. Captain Johnny Watts of the RAOC.' He smiled. 'Still, I dare say these will come in useful as a check, sometime or other. Pity some of the dimensions have been smudged.'

It was three hours later that Blake, who had eaten nothing all that day, was shown into the office above blacked-out Oxford Street by Major Hesketh.

Three men with red-tabbed lapels sat behind the big desk – the august figure of Lord Trenchard flanked by the major-general and the brigadier.

The brigadier raised his head as they came in. 'You took your time, Blake,' he said.

OTHER TITLES IN SERIES FROM 22 BOOKS

Available now at newsagents and booksellers
or use the order form provided

continued overleaf . . .

All at £4.99

All 22 Books are available at your bookshop, or can be ordered from:

22 Books
Mail Order Department
Little, Brown and Company
Brettenham House
Lancaster Place
London WC2E 7EN

Alternatively, you may fax your order to the above address. Fax number: 0171 911 8100.

Payments can be made by cheque or postal order, payable to Little, Brown and Company (UK), or by credit card (Visa/Access). Do not send cash or currency. UK, BFPO and Eire customers, please allow 75p per item for postage and packing, to a maximum of £7.50. Overseas customers, please allow £1 per item.

While every effort is made to keep prices low, it is sometimes necessary to increase cover prices at short notice. 22 Books reserves the right to show new retail prices on covers which may differ from those previously advertised in the books or elsewhere.

NAME ....

ADDRESS ....

....

....

☐ I enclose my remittance for £ _____
☐ I wish to pay by Access/Visa

Card number

☐☐☐☐ ☐☐☐☐ ☐☐☐☐ ☐☐☐☐

Card expiry date

☐☐ ☐☐

Please allow 28 days for delivery. Please tick box if you do not wish to receive any additional information ☐